Devin's Dilemma

Devin's Dilemma

The Victorians Book 2

Simone Beaudelaire

Chapter 1

"arry! Harry, please come here. I need you."

With a sigh, Harry put her book aside and rose to stand. Her feet ached in her cousin's too-large boots and her second-hand petticoats drooped to the floor. *I have to make time to alter this monstrosity.* But she knew better. The petticoat had been tripping her for months, and yet, when she had a chance, it was a novel, not a needle, that drew her attention.

"Harry, please hurry!"

Harry hurried down the hall from her small bedroom under the eaves to her cousin's larger room on the second floor, careful to keep her noisy boots confined to the soft black and red runner, lest they boom like thunder on the floorboards. A racket like that would certainly draw Uncle Malcolm's attention... again. *That's the last thing I want.*

She wrestled the cranky crystal knob on her cousin's bedroom door until the catch conceded to release and slipped into the room.

"What is it, Fanny?" she asked. But even as she spoke, Harry knew the answer. Her cousin, Fanny, stood in the center of her room in her underwear, muttering under her breath as she laced her corset to the carved mahogany bedpost. Her pale forehead shone with sweat and her black hair clung to it.

"Fanny, stop," Harry urged. "We tightened that thing already, remember? You don't need to do that."

"It's not enough," Fanny whined, her rosebud lip poking out into a pout.

"Why not?" Harry crossed the floor and smoothed Fanny's hair back. "It's not necessary to turn yourself inside out, you know. You have an enviable figure. Why tight-lace?"

Fanny looked down at her generous bosom, her tiny waist, artificially narrowed by years of tight-lacing, and her perfect, round hips. "Once William proposes to me, then I'll loosen my laces, but until then... I can't let my guard down. What if I have to make another match?"

Harry closed her eyes and took a deep breath. Her own, much looser-fitting garment restricted her, but not to the point of dizziness. "You won't," she insisted. "William adores you. He has your father's permission to court you. You'll be his bride before you know it, but what happens if you pass out tonight? You'll miss all the fun, and they'll have to loosen your laces anyway."

Fanny's pout in no way diminished. "That's easy enough for you to say. You don't have to worry about finding a worthy husband."

Harry bit her lip. "You're right." *And how kind of you to remind me I've gone from a poor relation with few prospects to a domestic with none.* Then she sighed. Fanny's comment had not been made from cruelty. "At any rate, I still think you'll be fine with it the way we had it. And you won't need to worry. Heaven forbid if something were to happen to William, you'd have a line of suitors waiting to claim you whether you tight-lace or not."

"Do you really think so?" Fanny's huge blue eyes widened until they seemed to swallow up all of her pale, heart-shaped face.

"I know so," Harry replied, patting her cousin's shoulder. "Now, why not bathe your face in some cool water and let's get you dressed. You have a big night tonight."

Fanny beamed, no doubt thinking of her beloved William, and Harry relaxed. Her cousin's obsession with her looks bothered the bookish young woman, but she had to admit, they were more likely to win her a comfortable existence than any tome ever written. *It's not like you would have been popular anyway, Harry Fletcher. Not with your...* she let the dangerous thought trail off. Taking slow, deliberate steps, carefully placing her boots on the floorboards so as to avoid stomping, she approached an ornately-carved wooden wardrobe. Red-paneled doors gave way to rows of hanging dresses, each one worth far more than she earned in a year. Harry pulled out the midnight blue and lace ball gown her cousin had commissioned for tonight's dinner.

"It's dreadfully hot," Fanny commented as she splashed cold water on her face.

"It is," Harry agreed, carefully removing the dress from the wardrobe and laying it out on the gold brocade bedclothes. "Did your father say when we're leaving?"

"To Brighton?" Fanny turned away from the ewer on her mirrored commode and approached the window, parting the curtains a crack to peer out onto the loud and dusty street. "He said it depends on me. If I can bring William up to scratch in the next week or so, we'll have to wait until all the arrangements are made. Otherwise, we'll leave next week, and he'll have to catch up with us there... or wait until next season."

Harry grimaced. Fanny certainly would not like either of those options. *I suspect there's to be a great deal of pouting in my future.*

Fanny turned from the window and Harry carried the corset to her, settling it around Fanny's perfect figure and beginning the laborious fastening process. *Thank goodness she didn't tighten it more. That can't be healthy.* But Fanny didn't worry about her health, only about her beauty, so Harry had no choice but to accommodate her.

* * *

Devin tossed the document onto his desk with a sigh, then threw his hands into the air, upsetting a cup of tea, which spilled over his paperwork.

"Damnation," he growled, flinging himself to his feet and sweeping away as much of the tepid beverage as he could before it stained the wood. The will he'd been drafting was ruined and he'd have to start over. "I love my job. I love my job. I LOVE my job!" he reminded himself. "Anything is better than that noisy, sweaty factory with Father and Chris telling me what to do."

Taking a deep breath, Devin screwed up the paper and tossed it into the bin. *At least you didn't upset the inkwell, dolt.* Too aggravated with himself to restart the document that had taken him several hours to prepare, Devin rose carefully, managing for once to avoid hitting his head on one of the low rafters, and ducked into the out-of-doors in search of a cup of tea that didn't endanger his paperwork.

Exiting his place of business—little more than a box hung with brown brocade curtains—Devin blinked in the sparkling June sunlight and rambled down a street lined cheek by jowl on one side with a row of brightly colored but narrow homes.

On the opposite side, adjacent to the building in which his office formed a small portion of the first floor, other shops and businesses competed with each other by decorating picture windows with gaudy displays of lace, hats, toys, cigarettes, and other goods and services, just waiting for the first influx of holidaymakers from London.

Après moi, le déluge, Devin thought irreverently. Not that he was going anywhere. His business remained fairly steady regardless of the socialites who tended to flood Brighton after Midsummer's Eve.

Only a week to go now. A week and the lovely solitude of the coast, which refreshed him after long hours hunched over his too-small desk in the semi-darkness, would be crowded with pretty and expensive-looking young ladies, trying desperately to be noticed by a gentleman who was titled, wealthy, young, handsome and kind. In short, a phantasm.

Devin sighed again, the cool ocean breeze insufficient to lift his melancholy. *Only a week until that damned Sir Fletcher will arrive and demand his will… which I just ruined. If he likes it, all's well and I can draw up a marriage contract for his daughter. If not, I'll lose the most lucrative client I've ever had.* Recalling the pressure that cramped his back and hands until he felt as though he'd tripled his twenty-five years, Devin's comforting sunlit walk began to feel like a dangerous indulgence. *Must get back to the will.* Ducking into his favorite tea house, he took a seat and awaited the arrival of the owner, his favorite lusty widow, Mrs. Murphy. As he waited, he scanned the stuffy interior. Suffocating pink striped fabrics billowed from the tables and clustered around the windows, as though trying to smother the diners with their aggressive cheer.

Sure enough, Margaret Murphy arrived at his side in a moment, with two cups of steaming tea and a plate of scones.

"Hullo, Mr. Bennett," she said in the impartial, businesslike voice that always startled him as she took a seat by his side. *How can such a passionate person feign coolness so well?*

"Mrs. Murphy," he replied in a parody of blandness.

Her emerald eyes twinkled with humor at their discreet exchange.

"How goes the legal world?" she trilled in her captivating brogue.

"Well enough," he replied, not wanting to talk shop, "and the world of business?"

"Slow." She sighed. "I'm looking forward to next week, even if I do have to work like a dog when they come."

"I understand," he replied. His eyes dropped to the hint… well, more than a hint… of cleavage revealed by her replica of a fashionable dress, and then returned to her eyes. He drank his tea and nibbled the scone while their gazes spoke words that could not be uttered in public.

"Will you be needing any help with the pavers in your garden tonight?" he asked at last, in an undertone, though the only other patron in the shop was an old woman so deaf, even shouting failed to capture her attention.

"Yes, I think so," Mrs. Murphy replied, biting her lip to contain a laugh. "An old widow like me should count herself blessed to have such a tall, strong young friend to help me with my gardening."

Gardening? Is that what we're calling it now? Devin grinned. *No seeds will be sown, to be sure, but no matter. It's as good a metaphor as any.*

"I'd better get back to work," he said, setting aside his cup. The scone, though flaky and tender as always, had seemed to stick in his throat, and lay half-eaten on the plate.

Mrs. Murphy nodded, frowning at the abandoned pastry.

"I'll see you at seven."

He winked at her, restoring her grin, and left the shop. *Finish that will, Bennett, and you'll earn a relaxing turn in the sheets with your favorite redhead.* Grinning, he ambled back down the sunny street and into his office, where his now-dry desk awaited. *I* will *finish this time.*

Chapter 2

ARRY perched on a straight-backed wooden chair with an embroidered cushion. The boning in her second-hand corset scratched and teased her under the arms and one particularly aggressive corner seemed intent on taking as much skin as it could. *I wish I could change into my nightgown. It's past three in the morning.* The late hours kept by fashionable people did not suit Harry particularly well, especially as she was obliged to remain, not only awake, but also dressed, until her cousin's gown had been safely ensconced in the wardrobe, her jewelry carefully placed in the safe, her shoes brushed, and her stockings sent for cleaning. And that was if Fanny decided to let her work. Tonight, as was no surprise, she wanted to recline on her bed in her chemise and pantalets and regale Harry with a detailed account of the evening.

"And so, once the announcement was made, Father stuck to my side the whole evening. I didn't have a single moment to spend alone with my betrothed. It was beyond silly. If they think Will and I have never kissed, they're dreaming." She flopped onto her back, rubbing her skin where her own corset had pinched her.

Harry grinned. "They only want to prevent a scandal, you know," she said, examining one of Fanny's dainty white dancing shoes for stains or dirt. *Looks pretty good, but I'll have to go over them more thoroughly in the light.*

"A man kissing his intended is hardly worth more than a giggle, unless you're the worst kind of stuffy old prude," Fanny complained, rising up on one elbow and pulling the pins from her shiny black hair.

"Unfortunately, the stuffy old prudes run the marriage mart," Harry reminded her cousin.

"I can't wait to be married," Fanny said, abandoning prudes in favor of dreamy future-gazing. "Then no one can tell me not to kiss my William."

You'll have to do a bit more than kiss him. I hope someone explains it to you before the wedding, or you're in for a nasty shock. Too bad your mother is deceased. I don't know enough to explain. "It's true," Harry agreed, "but people will still frown on you doing so in public."

"Bah." Fanny dismissed the comment with a wave of her hand. "I won't need to in public. We'll have all the privacy we need, once we're married."

"That's right," Harry agreed, rising from the chair with a groan and tucking the shoes into the wardrobe before turning to Fanny's abandoned corset. *Still looks fine. I think I can just put it away.* "Did you discuss when the blessed event will take place?"

Fanny sighed. "Father isn't ready. He's quite insistent no plans be made until the settlement documents are prepared and signed."

"I see," Harry agreed. "And how long do you think that will take?"

"I don't know!" Fanny cried, dramatic as always. "He muttered something about 'that young solicitor in Brighton,' but I'm not sure what he means by it."

Bemused at her cousin's featherbrained comment, Harry explained. "After your father's previous solicitor, Mr. Phillips, passed away, he's been searching for a replacement. He asked a young man in Brighton to draw up a will for him, and if he likes it, he'll retain the man permanently, to create all legal documents for the family. So at a guess, I'd say when we leave for our holiday by the sea, he'll be checking in with the young man and, if the work is satisfactory, your settlement will be next."

"But... but... that's another week!" Fanny wailed.

Harry snatched a nightgown from her cousin's bureau and carried it to the bed. *I won't tell her that if he agrees to draw up the documents, a week is only the beginning of the wait.* "There, there." She handed Fanny the nightgown and patted her arm. "All will be well, you'll see. Your father only wants to protect you and your interests. You and William will be married before you know it. Now you should turn in. If you want me to be awake to pack your clothes for the trip, I need to get some sleep."

Fanny's pout turned to a laugh. "You're such an old lady, Harry. All you think about is sleep."

Because I don't get to sleep half the day away, you goose. But Fanny wouldn't understand, and Harry didn't want to get into yet another long discussion. With a tight smile, she excused herself for the night.

* * *

Devin groaned deep in his throat as ecstasy washed over him like ocean waves on the pebble beach. Warm, voluptuous female flesh compressed beneath his body and soft, breathy cries of pleasure mingled with his. As the pounding in his head decreased and awareness returned, it was to the image of Margaret Murphy's pretty, freckled face, her green eyes soft with pleasure, her pink lips relaxed and ripe for another kiss. He lavished it on her with generosity. She hummed into his mouth. He relaxed onto her, bracing the bulk of his weight on his arms so as not to crush the curvy redhead beneath him.

"Margaret," he said gently.

"Hmmmm?" She shifted beneath him.

Fearing a leakage, he reached down to grasp the French letter that protected their activities and slipped from her welcoming body. "Awwww," she whined.

"Sorry. I'm spent." Removing the linen sheath from his softening erection, he rose. "I needed to tell you... We'll have to lie low for a while now."

Margaret rose up on one elbow, a move that did interesting things to her plump breasts. "What's going on, love?"

Though he knew she called everyone that, it still bothered Devin. What they shared was a pleasant friendship with a few interesting perks, not love. Still, it hardly seemed worth fussing about. Disposing of the condom, he began to pull his clothing on. "I have a new client coming to town. Actually, he's not a client yet, but if I play my cards right, he might just become the opportunity of my career. Wealthy. Lesser title. Lots of legal documents needed."

"Don't rush off," Margaret urged. "Stay a minute and explain why this fellow means I can't play with my favorite toy anymore."

He rolled his eyes. *Favorite toy indeed.* Slightly insulted by her failed endearment, he replied, "He's known to be a bit of a prude; doesn't like scandal or gossip or any other 'unseemly' things. In fact, the man is so stiff, I think he starches his spine. He'll not be interested in a solicitor who spends time with naughty women."

To soften the sting, he placed a knee on the bed and leaned over, kissing the end of Margaret's freckled nose.

Margaret twisted her lips but made no move to deny the allegation. *And rightly not. I'm far from your only 'toy'.*

"Very well," she said, and her green eyes took on a calculating look. *I suppose she's wondering who can fill in my Tuesday spot while I'm occupied.* Shrugging, he sat on a white carved boudoir chair with a pink embroidered cushion and bent down to pull on his shoes. From this angle, the suffocating coziness of the pink and white lace bedroom seemed to close in on him, stealing his breath. *Margaret's room matches her personality—a smothering cross between overprotective mother and clingy lover.*

The realization dawned on Devin that their affair, such as it was, seemed to be waning. *I hope I can remain her friend, but this intimacy no longer makes sense.* Not sure what had prompted the change, he nonetheless couldn't deny his interest in Margaret's body had become a fraction of what it once was. *And why not? There's never been a hope of anything more, not from you or her. It was meant to be temporary.*

He opened his mouth to speak, but the words abandoned him, so instead, he departed.

Devin ducked into the alley behind her house and made his way quietly to an innocuous and empty public street, lined on both sides with silent shops. The display windows seemed to watch him with a condemning glare, their contents obscured by darkness.

Shivering, he pressed on, emerging from between the buildings to a path skirting the beach. From here, he could perceive the irregular growl of the sea over the beach, the quiet conversation of springtime insects and the shrill cry of a night bird. Nature, always faithful, achieved what sex had not, soothing away the stress of Devin's job and leaving him relaxed and peaceful.

As he walked, he imagined all the documents dripping from his fingertips into the ground and being absorbed by the earth. Overhead, the stars twinkled, laughing at his guilt. *Silly man,* they seemed to say, *easing your urges with a willing female is natural.* And yet he'd been taught love was the better way. That marriage, not shallow affairs, led to true happiness.

His parents proved it with their behavior every day, his brother as well, and yet he had not quite managed to find peace with the demands of his body. Being caught between middle-class morality and the lustiness of youth left him perpetually both unsatisfied and ashamed of himself. *I suppose Mother would say I should find a wife, and she probably has someone in mind, but I'm not Christopher, and I'm not ready.*

Shrugging off his unproductive musings, he returned his focus to releasing his hours of work. Blank pages floated up to the sky to be forgotten. Ink oozed from the toes of his boots. As he walked, weariness replaced his restless agitation. *Good. I should be able to sleep tonight. No need for whiskey.*

At last, just beyond the edge of town, a tiny cottage loomed up in the darkness. He'd sacrificed both size and proximity to town to have a home on the edge of the sea, and he'd never regretted it. The miniature structure, charming in stone and ivy, had roses blooming in profusion around the foundation. Though the dark had faded all colors to shades of gray, the fragrances of sea, flowers and home remained as bright as ever. Devin inhaled and smiled. Then he proceeded up the walk to the door, entered and wandered down the hallway, happy to clean up, stretch out on his clean, white sheets, and drift off to the sound of the sea through the open window.

* * *

All the luggage had been stowed. Fanny had fallen into a light sleep, her head pillowed against the arm she had propped on the window, as the countryside flowed past them. Uncle Malcolm had finally stopped fussing and retreated to his own compartment, leaving the girls in peace and privacy at last.

Harry settled into her seat and pulled her novel from her own satchel. Soon, the lyrical prose of Jane Austen drew her out of her own difficult circumstances and into someone else's problems. Problems solved by a dreamy romance bigger than life. *Bigger than my life anyway. No romantic hero will tease and banter with me, and finally save me from my life of drudgery.*

Her best hope for the future was to accompany Fanny to her married home and continue to serve her. *At least I wouldn't live in constant fear of upsetting Uncle Malcolm. William seems like a calm, kind man. That would be an improvement of sorts.*

Sighing, she settled back against the blue brocade upholstery and let her imagination take her away. The ride would only last a short time, and then it would be back to work. *I'd better enjoy my quiet moment while I can.*

Chapter 3

EVIN stared up at the imposing white edifice of the Mercury Hotel. This monstrosity of a building strove, not to allow the wealthy to enjoy the natural beauty of the shore, but to bring their ideas of luxury with them to it. It spoiled the view from three blocks of town. He considered it an eyesore, but most of the locals welcomed these wealthy, if difficult, guests for the money they brought to the town. *And I'm working for one, so I don't get to be choosy.*

Mounting the steps to the two massive red doors, flanked by imposing columns, he entered the grand and opulent foyer. Plush carpet in tones of tan and red threatened to turn his ankle with every step. Everywhere he looked, white wooden panels divided and decorated the space. He checked his note again for the number of the suite where his illustrious guest awaited him and mounted the stairs to the left.

More of the overly thick carpet formed a colorful runner up the center, so he carefully placed his feet on the pale wood at the edge, clinging to the ornate cast-iron balcony for balance. Upward he climbed, until looking over the railing made him quite dizzy, and he decided to keep his eyes on the tread in front of him, until at last, panting and wheezing, he reached the fifth floor.

He quickly located the suite the Fletcher family had rented for the summer and knocked. A stuffy-looking manservant opened the door and ushered him through the sitting room and into an office dominated by an imposing desk. The man himself, Sir Malcolm Fletcher, sat behind it, easily claiming the throne-like structure. His lack of height and heft struck Devin, and yet, for all his slightness, the man possessed an imposing presence.

"Sir Fletcher," Devin said politely.

"Have a seat, Bennett," his prospective client urged, indicating a small chair across the desk. Devin suppressed both a grimace and a sigh as he squeezed his oversized frame into the too-small seat. The back barely supported him, and the wood groaned under his weight. Alarmed, he decided to sit as still as possible. He extended the portfolio and watched as Fletcher opened it and examined the contents.

"Well, Bennett," he said after a brief perusal, "I must say these are well done. I've had the same solicitor for years, and you've managed to find clearer wording than he did. No one would be able to contest this. Excellent."

Though the words might have seemed enthusiastic, Fletcher's deadpan delivery left Devin a bit uncertain where he stood. "Sir?"

"This is only part of the job, Bennett. I had to be sure of your ability before I trusted you with full disclosure."

Oh, Lord. What now? "How can I help you, sir?"

"Can I count on your utter discretion?" Fletcher demanded, his eyes boring into Devin's with painful intensity.

"Yes, sir. I wouldn't be much of a solicitor if I couldn't keep my clients' private matters private, now would I?" He leaned forward, intending to prove his sincerity. The chair gave an ominous creak, and he froze.

Fletcher considered him, and then opened his mouth to speak. At that moment, the door burst open and two women bustled into the room. Devin rose to greet the arrivals.

One, tall and stately with an admirable figure and masses of black curls regarded him with wide blue eyes and a hint of a smile lingering around her lips. The other hung back, small and drab in a brown dress, which suited neither her dark hair nor her olive-toned skin and tried to look invisible.

"Sorry, Father," the taller girl chirped. "I just wanted to let you know I'd be taking a walk on the seashore to enjoy the afternoon sun."

"Be careful of your complexion, my dear," her father urged. "You know how badly you freckle."

The girl indicated a lace parasol that matched her frilly dress and he nodded, a half-smile curving his mouth and compressing his cheek. "Very well then."

"Father, where are your manners?" the girl cried. "Who is this tall and handsome gentleman?"

A blush, the redhead's curse, heated Devin's face.

"Of course. Fanny, this is Mr. Devin Bennett, my new solicitor. He'll be drawing up your marriage contract. Bennett, this is my daughter, Miss Fletcher, and her companion… um… also Miss Fletcher."

Interesting. He looked like he'd bitten a lemon when he spoke the companion's name. "A relative?"

"In a way," he replied, "but never mind about her. She's only a servant."

Now the smaller girl's cheeks heated, and her dark eyes snapped with displeasure. *And no wonder. What an unkind comment. Nothing wrong with working for a living.*

"Pleased to meet you, Mr. Bennett. We'll be back later, Father."

"Off you go, then," Fletcher urged. The girls turned and left.

Devin watched them until the closing door blocked his view completely, then he turned back to his client. Fletcher was still smiling. Something about his expression made Devin uncomfortable.

"So, a marriage contract?" Devin asked.

"Yes," Fletcher replied. "It's a bit of a poor match, I'll admit. The boy is only a younger son of a yeoman, and a professional man at that, but he's been so kind and tolerant of her. In the end, I couldn't say no. Her happiness means more than some title."

This made Devin like him more. *Guess he's not as stuffy as I thought.* "What profession?" Devin asked.

"A physician," Fletcher replied. "Why do you ask?"

Idle curiosity. "If he were also a man of law, it would affect how I write the contract," Devin explained.

"Ah. Well, my one demand, which the lad is already aware of, is he must accept the contract exactly as I lay it out. No exceptions, no substitutions, no prevarications. If he objects, no wedding."

"Interesting," Devin replied.

"Don't mistake me," Fletcher continued. "I don't intend to cheat him. It's only that my Fanny has enjoyed a certain lifestyle, and I don't want her reduced to a pauper because of her marriage."

"I understand," Devin replied. *This man is so hard to read.*

"Won't you take a seat? You can write up the contract first. The will might take a bit longer."

"I'd rather stand," Devin replied. "I don't think the chair will take my weight."

Fletcher chuckled. "Very well then. Let's get started."

* * *

"Did you see him?" Fanny asked, her eyes wide, as she practically danced along the path leading from the hotel down to the seashore. The sea-tangy breeze teased strands of Harry's dark hair loose from its modest chignon, even as the sun kissed her cheeks and the end of her nose. Fanny's umbrella had slipped over her shoulder, no longer protecting her from the sun.

Harry indicated the parasol with a pointed look. Fanny stuck out her tongue but obediently shaded her face, nonetheless. "You're such an old lady, Harry!"

"I know," she replied. "I don't like it when your father scolds me, so have pity on me, please. And yes, I saw him. He's quite tall, as you said."

"Tall and *handsome*," Fanny insisted. "That face." She sighed dramatically, resting the back of one hand on her forehead.

"I suppose, if one fancies gingers," Harry muttered.

"And why not?" Fanny demanded. "Handsome is handsome, regardless of hair color."

Harry nibbled her lower lip but did not reply. *She's not wrong. That strong jaw, those broad shoulders… but my favorite part was the intelligence in his eyes. Brown eyes with red hair is such a striking combination.* And his fair skin had a golden glow that suggested many hours spent out of doors. *I wonder how he does that when he spends so much time hunched over a desk.*

With a sigh, she released thoughts of the solicitor to float over the heaving sea and concentrated on walking, not wanting to step from the path and sink her floppy boots into the pebble-laden sand.

"And did you hear what Father said?" Fanny chirped on. "He's going to be drawing up the marriage contract. I'll be wed to Will in no time. I can't wait!" She actually kicked up her heels.

"Settle down, Fanny," Harry urged. "It will be months before a wedding can be planned in full. You're getting worked up over nothing." *Heaven help me when we're almost there.*

"Spoilsport." Fanny stuck her lower lip out. Harry shrugged as the two continued their walk, enjoying the sun and the salty, fishy tang of the air. Harry longed to close her eyes and experience all of nature through her other senses. The whoosh of the tide over the beach. The cries of gulls and curlews along the shore. The salty savor of the humid air. All bespoke a different way of life than the crowded, dirty streets of London, and it was a change she adored. *I could stay here forever.* Despite all the work involved in travel, she didn't regret having come.

Chapter 4

VERY day they spent in Brighton, some of the isolation and stress of Harry's uncomfortable station seemed to slip away. Here, under a bright sun, kissed by sea breezes, the future seemed less bleak and hopeless. The eternal roar of the sea filled her mind with a sense of wistful expectation.

Here, the impossible seemed possible. *Anything* seemed possible. As she walked down the beach path with Fanny on the third day of their visit, Harry half-listened to her cousin's piping chatter, focused instead on soaking in as much natural beauty as possible. Last night, she'd opened the little window of her tiny servants' room in the attic of the hotel and listened to the sea as she fell asleep. A salt-scented breeze had teased her into dreams of mermaids singing on rocks far out in the sea. A ship had sailed past and a tall pirate, his burnished hair gleaming in the sun, had dived into the water for a closer look. Only, as he heaved himself onto the boulder, had she realized she was the mermaid, naked and seductive, her dark hair swirling around her shoulders but leaving her breasts bare.

"Will you lure me to my doom?" he'd asked in his shiver-inducing voice.

"Depends on what you mean by doom," she'd quipped back, moments before he joined her on the sun-warmed stone and took her in his arms.

And then Harry had learned, to her sorrow, one of the costs of sleeping with the window open as a noisy gull perched on the sill and demanded food with a raucous screech.

It was just as well he did. I almost overslept.

Trying again to focus on Fanny and forget her dream, she almost shrieked in terror as a massive shadow blocked the sun. As it was, a gasp of surprise led to a clumsy stumble.

"Sorry," a masculine voice cut into her awareness as a warm hand closed around her arm.

She blinked and inhaled as deeply as her corset would allow, before raising her eyes to meet a warm, brown gaze, filled with concern. The backlighting of the sun turned his hair to a living flame and the freckles on his nose seemed to dance in a golden sea. Her pirate had come to her from the depths of her dream, as though her thoughts had summoned him.

"Mr. Bennett," she said, pleased her voice only wavered a trifle.

"Miss Fletcher." He turned his attention to Fanny. "And the other Miss Fletcher. Goodness, how do you ever keep each other straight?"

Fanny laughed. "We know who we are, nitwit," she teased.

Harry ground her teeth. "He's joking, Fanny."

"I know," the black-haired beauty piped, and her high-pitched giggle, for the first time in Harry's life, seemed to grate on her senses. "I'm playing along."

"I can hardly blame her," the man said, pursing his lips. "It was a terrible joke. I deserve to be called a nitwit."

Fanny laughed. Harry scowled.

"Now, please, my lady, don't frown so. Listen, I'll stop joking and be serious. Will that please you?"

"Don't do it, Mr. Bennett," Fanny urged. "Harry is turning into a sour old woman. She needs to cheer up, even if terrible jokes are required."

"I'll keep it in mind."

Harry stood mute, overwhelmed by the rapid banter, and uncertain of what an appropriate response would be. She inhaled to clear her head and noticed, for the first time, how lovely Devin smelled, like fresh air, crisp, clean cologne and the most enticing man.

She shook herself and stepped back. "Never let it be said I can't appreciate a joke, even a silly one. I was startled, that's all. It's good to see you again, Mr. Bennett."

"Ah, she speaks. I had so worried my antics had forever sealed your mouth in prunish disapproval."

"Oh, please," she replied. "An old lady's maid like myself would never bother with prunes. Lemons are so much more effective for wrinkling the lips."

He stared at her for a long moment, and then erupted in a bark of laughter.

Fanny tittered. "Well done, Harry," she squealed, clapping her hands together. "I haven't heard you joke in ages. I was so worried about you."

Oh dear. I'll have to try harder to hide my feelings. "No need to worry. I've only been tired from waiting up for you after so many parties. But once you're married, I'm sure I'll catch up on my sleep."

Devin looked from one lady to the other. "Do you two mind if I walk along with you? Sorry to be so forward, but I normally take a bit of fresh air at this time of day, and it would be... nice to have some company for once."

"N–" Harry began, but Fanny interrupted her.

"You may," the girl said. "After all, this is a public walk. No one can stop you. Besides," she slanted a glance at Harry, "I haven't seen my dear cousin this animated in ages."

"Quiet, you," Harry snapped, pressing her hands to her overly-warm cheeks. *That's not the sun.*

The three of them moved into position to continue down the path. All around them, people walked and talked, approaching each other and parting. The seaside formed a perfect place for casual—and per-haps pseudo-casual—meetings. *I wonder if any lovers are meeting by accident on purpose.* Grinning at her overwrought imagination, Harry ambled along, keeping part of her awareness for her shoes, but turning the greater part to their unexpected companion.

Devin Bennett. Such an unassuming name for a man who stands out in every possible way. Tall, so tall. Like a giant. Muscular—I thought someone who worked behind a desk would be soft, even fat—but his bulk is pure strength. Chiseled features. Full lips. Those warm brown eyes. And that hair... in the full sun, she was able to consider its exact shade. *Like brandy, a gleaming mélange of red, brown and gold.*

Harry's smile deepened. *I'm attracted to him,* she acknowledged. *How lovely to have a feeling like this.* He turned in her direction, meeting her eyes with a warm smile. She blushed and turned away, embarrassed to have been caught staring, but when she glanced back in his direction, his eyes remained fixed on her. Fanny's chatter faded into the sound of the waves and the world shrank, drawing inward until all became Devin: his scent, his eyes. Harry could think of nothing else and found no reason to try.

* * *

Devin lay in his bed, heels perched precariously on the lower edge of the too-short mattress. The open window admitted scents of roses that normally soothed him, but tonight he scarcely noticed. Tonight, his mind had flown far away.

Who knew small and dark would capture my attention, especially after the 'Irish Rose' I've been with? He pushed thoughts of Margaret away. They no longer enticed him. *Mother would say it's because you've met a decent girl.* He waited to feel foolish, to realize he was putting far too much emphasis on a random encounter, but the feeling never came. *Talking to Miss Fletcher felt... good. I hope I run into her again.*

Chapter 5

N the days that followed, Devin did run into the two Miss Fletchers frequently, nearly daily. He seemed to have developed some sort of magnetism that allowed him to know when the ladies would be outside and where to find them, and when he did, they never refused his company.

While Fanny laughed, joked and bantered, the quieter, more intelligent comments her companion provided captured him far more. Her mind entranced him. In some ways, she reminded him of his brother's wife, Katerina, who was also smart, quiet and a bit shy, though much taller and slenderer. Harry's curves made his head spin.

After a week of conversation, he hadn't begun to plumb the depths of her... and he loved it. Though he could see her equal infatuation, the way her eyes lit up when he approached, the glow in her cheeks when he complimented her, they never spoke of their growing attraction, interacting in the highly proper manner of casual acquaintances. He felt no impatience. They had all summer for their connection to grow, and there was no need to rush.

Well, almost none, he admitted as he grasped her gloved hand and gently kissed the back of it. For such an innocent gesture, a ridiculous amount of heat went shooting directly to his groin. *This is the downside of a proper courtship. Long, slow and no relief in sight.* Not that it actually mattered. Deprived of its normal source of satisfaction, his body had decided to release the pressure while he slept, enmeshed in dreams of the lovely Miss Fletcher, of eager, innocent passion. *Like a damned adolescent.*

Regarding her with a heated gaze, he caused her sun-pinkened face to darken further. He smiled. *I love how easily you blush... without stammering or acting as though anything awkward were happening.*

The sun had darkened the olive tone of her skin slightly, making her look exotic, almost foreign. It meant she fit perfectly under the summer sun, on the walk beside the sea.

"How is my marriage contract coming along, Mr. Bennett?" Fanny asked, drawing his attention.

"Quite well, if slowly," he replied. "Sorry for the delay. Your father is determined to make it exactly as he wishes it to be."

"I'm sure," Fanny said, pouting.

"Don't be sad, Miss Fletcher," he urged. Despite how featherbrained she seemed to be, he didn't dislike Fanny. "Your father only wants what is best for you."

"I know." She rolled her eyes. "But his view on things is not quite the same as mine."

Devin didn't point out that her view on things might, perhaps, be founded on something less than full wisdom. Biting his tongue, he waited for the friendly young woman to say something more. He did not expect a growling sound to interrupt the conversation. A slender figure of a man bore down on them, interrupting the conversation.

"Just as I heard, though I could scarcely believe it," the fellow snarled in a vicious undertone. "You, sir, are out of order."

"I beg your pardon?" Devin stared.

"I've heard nothing for the last week but that my betrothed was spending all her free time with an eligible bachelor. Are you attempting to poach what is mine?"

"William? Here, now?" Fanny, stammered, her mouth opening and closing like a hooked fished. Then she steeled herself, finally finding her voice. "William, listen..." She laid a hand on his arm.

He shook her off. "I'll deal with you later."

"Deal with… William, you have it all wrong. Listen!" She gripped his arm again, with greater force this time.

"Fanny…" the look he turned on his intended was one of pure pain. It twisted Devin's heart to see it.

"Yes, listen," Devin urged, drawing the man's attention back to him. "I have no designs on your intended. I swear."

"But… but…" William stammered, looking from one to the other.

"He's not interested in me," Fanny said matter-of-factly. "In fact, for once I'm here as chaperone."

As one, three sets of eyes turned to Harry. She seemed to shrink from their gazes.

"You mean…" William trailed off, clearly stunned.

"Yes, that's right," Devin replied in a calm, unwavering voice as he held out a hand in Harry's direction. "It is this Miss Fletcher, not your fiancée, with whom I'm spending time."

William opened his mouth and closed it several times without uttering more than a few incoherent sounds. He removed his bowler hat and raked his fingers through a nimbus of blond curls that should have graced a painting by that damned Pre-Raphaelite, Dante Rossetti. *Well, they make a striking couple,* Devin thought, eyeing them. Seeing the infamous William made the contract he was constructing suddenly seem completely different. *He loves her. Loves her enough to leave his practice a week early and hurry to the seaside and confront his supposed rival, and even though I'm so much bigger than him, he didn't hold back.* Pleased his new friend had a promising protector, he extended his hand.

William's pale cheeks flushed scarlet, but he took the offer without hesitation.

"There, now," Fanny said. "William, my love, let me introduce you to Mr. Devin Bennett. He's the solicitor who's preparing our marriage contract."

The flush in the young man's cheeks darkened to a painful shade of purple.

"Don't worry," Devin said, "I won't hold it against you. I quite understand. Now then, I have work to do, and the morning is passing. What do you say we walk?"

Fanny giggled and took her fiancé's arm. The two of them led the way, speaking in an undertone together.

An excellent notion. He extended an arm in Harry's direction. She regarded him uncertainly.

"Come on, Miss Fletcher," he urged. "I won't bite, I promise."

* * *

Cautiously, Harry stepped close to Devin, closer than she usually let herself go, until his enticing scent washed over her, drowning her resistance. She linked her arm through his. Though in no way was one iota of skin touching, something about the contact still felt beautifully, uncomfortably intimate.

Could I be falling in love? she dared to wonder. Her eyes trailed up the length of Devin's brown suit coat, to his face. She met warm brown eyes that captured hers. *I might be. I feel like I've swallowed a live eel. And he certainly made no secret of his interest. Declared himself in front of witnesses on a public street... how I wish we could have a private moment.*

A soft touch drew her attention back to the place where their arms joined. He had covered her hand with his and was rubbing his thumb over her glove in an unmistakable caress. Harry closed her eyes, enjoying the sensation. *I don't think privacy is needed after all,* she thought. *This is enough for today.*

* * *

Sighing, Devin crumpled up yet another half-prepared document. His attention lately had been poor, and today, since he'd expressed his interest in Miss Fletcher—*Harry, her cousin calls her. Must be short for Harriet*—he had become basically worthless, blotting ink and misspelling words like a primary student. *Pull yourself together, man,* he urged his wandering mind. *If Fletcher becomes displeased with your work, he'll find a new solicitor. Then not only will you delay Fanny's marriage, which will certainly upset Harriet, but you'll have a much harder time convincing… anyone… that you're financially solvent.*

Devin took a deep breath, rose from his chair and stretched, trailing his fingertips over the plaster ceiling of his office. Outside, the sunlight had changed, dimmed. *How much time have I wasted woolgathering?* Aggravated with himself for letting a very new infatuation drag his mind away from his work, he retrieved a fresh sheet of paper from his desk drawer, and with practiced precision, sharpened the nub of his pen, determined that this time, the notes he'd taken after his last meeting with Fletcher would become a flawless document.

The knife slipped, cutting deep into his thumb and spraying the pristine, unused paper with blood.

"Damnation," Devin roared, tucking his thumb into his mouth. *You'd better go home, man. You're worse than useless today. Sleep off your distraction and get a fresh start.*

Such advice had the sound of his mother about it, but he knew it was futile. He would never be able to sleep. *Like last night, and the night before… not when this dark-eyed siren keeps haunting my dreams.* He needed relief, but what could he do? Proper courtship provided no such opportunities.

Margaret. The thought burst into his mind. *She would be willing.*

Desperate to quench the burning in his loins, he left his office, locking the door and heading down the street in the same direction he always took to go home. *Still have to be careful not to create any scandals. I might lose more than a client if someone took offense. I might lose my license to practice.* At the mouth of the alley that led to Mrs. Murphy's house, he took a sharp left turn, then crept down the darkened little street, stepping quietly on the stone pavers so as not to raise a clatter.

Her back garden was encircled by a high stone wall, but he knew where she hid the key to the gate. He reached for it but suddenly noticed the gate had been left unlocked. *Is this a sign?* He slipped through and pulled the gate shut behind him. In the burnished light of the setting sun, the garden seemed to be made of glowing gemstones. Emerald grass waved in a soft breeze beneath his feet. Strawberries like shaped rubies grew thick on short stalks. Bright blue flowers—Devin didn't know what they were called—seemed to reach for him from the fence where they clustered in sapphire profusion.

He moved carefully through the garden to the rear entrance of the house, intent on his goal, when a sound interrupted him. *I know that noise. What is it?* It seemed to be coming from an open window at the back. *The window into Margaret's bedroom.*

Feeling like a voyeur, he nonetheless peeked in… and frowned. Margaret lay sprawled on her bed, eyes closed, while a dark-haired man buried his face between her thighs. One rough, calloused hand caressed her naked breast, plucking the nipple. She bucked her hips and squealed.

Ardor deflated, Devin fell back from the house before the coupling pair could see him. He let himself back out into the alley and hurried down to the street, but instead of going home, he headed to the beach, wanting to soothe his frustration with the sea and evening sky.

You got what you deserved, his long-ignored conscience woke up to nag him. *Just what the hell were you doing anyway? You're infatuated with a decent girl. What could have possessed you to betray your promising new romance with an easy woman?*

"I needed relief," he whispered, and the murmuring sea took his words away before anyone on the mostly deserted beach could overhear them.

Self-control, the voice in his head sulked. *You learned it in school. You use it every day to do your work when the out-of-doors is calling. Now, you have a new reward waiting. You know she wants you just as badly as you want her. What's wrong with you that you're considering betraying her by bedding a tart, one you already know you're losing interest in?*

Devin closed his eyes, acknowledging the truth of the thought. *If your mother knew…* He ground his teeth. Even at twenty-five, the threat of his mother's disapproval remained potent. He'd inherited her red hair, and her temper, which she could bring to bear as icy disapproval of her son's shenanigans. She would like Harriet. Of that he was sure. *Then don't jeopardize it.*

Heaving a noisy breath, Devin turned his eyes to the horizon. The sun sat on the sea, turning the pale gray-green water to pulsing blood. *Throbbing like my heartbeat.* At last, he noticed what the initial rush of emotion brought about by his thwarted plans had subverted. *She doesn't even look appealing. I don't want her anymore. If I bedded her, I would be using her—with someone else on my mind. Margaret deserves better.*

Feeling frustrated, embarrassed and deeply ashamed of himself, Devin stumbled home. The cottage welcomed him like a warm embrace, soothing his flailing emotions. *You were lucky. You without being hurt, and without anyone knowing. Take the lesson to heart with thankfulness.*

"Shut up," he urged his conscience. "Enough is enough."

Thankfully, the nagging voice fell silent as Devin considered his options. *So what I want from Miss Fletcher precludes any kind of sexual release, either from her or from anyone else. Does this mean I'm in love with her?* Certainly, she had created the urge for him to become a better man. *Damn it.* But love? *It's too soon. I've known the girl a week.* Well then, it could become love. *Hmmm. That sounds right.* Devin poured himself a glass of port from the sideboard in his parlor and reclined on the striped tan and silver upholstery of his sofa.

Letting his mind wander, Devin was unsurprised when his thoughts turned to Harriet once again. *I wonder if she would like this place... someday. It's small. She's used to luxury. I wonder what she would make of a single parlor/library, a plain simple kitchen and two bedrooms. Even the toilet is barely attached, built into that lean-to on the back. And no bathing room like that fancy hotel has, only a slipper tub stored in the kitchen. It's such a common house, though pretty.*

He loved his home but looking at it from another perspective made him doubt himself. *She's used to luxury.* "Wait, she's used to being a *servant* in all that luxury. This is a small home, but she'd be the lady of the house, not the lady's maid." Realizing the futility of his thoughts—how could he know anything about how his home would look to a woman he was still scarcely getting to know? —he tried to find another topic… and failed.

I'm fixated. He frowned. *If infatuation is this distracting, what will happen to me as this develops? No wonder people want to rush through courtship.*

Shaking his head, Devin decided to give up and go to bed.

Hope I can sleep for once.

* * *

Harry lay on her back on her small, hard bed in the attic of the hotel, staring at the cracks in the plaster ceiling as her mind wandered. Beside her, an elderly cook-maid called Mrs. Roundtree snored loudly in a matching bed. Her snorts and gurgles had been adding to Harry's sleeplessness since her arrival two days before.

Of course, I wasn't sleeping well before then. Not with images of a towering, red-haired pirate of a solicitor weighing on her mind. Her arm still felt warm in the memory of his touch. At the time, she'd been forced to lean on him for support, as the scent, sight and feel of him had rendered her limp. *This is too overwhelming. And yet, how can I complain? He seems as interested in me as I am in him.*

Wonder blossomed like summer roses in a heart shriveled by too much deprivation. *I wonder where it will lead. Will he try to kiss me? Will I let him?* As if any question existed. If he reached for her, she would allow it. She tried to imagine it, the warmth of his lips, their firmness. *He's the sort to take charge, I think.* Those powerful arms would hug her tight, blocking the chill of the sea breeze. *And warming me from the inside too,* she realized as arousal heated her body. *If this works… I could be his wife. Share his bed. How wonderful it would be.*

A little thrill fluttered like hummingbird wings in her belly as she imagined herself stretched out on a more comfortable mattress, Devin's bulky body pressing her down as he pushed deep inside her. *Will it hurt, as these English ladies say, or will it feel good, the way I always heard it would before?* She hoped for the latter. It seemed likely if the tingling emptiness in her belly was any indication.

Blushing at her own wanton thoughts, Harry rolled to her side, squeezing her thighs tightly together. *Sleep, Harry. Sleep. You have a big day tomorrow... and if—when—Devin turns up for your morning walk, you don't want to have bruises under your eyes, do you?*

Sadly, willing herself to sleep did not prove to be a successful effort. Long into the night, she lay staring at the dark, shadowy wall, listening to her roommate snore and wishing sleep would claim her.

Chapter 6

ou look terrible," Fanny said with her usual artless candor. She, of course, looked flawless, a faux-casual black curl escaping from her chignon, her enviable figure laced, as usual, into a tightened corset. She pulled a pair of lace gloves from the steamer trunk at the foot of her luxurious hotel bed and slipped them onto her hands.

"I slept badly," Harry muttered, rubbing at her aching eyes.

"Oh?" Fanny raised one black, delicately arched eyebrow at her cousin. "Were you dreaming of a certain towering solicitor?"

"Hardly," Harry admitted. "You have to sleep to dream. Fool that I am, thinking about him kept me awake all night."

"That's not foolish!" Fanny exclaimed, clapping her hands together. "You're in love. I knew it."

"I think it's a bit soon to talk about love," Harry groused. "It's been a week since we met. I barely know him."

Fanny leveled her with a speaking look but said nothing.

"All right. I feel something… something that might become love someday."

"Will become," Fanny corrected. "Unless he turns out to be a beast, I think you're doomed."

"I fear you're right," Harry admitted. "Who would ever have guessed it?"

Fanny shrugged. "Why not? You're a nice person, Harry. You work hard, you're smart and you're pretty. Why wouldn't a man want you? And because you're not... flashy, it would have to be a man of substance. And you certainly found one. Oh, Harry, I'm so happy for you." Fanny grabbed her in a tight hug and whirled her across the room, nearly knocking her off balance.

"Don't rush so, Fanny," Harry protested. "Yes, this... friendship is quite promising, but there are many, many steps before it's even worth dreaming about."

"Yes, falling asleep would be the first one," Fanny quipped. She sank onto her chaise and opened her fan, fluttering it in front of her face. "But seriously, Harry, don't hold yourself back. Devin Bennett is quite a fine figure of a man, smart and funny and kind. I think you'll be his and won't that be lovely... except..." she trailed off. "Never mind," she rushed on, cutting off Harry's question. "Just concentrate on putting yourself squarely in the center of his thoughts, and all will be well."

"I'll try," Harry said, though she had to admit all the novels she liked to read didn't give her much information about how to conduct a proper courtship.

"Now then, let's stop woolgathering. A fine summer day is calling us outside. Let's go. Perhaps a pair of handsome gentlemen will appear to escort us."

"I think we can count on it," Harry mumbled, but allowed her cousin to drag her out of the room and down the lushly carpeted staircase to the lobby, and then into the street.

A chilly sea wind sliced through the late June sunshine and right into Harry's flesh. She shivered. "It's cold today, Fanny," she said, crossing her arms and wishing she hadn't sent her gloves to be washed.

"Can't have that." A warm hand captured each of hers, warming them. That first touch of skin on skin caused a bloom of heat that started in her belly and welled up to every finger and toe. Her scalp tingled.

"Mr. Bennett." She intoned the words softly.

"Miss Fletcher," he replied.

For a moment the world seemed to shrink down to only the two them, with the sun on their heads and the breeze ruffling their clothing.

Then, Devin took Harry's hand and wrapped it around his bicep again. This time, he covered it with his own, maintaining the contact.

Harry's powers of speech abandoned her, and if anyone spoke to her, she had no idea, focused as she was on the touch of Devin's fingers on hers. Her heart pounded and a strange sensation fluttered in her belly. Her whole body seemed to be responding to the delicate contact.

"Devin!" A female voice broke into the moment of intense connection, shattering Harry's focus. She turned to see a tall woman with dark hair hurrying down the sidewalk in their direction, clutching the hand of a little girl.

Not certain who this woman might happen to be, or why she was speaking in such a familiar way to Harry's suitor, the girl frowned at the approaching mother and child.

"Katerina!" Devin replied, his eyes lighting up and a broad smile spreading across his face. His obvious joy at the sight of this woman tightened down Harry's jealousy even further. "And Sophia. How are you today, my dears?"

The child, who matched the woman in nearly every detail, as though she'd been drawn in miniature, dropped her mother's hand and raced to Devin in a flurry of short, ruffled blue skirts. He dropped Harry's arm to scoop her up.

"I had no idea you two were coming to town so early," he continued, squeezing the child until she squeaked dramatically, and then giggled. She threw her arms around his neck and planted a wet-sounding kiss on his cheek.

Befuddled, Harry could only stare. Up ahead, it appeared William and Fanny had taken advantage of their chaperone's distraction to duck out of sight for a rare private moment. Harry didn't have the faintest clue where they'd gone.

"It was beastly in London," the tall woman explained, "and a stench like the grave was rising from the Thames, so Christopher said we should head this way early, and you would keep an eye on us. He sent a telegram."

"I never received it," Devin explained. "But it's certainly no problem. When will the old man be coming himself?"

The woman giggled, but her eyes grew fond at the mention of 'the old man'. "Another week," she explained. "They've ordered dye from a new distributor and Christopher wants to see it used on a large scale before he approves it for regular purchase."

Devin made a face and rolled his eyes but said nothing.

"Mummy, can we go now?" the little girl asked, wriggling. Devin set her on her miniature black boots, and she reached for his hand and her mother's, linking the three together.

Harry's heart clenched at the sight. Though it was clear Devin could scarcely be the father of that girl, and the mention of 'the old man' seemed to confirm it, seeing him with a woman and child had a profound and confusing impact on Harry. Sense notwithstanding, hot, boiling jealousy made her feel nearly ill. Though this woman was clearly not intimately connected to Devin, something about his expression revealed he'd once had feelings for her. It lingered in his soft gaze and the tiny smile curving his mouth. On a deeper level, she recognized that at the moment, he was treating her, Harry, as though something like this could be their future. She could easily picture herself linked to him by a small person who resembled them both.

She opened her mouth to say something, but no words coalesced, so she closed her lips again. *Damnation, Harry, you look like a codfish.*

"But who is your companion, Devin?" the woman asked at last, eyeing Harry without a hint of judgment on her pretty, olive-skinned face.

"Oh, I beg your pardon." He cleared his throat. "This is Miss Harriet Fletcher. Miss Fletcher, my sister-in-law, Mrs. Christopher Bennett, and my niece Sophia."

Sister-in-law? Harry nodded and took the woman's proffered hand. *That explains a great deal. 'The old man' must be Devin's brother. Older brother, if the age of the child is any indication.*

"It's a pleasure to meet you, Miss Fletcher, but please, call me Katerina," Mrs. Bennett said kindly, a gentle smile curving her lips. "I didn't realize Devin had made a new friend."

He cleared his throat. "Yes, well… it was bound to happen sooner or later, right?"

Katerina laughed. "Indeed."

Pull yourself together, Harry told herself fiercely. "Pleased to meet you, Mrs. … Katerina. Isn't it a lovely—if chilly day?" *The weather? How boring can you be?* Harry longed to slap herself on the forehead. The heat in her cheeks did not seem to be windburn.

"I'm relishing the coolness," Mrs. Bennett replied. "As I said, London has become unbearable. I feel for those who have no escape. I used to spend every summer in the city, and now I find the chance to visit the sea quite a luxury."

"Mummy, can we please go now?" the child begged, tugging on her mother's hand.

"Now, Sophia. Don't pester," the woman admonished gently. "I told you we'd get a bun, and we will."

"But I'm ever so hungry, Mummy. Please?" The child's large brown eyes turned sad.

Devin split the morning quiet with a bark of laughter. "This one is bound for the stage. But we can't have my favorite niece going hungry. Mind if Miss Fletcher and I tag along?"

"You go, Mr. Bennett," Harry insisted. "I need to catch up with my cousin. Some chaperone I am, if I allow her to sneak away with her intended."

"I'm afraid the deed is done, Miss Fletcher," Devin replied. "They've long since vanished. And you may have the job of chaperone, but it won't do to leave you all alone either. Won't you please join us?"

Harry's eyes met Devin's, saw the plea in those warm depths. *He wants me to stay and spend time with his family. That's actually quite a declaration.* She looked to Katerina next. The woman smiled encouragingly. Last Harry regarded Sophia.

"Please come, Miss Fletcher," the child begged.

Though not sure why everyone wanted her with them, Harry had no choice but to comply. "Very well."

"Hooray!" Sophia shouted, and a flock of startled pigeons scattered on the morning breeze.

"Decorum, love," Katerina urged with a laugh.

Sophia wrinkled her nose. A moment later she was tugging her mother down the street. Devin tucked Harry's hand back into the crook of his arm and the two of them brought up the rear, Harry still a bit lost in conflicting emotions.

"Are you in there?" Devin asked quietly.

"Pardon?" She looked at him with wide eyes.

"You haven't been this quiet since the day we met."

Harry felt her face color. "Sorry."

"Is anything the matter?" he asked, his fingers stroking over hers.

"I… no, nothing," Harry said, not sure how to put her uncomfortable feelings into words… or even if she should. *Don't give away too much.*

"Doesn't seem like 'nothing'," Devin commented. "But if you're sure you're quite all right?" He met her eyes, even as they walked forward.

"Yes, quite," she said.

* * *

Women always say they're all right even when they're not. Looks like Harriet is no different, Devin thought with amusement. Her soft, deft hands felt rigid under his, though her stiffness faded with his gentle stroking.

He had seen the play of emotions on her pretty face and had some idea what they meant. *She's jealous of Katerina.* He couldn't help but smirk, but his smug feeling quickly disappeared under a wave of guilt. *She shouldn't have to feel jealous. It's time to move this forward a bit.* All his insides seemed to tighten down at the thought, and yet excitement welled. He wanted it. *There's so much potential here. I don't think I've ever experienced a connection like this. It goes so far beyond her prettiness.*

The seashore had given way to an area of shops and business. Ahead of them, a familiar green-striped awning caused a different sort of squirming in Devin's guts. *Now, she would have reason to be jealous of this.*

"Katerina, Sophia, if you two will excuse us... I don't feel like sweets today, and I'd like to talk to Miss Fletcher alone."

"Of course." Katerina winked and let her daughter drag her into Margaret's shop.

Sighing in relief, Devin led Harriet into an empty building nearby.

She looked at the shabby and cobweb-laden interior. "Why are we here, Mr. Bennett?" she asked.

Damn it, Devin. This is hardly the place to declare anything. What a terrible ambiance. "Sorry," he said. "I couldn't think of any other private place. I do hope you'll forgive the surroundings. And..." he gulped. "I do hope you'll consider calling me Devin."

Her plump lower lip drooped in surprise. "Do you mean it?"

He nodded. "Of course I do. Surely this comes as no surprise, my dear. I mean, we haven't known each other long, but..."

"But there's something here," she finished for him, her dark eyes shining in the dim light filtering past the shuttered-up windows. "A lovely friendship..."

"That could easily become so much more." He moved closer to her, so her skirt swirled over his boots. She looked up into his face. Deliberately he placed his hands on her hips, cursing the thick boning of the corset that separated his touch from her curves. "Am I wrong?"

She slowly shook her head from one side to the other. "Not wrong."

"Then may I... may I call you Harriet?"

"No," she replied, and her pale, unpainted lip found its way between her teeth.

I'd love to nibble that. Then her response registered on him and he frowned. "No?"

"No," she reiterated. "I would prefer... if you called me Harry. Only people who don't like me call me Harriet."

"Harry." He couldn't help but grin. *She invited me to such a great intimacy. I'm honored.* "All right then. I think…" He trailed off, not knowing how to say what was swirling around in his mind. He tossed his hat aside and raked his fingers through his hair. Tentatively, Harry reached up and ran her hands over the burnished strands, smoothing them into place. *Something a wife would do.* For a moment, the rest of Devin's life loomed in front of his face in a dizzying swirl of half-realized images.

She didn't seem to find his lack of eloquence upsetting. Her fingers trailed down his cheek, feeling smooth skin give way to prickly stubble. Her touch made him tingle. *Amazing.* "Harry, I…" he began again and again words failed, so instead, he turned his head and nestled his lips into her palm.

Harry drew in an unsteady breath, her dark eyes growing large as she seemed to look deep inside him, drawing directly from his heart the message he couldn't express.

"Devin." The word emerged in a puff of clove-scented breath from lips he suddenly couldn't stop staring at.

"May I…"

Her eyes turned downward, shutting out the light that had dazzled him. Then, before he could even register disappointment, she looked back up at him through her lashes. The image of her shy flirtation riveted his attention, as did the dainty way her lip crept between her teeth.

She's still touching my face, he realized.

He moved closer to her, leaning in.

She pursed her lips slightly, not enough to look foolish, just enough to offer the invitation.

His mouth curled into a smile as he kissed her.

Harry's eyes slid closed at the touch of his lips, and he shut his eyelids a moment later, wanting to experience her with every sense. The tang of spices lingered about her lips, which compressed, soft as pillows, beneath his. A scent combining fresh air, rosewater and something harder to place engulfed them. As arousal heated their bodies, her scent sharpened, mingled with his. He drew in the fragrance, deep inside him. Too much fabric and boning blocked the softness of her body, but her warmth remained potent, nonetheless. Gentle fingers toyed with the soft hair at the nape of his neck.

"Harry," he breathed, releasing her lips with regret.

"Hmmm." Her eyes fluttered open.

"Will you allow me to court you, Harry?" he pleaded. "I don't know whose permission to ask, but will you consider it?"

"I don't think you need anyone's permission but mine," she replied. "I'm twenty-three years old."

"So Fletcher is not your guardian?" he asked, puzzled. *This family is surprisingly complicated.*

"Not in a long, long time," Harry replied. "He's my employer, and I think it's likely he'll welcome any opportunity to wash his hands of me, especially as Fanny is marrying soon."

"Well good," Devin replied. "So then, what do *you* say, Harry? Are you interested?"

"You know the answer," she replied. And then she tugged him down for another luscious kiss.

Chapter 7

YING back on the bed, listening to Mrs. Roundtree's soft snores, Harry relived the day over and over. The morning walk. Meeting Katerina and Sophia. *How I like that serene woman.* Though Devin had nearly drooled over his sister-in-law, which set Harry's teeth on edge, in the end, he had redeemed himself by bestowing on her the most perfect, beautiful kiss she had ever imagined. *Some might say it's too soon, but I love him, I truly do. He seems like a good, gentle man. A man who would never harm a woman. A man worthy of trust like...* Her thought trailed off, avoiding dangerous territory. Squeezing her eyes tightly shut, Harry willed herself to fall asleep. Relaxed by an enjoyable day, secure in her relationship with a man she could scarcely have dreamed, and exhausted from too many sleepless nights, Harry finally dozed off.

* * *

Harry opened her eyes to a room shocking in its familiarity. Heat unlike anything England had ever known made the air shimmer. She pushed aside a gauzy mosquito net and set her feet on cool wood. A sense of oppression more suffocating than the heat tightened her throat. Moving noiselessly along passages whose silence was shattered by the whine of flying creatures with too many legs, the furtive scrabbling of insect feet on the floor and the ticking of mice inside the walls, she walked, unafraid, past closed doors and covered windows.

Only as she drew near the main parlor did her heart begin to hammer and her stomach to churn. An ornate door handle surrendered to her hand and the heavy carved-wood panel swung wide. Harry hesitated in the doorway, her eyes skating away from the sight of a mahogany box in the center of the room.

"Harita." A soft voice called her name.

Harry gulped.

"Harita!"

Though her feet felt like blocks of solid lead, she stumbled forward until she found her belly pressed against the box. Unwillingly, her eyes turned downward, and her breath caught on a sob. Brocade draperies and sheet-covered furniture loomed like ghosts in her peripheral vision, but her entire focus had been snared, riveted by the lovely, dark-haired woman lying before her. Crinkles at the corners of her tightly shut eyes and grooves around her full, pale lips in no way detracted from her beauty, nor did the ugly bruises on her face, visible under a thick coating of cosmetics. Her hair had been styled strangely to conceal a gash Harry happened to know marred her forehead.

"Mama." Harry formed the word out of a whimper. "Mama."

She reached out one small hand, nails bitten to the quick, but couldn't bring herself to touch the ashen skin.

The corpse opened its eyes and regarded Harry, sorrow gleaming in the emerald depths.

"Mama? Mama, please don't leave me," she whispered.

"I didn't mean to," a well-loved voice, harsh with regret, filled the silent room with unexpected sound. "You have to be strong now, Harita."

"I can't." Her voice broke. "He knows. What will become of me?"

"I will watch over you," her mother said. "I will protect you as best I can. Farewell, my dear one."

"Mama!"

The eyes and lips closed, this time for good.

A fat fly buzzed his wings, loud in the too-silent room. He landed on Miranda's lips and crawled inside her left nostril.

Harry gagged.

A large, dark hand, thick with callouses, slipped into hers. "Kumar," she said without looking.

"Come, Harita," he replied in his carefully accented English. "We must go."

He tried to lead her away. She planted her heels and resisted. "No, I won't leave Mama."

A strange, smoky vapor, reminiscent of a cooking pit, wafted through the room.

"Come," Kumar urged, this time grasping Harry around the waist and lifting her over his shoulder.

Moving quickly, the tall manservant carried Harry down the mosaic tiled floor, through thickening smoke, and out into the cooler, fresher air of the garden. He hoisted her high and set her atop the stone wall, her back to the sea.

"What's happening, Kumar?" she asked, wiping smoke and tears from her eyes.

He turned to her, his craggy face wet and his eyes glowing red like coals. "It is the best way."

"What is?" she demanded. "What's burning?"

"All of it," he replied. "Your mother... she deserves the most elegant funeral pyre ever seen."

Harry closed her eyes against a fresh onslaught of tears and reached for him, hugging the man close. *Of course.*

"Another turn of the wheel is well worth it," he muttered.

Harry looked into his face, startled by the harsh determination that had supplanted his grief. Above his head, flames licked the windows and crept across the roof of the family's two-story home. In one of the upper windows, the silhouette of a man rose up and pounded the glass with his fists. A little tongue of fire crept downward from a burning drapery and seemed to stroke tenderly across the top of his head, leaving little sparks in his hair that quickly grew into a solid, blazing shroud.

With a shriek that could be heard from the garden below, the fists began to pound harder. Head alight like a torch, the figure disappeared and returned clutching a chair. One swing and the glass shattered. As air rushed into the room, the hood of flames flared into a cloak, igniting the man's dressing gown.

He screamed and jumped, landing with a sickening crunch and scorching the flower beds. Lurching to his feet, the burning man dragged himself forward, every step drawing an agonized howl from his throat.

He stopped in front of Kumar and grasped the bigger man's fore-arms.

Harry gagged and sobbed at the sight of his face, flesh bubbling like bacon in a hot pan, features half-melted, charring to ash. The stench threatened to overturn her stomach completely.

Kumar gritted his teeth. "May you return as a cockroach beneath my boots." Balling up a fist, he smashed the man's face over and over until he fell to the ground.

Kumar reached for Harry, and she could see the places where con-tact with the flames had hurt his arm and hand.

"Come, Harita. We must leave this place. If anyone asks, I took you out the front door. Do you understand?"

"Yes," Harry replied. "I understand."

"Do you understand why?" Kumar pressed.

"I do."

He took her hand and led her towards the gate.

Behind them, a strange hissing sound drew her attention and she whirled to see the burning figure lurching toward her, arms out-stretched.

"Bastard!" he screeched.

Harry screamed, sitting bolt upright in the bed.

"Fletcher? What is it?" Mrs. Roundtree stood over her, one fist clutching the sleeve of Harry's nightgown.

Harry pressed her hand to her heart, trying to still the pounding. She gasped through sobs, trying to force air into her laboring lungs.

At last, she managed to draw in a complete breath. She expelled the air in a noisy whoosh.

"Sorry," she said. "I had a nightmare."

"I should say," Mrs. Roundtree groused. "You've kept me awake with your whimpering for nearly half an hour."

"Sorry," Harry said again.

Grumbling, the old woman stomped back to bed.

Harry rolled over onto her side. She had begun trembling, not violently, but with painful, deep shudders. *It's been so long since I had the dream. What's happening? Could this be related to Devin somehow? Pray God he never finds out.*

Harry closed her eyes and pretended to sleep.

Chapter 8

NOTHER week passed in the popular town beside the sea. Devin spent his days struggling to focus on the demanding paperwork Sir Fletcher kept altering. He frowned at the will in front of him. The numbers weren't adding up. Neither inherited wealth, nor farming, nor even Fletcher's lucrative horse breeding program came close to equaling the amount he was leaving to his son in cash and unentailed properties.

Though he'd never met the lad, Devin had heard of him. Shrewd, clever and manipulative, or so their mutual acquaintances said. Benton Fletcher was respected, but not usually well-liked. *So much like his father.* Devin struggled to understand his employer, who clearly adored his children and spoiled them but treated another member of his family, Harry, like the lowest sort of scullery maid.

Worse than a scullery maid. There's nothing wrong with honest service. He treats her like a dockside whore. I'd almost think she'd committed some sort of indiscretion. And yet he knew better. She'd confessed, eyes shifting with nerves, that he'd not been her first kiss. Devin recalled that conversation. Setting his pen aside, so as not to splatter the document again, he let his mind wander, knowing he'd get nowhere forcing it away.

Ducking into the alley one block from where they'd left Fanny and William, with stern warnings that a five-minute limit would be strictly enforced, Devin wasted no time taking Harry in his arms. She'd gone so willingly, leaning her cheek against his shirt.

"Devin?" the sound of her soft voice enunciating his name sent a thrill through him.

"Yes, dear?"

"Kiss me." She rose on tiptoe, tugging him down. He went willingly. The flavor of cloves tingled on his lips and tempted him to deepen the kiss. He pressed against the seam of her mouth with his tongue.

Startled, Harry pulled back and leveled wide brown eyes on him. "What are you doing?"

He smiled. "All those novels you tell me you've read, and you don't know about deep kissing?"

She blinked. "Well, I never!"

"Never, Harry?" he asked. "You don't kiss like an absolute novice. Has someone made free with these lips besides me?"

Her cheeks flared and she looked away. *Silly girl, don't be embarrassed. A kiss or two is not such a terrible transgression.*

"Yes," she choked. "One of the footmen…" she scrubbed at her mouth with one hand as though to remove a lingering taint.

Instantly, Devin regretted his teasing. "You didn't enjoy it?"

She turned her gaze to him again. "I didn't want it. Would you enjoy someone grabbing you and…?" Her lips compressed as though she really had bitten a lemon. "…doing *that* while you struggle?"

"I'm sorry," Devin replied. Bringing up one hand, he caressed her cheek. "Kisses should never be forced. What a fool."

"Yes, I was." She closed her eyes.

"Not you, Harry," he replied quickly. "I know sometimes girls can't get out of the way fast enough to avoid people like him. I meant him. Those who don't respect others ruin special moments. But… I really don't think it counted since you didn't want it."

"Really?" Her eyes, when she opened them, had such a look of haunted regret, he couldn't help hugging her a little tighter.

"Really." To prove it, he leaned in again, tasting her lips and telling her without words that he greatly appreciated her willingness to share herself with him.

Banked heat rose between them, and without urging, she parted her lips as though in invitation. *I love your curiosity.* He rewarded her with a gentle glide, slipping his tongue into her mouth and tasting deep of spicy warmth. She accepted the touch this time, shyly coiling her tongue around his, and then sucking in a deep breath as the touch delivered a magnetic pulse of arousal. *I have to have this woman,* Devin thought. *When have I ever wanted a decent girl? And yet I can't get these thoughts out of my mind.* Though he recognized his desire for what it was, he couldn't quite bring himself to form the thought fully. *No rush. Enjoy each moment. The time will come.*

He lifted his head. "We'd better stop for now," he said, pleased his voice only sounded slightly breathless.

"I suppose," she agreed, and he loved the reluctance in her glum tone.

"Harry, don't worry. I'll kiss you again tomorrow, and the next day... and the day after as well. You'll not be getting rid of me easily."

She laid her head against his chest. "I have no desire to get rid of you at all."

"Good. That's how I feel as well."

One more quick smudge of his lips over hers and they'd gone to collect their companions, who were also looking a bit rumpled and stung around the mouths.

Sighing, Devin put the memory aside and collected his pen, carefully inscribing another line of text. *If I can alternate between wool-gathering and work, maybe I'll finish this document on time.*

* * *

"What have you got there?" Harry asked, looking up from the novel she held in her lap.

"A note," Fanny replied.

"I can see that," Harry said dryly. "Is it anything I should know about?"

"Perhaps." The girl's pretty face took on a perplexed expression. "Do you know anyone by the name of Mrs. Christopher Bennett? Is she related to your Mr. Bennett?"

"Yes," Harry replied. "She's his sister-in-law. Why do you ask?"

"Well, she's invited us to tea in the parlor this afternoon."

Harry blinked. "She has? How interesting."

"At a guess," Fanny said lightly, "I'd say she's matchmaking."

Harry smiled. "I don't mind."

"Of course not. So would you like to go? What if Mr. Bennett doesn't come with her?"

Harry shrugged. "She's a kind, friendly woman. I would have no problem spending a few hours with her."

"Especially if she might become *your* sister someday," Fanny pointed out.

"Please." Laughing, Harry waved her book in the air, as though to dispel the foolish words. "We've known one another less than two weeks. We're nowhere near ready to talk about such things."

"What of it?" Fanny demanded, fixing her blue-eyed stare on her cousin with unexpected intensity. "I knew my William was the man for me immediately. The courtship period was only a formality."

"Fanny," Harry said gently, "you were very, very lucky. That kind of love at first sight is rare. It's better left to novels. In real life, people aren't always what they seem. Devin *seems* wonderful, and rather like a perfect match for me, but that doesn't mean he actually is. There's so much I still don't know about him."

"And as you learn, you'll draw closer together, Harry. You'll realize he's loved you all along."

I wish I could believe it. "What time is the invitation for?" Harry asked, changing the subject.

Fanny pursed her lips but answered, "Four." Then she turned to the window, ending the conversation in irritation.

Harry wanted to apologize, though for the life of her she couldn't imagine what she had said wrong.

* * *

Harry tugged uncomfortably at the collar of yet another oversized hand-me-down dress. Though she'd been to the parlor before, her role had been to sit to one side and observe her cousin, not take part in the conversation. In truth, she'd been glad. Trying to keep up with Fanny's chatter left her a bit dizzy, and she much preferred to focus her attention on an embroidery hoop and keep watch. *Good thing Fanny prefers socializing to shenanigans. I've had a pretty easy time of it, all things considered.* But today she would be expected to join in. Katerina had specifically invited her, along with her cousin.

Exhaling a nervous breath, she entered the room, wincing at the busy blue wallpaper that adorned every angle and line of the wall from the top of the polished wainscoting to the edge of the molding adorning the ceiling. Thankfully, the furnishings were less ornate overall, consisting of low tables, high-backed chairs and one blue velvet settee. Perched on the soft upholstery were Katerina, looking lovely in a pale blue gown buttoned high on her long neck, and her daughter in short ruffled pink skirts and miniature white boots.

"Hello, ladies," she said softly, rising to meet them. She took Harry's hands in both of hers and looked her up and down. "I'm so glad you decided to join me."

"Thank you for the invitation," Harry replied, feeling awkward. "I don't receive many."

"I know what you mean," Katerina said. "Before my marriage, I was a veritable wallflower. I never received invitations to anywhere. It wasn't until I met my Christopher that my world began to open up."

Harry considered whether to mention that her lack of socializing was due to her being in service more than natural shyness but decided against it. *She gave me a means of escaping from judging eyes. I'll just be grateful.*

"And is this your cousin?" she asked, turning to Fanny. "Devin mentioned you. What a lovely dress you have on."

Fanny preened as always under the compliment. "Thank you. I should say something like, 'this old thing'? But I don't want to. I like this dress, and I'm glad you do too."

Katerina smiled at the artless reply.

Fanny gets a lot of mileage out of laughing at herself and the rules. I suppose it's part of her charm. She's neither conceited nor rebellious but plays at both. Harry admired her cousin's easy way with the public but had little desire to emulate it.

"Fanny, this is Mrs. Bennett, Devin's sister-in-law, and her daughter, Sophia," Harry explained.

"How nice to meet you both." Fanny stooped to take in the olive-skinned child. Today it appeared Sophia felt shy. She met Fanny's eyes without the squirming exuberance she had previously displayed. "You're very pretty," Sophia said at last.

"Thank you, my dear," Fanny replied. "You are too." They exchanged smiles and then Fanny groaned and hoisted herself upright, fighting the confining whalebone of her corset.

"Shall we?" Katerina indicated a table on which sandwiches, cakes and tea had been laid out, enough to satiate a small army.

Fanny joined their hosts on the settee, but Harry preferred one of the hard, high-backed wooden chairs. The rigidity helped her with her posture, which minimized her own corset's devilish desire to dig into her flesh again.

"I suppose you two are wondering why I invited you," Katerina said as she handed her daughter a plate with a delicate sandwich on it.

"Not particularly," Fanny replied. "I figured it out pretty quickly. Since Mr. Bennett is your brother, and he's clearly madly in love with Harry, and she's madly in love with him, you must want to be certain my cousin is a good woman and will make a good wife for Mr. Bennett, which she will. I also deduced that since Harry is technically in service, you included me in the invitation so you would have a plausible excuse to invite her without seeming strange." Fanny took a bite of her cake, a smug look on her face.

Katerina stared at the girl in astonishment as Harry choked on a mouthful of tea. When at last she could breathe again, she said tartly, "Madly in love might be a stretch, Fanny. I'm… very fond of Mr. Bennett, and he has expressed similar feelings, but you've raced your horse a good way down the track."

"Nonsense," Fanny replied. "I know you better than you know yourself, Harry. But no matter. You'll arrive at the same conclusion when you're ready."

"Is she always like this?" Katerina asked, sounding stunned.

Fanny laughed at both of them and helped herself to more food. "You know I love a gothic novel when I have a spare moment. Father hates it. I don't think he wants me to think for myself."

Did I know she read them? Harry had no such recollection. *Could it be that I've been wrong about her?*

Beside her, their new friend let out a giggle, drawing Harry's attention

Katerina and Harry looked at each other for a long moment and then an inelegant snort rose up from the depths of Harry's soul and escaped through her nose before she could contain it. Her shoulders shook in an attempt to stem the laughter rising up within her, but she failed utterly. Fanny had once again demolished her dignity, but she could bring herself to feel no regret. She laughed, nervousness shattered, a deep, sincere chuckle. A moment later, Katerina joined them.

Together, the ladies put away far too many sandwiches and cakes while they chatted. As Harry had expected, Katerina proved to have a quiet kindness she found most appealing. *We could be friends… do I dare to hope sisters?* She realized she wanted that almost as much as she wanted Devin.

"Ladies, I realize it's a bit late, but do you think you might join me for a brief walk?" Katerina suggested. "I need to move and it's stuffy in this parlor."

"That it is," Fanny concurred. "Let's go. Come on, Harry."

Willingly, Harry rose to her feet and trotted along with the other three. She hadn't noticed the parlor felt stuffy until she stepped out into the refreshing sea air. Though their habitual walking path led to the right, from the front of the hotel towards the town, today Katerina led them left. In this direction, the seashore grew wilder, the buildings sparser, until only a few small cottages fronted the rolling sea.

Without the chatter of voices and the clatter of wagon wheels, the gulls screamed with even greater abandon, wheeling in the sky and diving toward the surf in ostentatious displays of acrobatic prowess. The rolling water clapped the shore, applauding the performance, and flung pebbles and shells high up onto the strand. Hanging low in the sky, the summer sun bathed the sea in a rich, blood-red tone that seemed to float on the waves, advancing and retreating with the movement of the water. Peace crept over Harry. *The sea has always been my friend. Even when it bore me away from home, it comforted me. No wonder I prefer Brighton to London.*

"Follow me," Katerina said, leading them away from the frothing surf up a path of small pavers leading toward two cottages. The smaller of the two, clustered with dense rose vines, seemed to exude an air of welcome.

"Where are we going?" Fanny asked.

"You'll see," Katerina replied, a hint of smugness in her voice.

Wondering what her companion was up to, Harry followed Katerina to the front door and waited while the taller woman knocked.

The door withdrew inward and Harry's jaw dropped. "Devin?" In her amazement, she failed to notice the knowing looks passing between Fanny and Katerina as they reacted to her use of her suitor's Christian name.

"Hello, Harry. Hello, ladies. Won't you come in?" He stepped aside, allowing them to enter.

"Surely this is improper," Harry spluttered.

"For me to visit my brother? With friends along?" Katerina laughed.

"No one will know," Devin added. "It's rather isolated here."

"It's beautiful," Harry replied, drawing a hint of a grin from his lips.

"Well, go in, you goose." Fanny pinched Harry's arm, sending her through the door and following close behind.

Devin pushed the heavy oak back into position, closing out the evening.

"What are we doing here?" Harry demanded. "Surely this is your home, Devin, is it not?"

"It is," he agreed amiably. "I enlisted Katerina and Sophia to lure you two here." He made a wicked face and then laughed at her alarm. "Such high drama. Surely you can guess I wanted to spend a private moment with my lady." He took hold of Harry's hand and tucked it around his bicep, and then covered her clinging fingers with his own.

Harry gulped. *It seems a bit dangerous, this idea. I'm not sure it's the best plan.* And yet, as Devin's warmth and scent washed over her like waves on the shore, she found her resistance melting away. After all, she had not one but two women with her, one a respectable matron, the other her cousin and closest friend. *And this is Devin. We're safe.*

"Katerina," Devin continued, "if I were to take a turn about the garden with Harry, how long do you think you'd give us before coming out to check we were all right?"

Katerina tapped her gloved fingertip on her lips. "Perhaps half an hour."

And before Harry could utter one word on the subject, he had swept her out the rear door.

Harry found herself in a walled garden clustered with flowers growing in wild profusion. The mingled scent of lilies and roses made her a bit dizzy.

"Are you sure this is wise, Devin?" she demanded. "We've had enough trouble controlling ourselves in public."

"Half an hour, Harry," he reminded her. "And really, I wanted to talk to you. I have no intention of causing harm to your innocence or reputation."

"I know, Devin. It's the unintended that worries me."

His lips twisted wryly, acknowledging the temptation they'd been skirting and toying with. "I'll be careful," he said.

"So, what did you want to talk about that couldn't be discussed in public?" she asked, still not certain what he was up to.

"It pertains to our courtship," he replied, and a sudden tension in the arm beneath hers betrayed his concern.

"In what way?" *Oh, please don't have decided against this, Devin. I care for you so.* She trembled at the thought that he might have drawn her outside to break things off in private.

"You know I have no issue with your being in service. It doesn't bother me in the slightest," he began.

Not sure where this was leading, she looked into his eyes, and the tenderness there soothed her ruffled nerves greatly. "I know. I appreciate it," she replied. "I might have worried I'd be beneath you, but you've never seemed to care."

"Nor will I," he replied. "I have no fear of honest work or those who engage in it. You being your cousin's companion is in no way off-putting. It does, however, present a practical problem."

"Oh? And what would that be, Devin?"

His face lit up like the sun illuminating their conversation when she spoke his name. "What will happen when your cousin marries? Do you stay with her or does your uncle retain your employment?"

"I suppose I will stay with her," Harry replied. "You've met William. He's a kind man and seems to have no prejudice towards me. At least, he's never been rude to me. Uncle Malcolm... I think he hates me. If I had a choice, I'd go far from him."

"He's a strange man," Devin replied, "and hard to read. But I think you might be right. There's venom in his voice when he speaks your name, which he rarely does. You're not mentioned in the marriage settlement, but it doesn't surprise me. You're not property, and as you've mentioned, not a minor either, so likely you'll have the choice to go with your cousin if she and her husband agree."

"They will," Harry replied. "Or at least I'm sure Fanny will, and it's quite clear her intended would do anything for her. Why do you ask? What has this to do with us?"

"A great deal," he replied. "Are you aware that ladies' maids and others in service often have half-days off now and again?"

"I've heard of such," she admitted. "Uncle Malcolm says since I'm a charity case, he's under no obligation."

"Charity," Devin scoffed, his lips turning downward. "Are you not providing a service he'd have to employ someone else to perform? Does he pay you?"

"A little," Harry admitted. "About five pounds per annum."

"Five!" he exploded. "That's robbery, Harry. You're working extra hours for less than half the pay of a lady's maid. Even a scullery maid earns more than twice as much. Sounds to me as though you're providing the charity to him, love."

Harry took a deep breath. "Perhaps, but what do you suggest I do? Ask him for a reference? He'd never provide it. This is the best position I'm likely to get."

"Sorry." Devin removed his hat and raked his fingers through his hair. The burnished strands glowed in the light of the low-hanging sun. "I dislike unfairness, and I became distracted. The reason I'm asking is I want to know how to proceed with our courtship. I assume you would like to take this rather slowly?"

Harry nodded. "I think that's best."

"Then likely your cousin will marry, and you'll go with her."

Again Harry tilted her chin downward.

"All right. I didn't fancy calling at your uncle's household as a suitor for you. The whole thing seems ridiculous. If you're with your cousin, it will work much better."

"I wouldn't mind being ridiculous for you, Devin," Harry admitted.

He smiled and ran a gentle finger over her cheek.

"So you're quite sure," she continued, "that you want a long-term connection? Don't forget, we'll be leaving here at the end of summer."

"I'm quite sure," Devin replied. "Don't tell me you feel any differently, Harry."

"Of course not," she insisted. "You know that."

"I do," he agreed. "So what I propose is this. We continue as we have been throughout the summer. Meet together. Walk. Spend time in private if we get a chance. When you go back to London... that will be hard, but we'll write to each other. I think it can work. And once your cousin marries and settles with her husband... it will be an excellent time for us to make more definite plans. By then, we'll have been courting about a year. I know it sounds long, but it's for the best. You know the saying."

"*Marry in haste, repent in leisure,*" Harry replied. "A year does sound long, Devin, but I see the sense in your plan. I think I can agree to all that." She didn't mention the thrill she felt at the implications for their future. *There's no need. It matches the gleam in his eyes.* "Does this ever just amaze you?" she asked.

He shook his head. "Not really. You should see my brother and his wife together. They met under the strangest circumstances. Everything about them should be wrong, and yet, they're the happiest couple I know... apart from my parents. You see, Harry, in my family, love is real, no matter how it comes about."

"Are you sure your family won't object to my being in service?" she asked, worrying a dry flake on her lower lip with her teeth.

Devin thumbed her lip out of her mouth and kissed her once, gently. "Not at all. Do you know what my family business is? I'll give you a hint... I'm the only man of law in the Bennett clan."

She replied with a silent appeal for information.

"My father owns a factory. My brother is in charge of repairing machines. My father's closest friend is the manager. Working people, Harry. Middle class, all of us. No one will worry about you working for a living. It's something we all understand. You've spent too much time among rich people."

She beamed, happiness spreading from her heart out to her every extremity until her fingers tingled with the desire to touch him. "What about Katerina?" she asked, mainly to keep the conversation going. "She carries herself like a queen."

He laughed. "Well, they say she's descended from the Medicis, but in reality, she's a mad musician who can't keep her hands off the pianoforte. She's also a perfectly lovely person."

"I agree," Harry replied. "I noticed that about her. And your reaction," she added.

She instantly regretted the comment as Devin's ruddy eyebrows drew together. "What reaction?" he demanded.

"Oh, nothing," Harry replied. "When we first met... something about the way you looked at her made me think... this is so silly..." she broke off, blushing.

"Go on. Think what, Harry?"

Don't look so serious, Devin, please. "I thought maybe you were in love with her." Harry toyed with the lapel of Devin's suit coat.

"You can see so much? Well then, there's no doubt we have to remain a couple. If you can read my history without me saying a word, it's too dangerous not to have you as my wife."

The word 'wife' twisted Harry's insides badly, but so did the implication that her guess hadn't been wrong. "So you do love her, then?"

"Harry, listen," he sighed, rather than spoke. "When I was seventeen, my brother up and married this beautiful Italian lady, with no warning at all. One day he was fussing with our mother about introducing them, and, no jest, they were married two weeks later. I couldn't understand it at the time. All I knew was that her quiet beauty bowled me over. I... became quite infatuated with her, to the point of being silly."

Harry closed her eyes.

"Want to know what happened, love?"

She nodded.

"I declared myself to her. Offered her... heaven only knows what. I was little more than a child. She was so kind. She told me she loved my brother, would never leave him, and someday I would understand why because I would truly love someone myself. I never did know what she meant by it."

Harry opened her eyelids and dared to voice a question whose power made her tremble. "Do you now?"

Slowly, Devin nodded. "I think I do."

Drawing in a shuddering breath, Harry stretched up to her fullest height and threw her arms around Devin's neck. "How can I be the one?"

His fingers trailed back and forth across her shoulders. "You make the sun brighter, the sea air fresher. You make the grass greener. I don't know how I lived before I met you, and I never want to know how I would live if you went away. Promise me, love. Promise me you'll be mine?"

"I promise," she replied.

Well, such a declaration had to be sealed with a kiss, and Devin did not disappoint, claiming Harry's lips in a kiss of such aching sweetness it brought tears to her eyes.

* * *

After a moment, Devin released her, though she tried to cling to him.

"See," he teased, "I know how to behave."

She nodded.

"Now then, you've been a bit gloomy today, love, which isn't your way. Is anything the matter?"

"I slept badly," she mumbled.

I understand. "So did I," he admitted. "I have for days. My mind keeps returning to a certain pretty brunette who has completely captured my attention."

"I had a nightmare," she replied.

Feeling a bit deflated, Devin nevertheless attempted to comfort his lady. "I'm sorry to hear that. What about?"

She hid her face in the coarse brown fabric of his coat. "I dreamt of my mother's death. I hate it when that happens," she gritted out between clenched teeth.

My poor darling. "I'm so sorry, Harry. Were you very young?"

"Fourteen," she replied. "I... I wasn't ready."

"Was she ill?" he asked.

Harry laughed bitterly. "No, ironically not. Despite the numerous plagues and outbreaks in Bombay, Mother never fell ill. Not once in all the time I can recall did she contract so much as a runny nose or a scratchy throat. No, it was... a terrible accident. She fell..." Harry swallowed so hard he could feel it through the layers of his clothing. "She fell down the stairs and... and hit her head. It was horrible."

"That is horrible," Devin tried to commiserate. *If anything ever happened to my mother, I'd be just as devastated.*

"My whole life ended that day. Before, I was... I was a normal girl. I had the same prospects as anyone. Her death... and my... my father's... they ended my hopes."

"What do you mean, love?" he asked. *I want to understand you, Harry. How did you get to where you are?*

He tucked one knuckle under her chin and raised her face so he could admire the haunted loveliness.

"My father was an officer in the British army. He earned an excellent salary and we lived well, in a nice two-story home by the sea."

"Did you say in India?"

She nodded. "I was born in Bombay, lived all my life there. My parents had friends. I had friends. Life was quite good for the most part, or so I thought. Until that day."

"Your father died at the same time?" he asked, trying to make sense of her comments.

"The next day," she replied. "There was a fire. He... he was trapped inside." She took a deep breath. "If I had been about two years older at the time, I might have been able to stay, find a husband, live with friends, something. But because I was only fourteen, I was sent to my guardian..."

"Your Uncle Malcolm," Devin guessed. At her nod, his lips twisted. "I think I understand the rest of the story."

"I imagine you do," she agreed.

"That must have been horrible," he said, "to go from the daughter of a relatively well-to-do man to a servant-girl in one fell swoop."

"I hate to say it, I sound so greedy, but I don't love this life. I mean, I have a roof over my head, food, and clothing. I have my cousin, and I love her dearly. She's my very best friend. Many people have far less, but…"

"But you want your old life back," he guessed. "Well, Harry, I can try to do it for you. I mean, I'll never be wealthy, but I do make a comfortable living. And I have this little cottage, which I'd love to share with you someday." *Maybe that someday should be sooner than I originally thought. I'll have to ponder this.*

"Time's up, lovebirds," Katerina's voice cut into their intense moment. Devin gave his sister-in-law a speaking look, kissed Harry on the forehead and led her back into the house. *Everyone was worried, and we really did only talk.*

Chapter 9

IGHT deepened. A bright sliver of a moon stared through Devin's bedroom window, illuminating his wide-open eyes. Sleep once again eluded him, tortured as he was by thoughts of Harry, of kisses that grew in heat and intensity with every passing day, of deepening feelings and tender memories. *Today we talked as though we planned to marry. How can I go so quickly from not wanting marriage anytime soon to thinking about nothing else? What changed my mind?*

Harry did. His sweet-faced, dark-haired lady had turned Devin's world completely upside down. *And I wouldn't change a thing.* Only one negative remained… an ache in his loins that wouldn't go away. *Another reason to consider moving this forward a bit faster. If she wants a fancy ceremony, I might be out of luck, but for something humble and small… On the other hand, I don't want to deprive her of anything. I suppose I'll have to ask.*

Regardless of timing, he had a lengthy wait, and his previous attempt to assuage his lust had lingered in his mind. He felt even worse than he had at the time. *As if dipping into any willing woman would satisfy my need for Harry.* His desire for her innocent sensuality would never be assuaged by a cheap liaison with an easy woman. *And it wouldn't be fair to Margaret either, bedding her in place of someone else.* Putting the idea out of his head, he pondered other options. *It's going to be a long time until I can bed Harry.* Sighing, Devin realized that if he wanted any sleep, he only had one option. *I hope I don't go blind,* he thought as he slipped his hand under his nightshirt.

* * *

"Come in," Malcolm said in a chilly, unreadable voice that made Harry's heart clench and a sick feeling tighten the pit of her stomach. "Shut the door."

Harry's hands began trembling as she stepped over the threshold into the close, stuffy environment of the room her uncle was using as an office here at the hotel. Shutting the door, she clasped her fingers behind her back. From beyond the gauzy draperies, the sun faded, perhaps behind a cloud. Shadows lengthened, casting a pall over the room.

"Yes, sir?"

"I have received word, Miss Fletcher, of some questionable behavior on your part." He steepled his fingers and leveled a speaking look in her direction.

"Sir?"

Fletcher slammed his hand down on the desk. "Don't play stupid with me!" he barked. "You were seen walking arm in arm with a man—with *my* solicitor. What do you have to say for yourself, wench?"

Harry took a deep breath and released it slowly. *Steady, girl.* "It's true," she said. "I walked with him... in public. Nothing untoward happened though. Fanny and I often run across him when we go for our walks. He has..." she broke off, considering her words. "He has expressed an interest in me." *Thank God Uncle Malcolm doesn't know about the visit to Devin's house.*

Her employer responded only with an audible grinding of teeth.

"May I ask what the matter is, sir?" Harry dared to query. "Am I not allowed to have a suitor?"

"You don't deserve one," he snapped. "Your whore of a mother made sure of it. Do I need to remind you what you are? No decent man would accept you as anything other than a mistress." Though he didn't shout, his icy declaration struck like hammer blows on Harry's heart. "I kept you out of Christian charity, but don't push my indulgence too far. If you bring one whiff of shame or scandal down on this family, you'll be out on your ear, you understand?"

Harry gulped at the burn in her throat and held her eyes wide to prevent tears from escaping. "Yes, sir."

"Now get out of my sight."

Harry fled like a startled hare, racing up the stairs at much too fast a pace for her ill-fitting boots. Under the eaves, even the milder heat of Brighton conspired with the burning humiliation to raise beads of sweat on her forehead and temples. Alone at last, choking on the unfairness of her fate, she burst into noisy sobs her pillow could scarcely muffle.

Images of Devin seemed to dance and shimmer on the insides of her eyelids. His russet hair, warm dark eyes, the faint smattering of freckles on his cheekbones, his dimple. The warmth of his hand on her skin. He had awakened something within her she never realized she possessed, and not merely desire. Hope. With Devin, for a moment, she'd dared to wish for a normal life. For love, family, a true place in this world not built around secrets and lies. She pounded the pillow with both fists. For years she'd served in silence and tried to remain invisible. She'd catered to her cousin's whims and lived in the uncomfortable space between family and servant. "Why is it so wrong to want a future of my own? Why am I condemned to this partial existence for someone else's sin?"

Neither answers nor solutions appeared before her.

"And how will I explain to Devin?"

At the thought of his enticing smile turning sadly puzzled, fresh tears welled up.

"Tell Devin what?" Fanny's voice penetrated Harry's misery.

"Your father has forbidden me to see him again," Harry explained, sitting up and wiping her eyes.

"And you're *this* upset? I don't think you can deny anymore that you've fallen in love with him."

"I think… this might be the beginning of love," she admitted, "but it's also everything else he represents."

"Shouldn't you just love him for himself?" Fanny asked, her face contorting.

"I don't know him very well yet," Harry reminded her. "He seems loveable. It's growing stronger every day. We have a beautiful future—or *had* one. Now I..." Her voice broke. "I'll never find out."

"Well this seems like a bit much for some conversation and an opportunity," Fanny said, raising one eyebrow. "You're not exactly in slavery, Harry."

"Aren't I?" Harry demanded, her earlier conversation with Devin replaying in her mind. "I work as hard as any servant but receive almost no pay. Your pin money far exceeds my salary. I have to answer to your father for everything *you* do, even though I have no authority over you, and I never even get a half-day off. Tell me how I'm not a slave."

Fanny's eyes widened. "Harry, I had no idea you felt that way," she breathed, tears glimmering in her eyes. "I thought you liked spending time with me."

Stung, Harry sat up and clasped her cousin's hand. "I do. The best part of this wretched existence is the time I spend with you. But, Fanny, you're on the verge of marriage. Can you understand my desire to be the lady of my own household, to have a husband of my own—and babies? I love babies."

"You and Devin would have such pretty ones," Fanny commented.

Harry's heart tore all to pieces as she considered an olive-skinned, russet haired baby. "I'll never know. Not about Devin, not about anyone. Your father will never allow me to have a suitor. He made it very clear."

"No, Harry," Fanny said, her normally dreamy voice hardening to determination. "Listen, you know I love my father, but I'll be the first to admit he's old-fashioned and a bit of a snob. I know he generally thinks the classes shouldn't mix, but he agreed I could marry William, even though he's technically beneath us. The thing to do is—keep seeing Devin. Let your love grow. Don't hold back from him. He's a man of law and can help you make an argument Father can't reject. After all, you're of age. Worst he can do is sack you, but if your beloved is waiting to marry you, that won't matter one whit. Think about it, Harry."

Harry did think. While sneaking around like an object of shame made her uncomfortable, and the fear of being caught turned her belly to a bowl of minnows, Devin's eyes seemed to shine in her heart; hopeful, kind and utterly captivating.

"What do you suggest?" Harry asked. "I can't be seen with him in public. I swear this town is filled with your father's spies."

"Leave that to me," Fanny urged, and the calculating gleam in her eyes alarmed Harry more than any other conversation they'd had to date.

Chapter 10

s he did most days, Devin began his morning with a cup of coffee and the mail. Leafing through a pile of envelopes, he set the bills in a basket. *Friday is for bills.* As the calendar suggested it was Tuesday, they could wait. Two invitations, one to dine at the home of friends—a barrister and his wife—who lived in town, the other from Mrs. Murphy, reminding him she would leave the back gate unlocked.

He tossed the invitation into the bin. Margaret Murphy no longer seemed appealing compared to the sweet, womanly scent and luscious warmth of Harriet Fletcher. "You do have it bad, don't you?" he asked himself, wondering how on earth this saucy little slip of a girl could have captured him. *She's pretty, though not as pretty as her cousin.* And yet, while he admired Fanny's beauty, it was Harry, with her witty conversation and the twinkle in her dark eyes, who kept him distracted day and night. "Especially at night." He groaned as the memory of erotic dreams tortured his sex, leaving him aching. "Damnation. How can slow and proper courtship not prove fatal?"

Shaking his head, Devin returned to his mail. One last envelope awaited him, this one in a frilly, feminine and unfamiliar hand. Curious, he opened the missive. A pretty but complicated cursive teased him, defying his initial attempts at comprehension, but at last the swirling curlicues resolved into words.

Dear Mr. Bennett,

I apologize for intruding upon your solitude, but a desperate situation has arisen with my cousin. I could not help but notice your interest in her, and I am in dire need of your help.

Devin rolled his eyes. *The girl should write gothic melodrama.*

My father, being a staunch and stubborn man, has refused to allow permission for even the possibility of a courtship between yourself and Harry, owing to the difference in your stations. Naturally, I cannot bear to see the future of my dearest friend—not to mention the course of true love—thwarted by such outdated conventions. Therefore, I feel we must meet to plan our future path. I entreat you to reply to this missive with all due haste. I eagerly await your reply.

Yours in secrecy,

Fanny Fletcher

While the tone of her note continued to grate on Devin's nerves, her message cut straight to his heart. *Fanny's right that we needed to meet, because not seeing Harry again will never do.*

Hurriedly, Devin scrawled a note to both Fanny and her fiancé, suggesting a time and place for their meeting.

* * *

A few hours later, a knock on his door revealed the face of the man everyone was concerned about. Sir Malcolm Fletcher stalked into the room with a sour scowl and a sheaf of papers in his hands. Devin tried not to roll his eyes. Standing, Fletcher presented an even less imposing figure than he had from his throne-like chair. *He's scarcely taller than his daughter, and scrawny as well as short.*

"Won't you sit down, sir?" Devin suggested, indicating a plain but sturdily constructed seat. "What can I do for you today?"

"For one thing, you can leave my damned employee alone," Fletcher snarled.

"I beg your pardon," Devin replied with a hint of sarcasm creeping into his courtesy. "I was under the impression that as a woman in her majority, the decision to accept a suitor was hers to make." Devin took a seat in his own chair and leveled an expressionless gaze across the table.

"I'd have a care for my position if I were you, sir," Malcolm replied. "I know she might have a certain... appeal, but don't be swayed by it. Never forget, if a man in your position causes some sort of scandal, you stand to lose a great deal more than my patronage."

Devin grimaced at the reminder of how precarious his license could be. "Perhaps you could explain more fully," he suggested in a neutral voice. "I've grown to care greatly for Miss Fletcher. Developing a relationship with the relative of a client, even if she is a working-class woman, doesn't sound all that scandalous to me. And we've behaved with the utmost propriety." *Don't strike me down, Lord. Surely a few kisses aren't that great a violation of convention.*

Fletcher made a growling sound. "You're putting me in a difficult position, man. Trust me, there are things about Harriet Fletcher you don't know. Things that would hurt both of you if you pursued this connection. I'm not trying to mislead you so much as to protect her, to preserve her reputation. If the truth about Miss Fletcher were ever to be known, she'd become a pariah, and you'd lose your entire situation. Leave her alone, for both of your sakes," Fletcher insisted.

Startled by the man's statement, Devin didn't reply for several long moments. While he longed to demand the truth, he could see from his client's stony expression that more was not to be forthcoming. *Not to mention, it's Harry's decision to tell you her secrets, not her damned uncle's.*

Devin made no promises one way or the other, and Fletcher leveled a hard, speaking look on him.

"I see you're angry with me," the man said. "I probably sound like some kind of archaic old ogre." He set his hat on the desk and raked his fingers through a sparse layer of steel-gray hair. "Can I still count on your discretion for the preparation of my documents?"

Devin swallowed hard. *Can I be that professional? I've never actually liked the man, but I need the money, especially if all I hope to accomplish with Harry comes to be.* "I suppose," he said at last. "I dislike wasting work."

"Very good." Fletcher broke into a tight grin… little more than a ticking of his cheek, actually.

Devin reached into the desk drawer to his left and brought out a small bundle of papers. Extending them across the table, he commented, "Here is your daughter's marriage contract. I've laid out everything exactly the way you suggested, and there should be no legal means of wriggling out of a single item."

Fletcher leafed through the document. "I continue to be impressed, Bennett, with your abilities. For being so young, so new in your field, you really do grasp the nuances of legal language with surprising insight. I accept this, and I won't attempt to change the price we've negotiated. Despite what you might think, I don't cheat people who work for me."

"Somehow, I don't think I agree." The words escaped before Devin could stop them.

Fletcher frowned. "Has that damned chit been telling tales?"

"Are they tales?" Devin demanded. *Too late to take it back. Might as well get the answer.* "Is it true she doesn't get her half-day off, and her pay is less than half of an average scullery maid? Don't you think that's a bit unfair?"

"No," Fletcher replied. "It's perfectly fair. She's lucky to have a position at all… at least one outside a brothel."

Devin blinked. *What the devil is he talking about? A brothel?* He shook his head.

"Now I've said too much." The man looked stricken. "Bennett, you're here to draw up legal documents, not question how I treat my employees. If she wanted a different position, she's not a prisoner. She chooses to stay, and I think it's because she knows how lucky she is to have honest, respectable work. But never mind about that. I'll not say another word. Let's stay on topic, here. Have you drawn up my will the way I asked you to?"

"Yes, sir," Devin replied coldly. No longer curious at the strange turn of conversation, he now felt truly angry.

"Well, good. Let me see."

Devin reached into his desk and produced a much thicker document. "I ran into some trouble I meant to ask you about," he admitted, struggling to maintain his professional demeanor. "I'm not satisfied with the wording about your overseas investments. Do you think you could be a bit clearer about what sort of business ventures you're leaving to your son?"

Fletcher leveled another seeking look at Devin. "Are you sure you're willing to be discreet and honor my confidence?"

* * *

By evening, Devin's head was whirling. A cyclone of unsettled thoughts, unfounded suppositions and unanswered questions threatened to turn him head over feet. He paced uncomfortably across his parlor, waiting for his promised guests to arrive.

A knock at the door brought an end to Devin's agony. He yanked open the heavy panel and ushered the young couple into the room.

"Miss Fletcher, Mr. Phillips, thank you for coming."

"I had to come," William replied, laying his arm across Fanny's back. "I have to protect my fiancée's safety and reputation."

"She's in no danger," Devin replied, "but I do understand. Won't you come in? Sorry, I haven't much refreshment to offer. Everything's been a bit... strange lately."

"I agree," Fanny said, flouncing to the sofa and perching primly on the edge with an unconsciously flirtatious adjusting of her skirt.

"How did you manage to get away from your father without Harry?" Devin asked. *It's not usual for a lady to be out at night with only two men for company.*

"Father's gone out to a friend's. I don't expect him back before the early hours of the morning, when he'll stumble to his bed, drunk, and sleep the day away. As for Harry... she looked exhausted and upset from crying, so I sent her to bed and told her not to come out until she'd rested."

Fanny's description hurt Devin. He could easily see Harry, upset over her uncle's unfairness, weeping in her bedroom. *Probably a servant's room in the attic, if Fletcher's behavior remains consistent.*

"Well, you said you had an idea," Devin stated. "What is it? And don't suggest I give her up. I won't agree to it."

"Nor should you," she replied. "Harry loves you, even if she pretends not to be ready for such a commitment."

"I know," Devin admitted, closing his eyes.

"Do you love her too, Mr. Bennett? Be honest now. I have to know if this is some kind of game you're playing, because the stakes are very high here. Far too high for any sort of shenanigans." Fanny nailed him with a hard-eyed stare.

Devin sank into his armchair as William joined his lady on the sofa.

"What do you suggest?" he asked the girl he had once thought ineffectual, who now provided his only link to the woman he was ready to admit—finally—that he loved.

Fanny pursed her lips at his attempt to steer the conversation. "Obviously, we can't allow Father to win this one. His argument makes no sense. Harry is a perfectly lovely person; kind, loving and generous. She's helped *me* learn to be generous, to think of others. I owe a great deal of my character to her, and the one thing I want most is for her to be happy. I didn't realize until earlier today how much she misses out on life because of her position. You've offered to change that for her, and I want you to do it, but only if you really mean it. So I'll ask again, do you love Harry, Mr. Bennett?"

He met their gazes with eyes that felt too hot. Behind them, almost disappearing into wallpaper dotted with owls, a clock ticked, ticked, ticked the minutes away. *Time is fleeting,* he thought, recalling one of the poets his brother had introduced him to, an American named Longfellow, *so I'd better let my heart beat stout and brave.* He drew in a deep breath and released it. "Yes, I love her."

Fanny nodded. "Good, because my father hates to lose. And…" she paused as though considering her words. "I think there's something else going on there. He keeps hinting Harry has some dark secret."

"He intimated as much to me," Devin replied. "Any idea?"

Fanny shrugged. "She doesn't like to talk about herself."

"That she doesn't," Devin agreed. "I only just found out about her parents' deaths. So tragic."

"Yes," Fanny agreed.

"Wait a minute," William interjected. His blond eyebrows drew together in the dim light of the lamps. "If she has some kind of dark secret, are you sure she should be coming to live with us?"

"Hush, love." Fanny patted his arm. "Yes. I'm sure. Whatever it is, it won't hurt any of us. You can trust Harry. She's a fine girl. Besides, I plan to have her married off to Devin as soon as possible." She turned from her fiancé. "Devin, do you agree?"

"I do," he replied in all seriousness. "At one point I was advocating a slow courtship, but I anticipated being able to call on her. Now?" He shook his head.

"We'll find ways to get you two together," Fanny promised. "Do you think your sister will help?"

"Katerina? Certainly, she will," he replied.

"All right then," Fanny agreed. "I'll correspond with her for the most part. If I meet with her, you'll be there?"

"Yes, but I must say, this is all very irregular," he protested.

"Father will never notice, though." She squeezed William's hand. "He never worries about me calling on other women and taking Harry with me. He never even asks where I'm going, if it's during the day. We'll make certain you two don't lose each other."

"Thank you, Miss Fletcher," Devin said earnestly.

"You'd better call me Fanny," she replied, a hint of her usual insouciance supplanting her serious demeanor. "We'll be family before you know it."

In spite of all they faced, the thought made Devin smile.

Chapter 11

"HERE are you going?" Fletcher demanded of his daughter as she breezed past the open door of his office. His growl made Harry flinch, even though he hadn't seen her. *Dear Lord, he's hungover. That's even worse.*

"I met a nice young matron in town. She and her daughter invited me to join them for ices, Father," Fanny explained.

"Step inside here," Malcolm snapped. "Shut the door."

Fanny obeyed, leaving Harry standing in the corridor alone. She took the opportunity to creep past the office while her employer couldn't see. Then, unable to proceed outside the suite until her cousin emerged, she examined the darkly stained woodwork of the door and window frames.

Every day, a chambermaid stopped by and polished the ornately fluted alder wood and the diamond-shaped leaded glass panes within. The floorboards matched in color, though they'd been sanded smooth and topped with a long runner featuring a red border within which a pattern of stylized vines and flowers seemed to meander at random until they finished where they started from.

It's from India, of course, she realized, *and how typical. Finding the end in the beginning. Returning and returning again to the start of all things. Repeating patterns over and over in a loop. Will I ever be free from the wheel? Will I ever escape?*

She sighed and tried to drag her mind away from Eastern fatalism. *Devin will find a way. He has to. I can't go on like this forever.*

Fanny stepped out of the office and collected Harry with a glance as she walked into the hallway outside the suite. Harry noticed she looked pale and was worrying her lip nervously between her teeth as she twisted her white lace gloves in her hands. Harry shut the door and followed her cousin down the many flights of steps toward the outdoors, which suddenly seemed much less free than it had.

"What happened?" she asked.

"I've never seen him like this," Fanny said, her forehead wrinkled with worry, her eyes as serious as Harry had ever seen. "What happened to you?"

"What do you mean?" Harry asked, and her heart began to pound so hard, she feared it might burst. *Don't let him have said anything. I can't bear it. If I were to lose Fanny's support now... or God forbid, Devin's. Please, Lord, if you're listening, let the secret be unrevealed. I swear I'll never ask for another thing.*

"He wouldn't say," Fanny replied. "He said it wasn't my business, but if I was encouraging you to seek a connection with a decent man like Devin, I was doing you both a disservice. I don't understand. Father has a title, and William doesn't, but he accepted him. Why is it so terrible for a man of business to fall in love with a lady's maid? He's not the crown prince."

"I don't know," Harry said, her shoulders sagging with relief even as she pronounced the lie. "I've never pretended to understand your father." *That much, at least, is true.*

"Well, I spoke with Devin last night, and he's not dissuaded in the least. If you're prepared to do some underhanded courting, he'll go along with it."

"That's frightening, Fanny. What if your father finds out? He has spies everywhere, I know it. Someone will see us and tell him. And then I'll lose my situation."

"And you'll be in the perfect position for Devin to rescue you, which I know he'd be willing to do."

Harry shook her head as the girls threw open the huge double doors and stepped out into the blinding sunlight. Fanny lifted her parasol over her head, for once without needing to be prompted. "No, Fanny. We already talked about this, you know, before. He wants a long slow courtship and for us to marry after you do."

"I know," she replied. "But that was before Father threw his tantrum. Now he's entertaining other possibilities."

Harry stopped dead. "What do you mean? And how on earth do you know all this? Did you say you'd spoken with him privately? When?"

Fanny grinned. "Jealous?"

"Insanely," Harry admitted. "Please, don't tease me."

"Well, then, my dear cousin, rest assured. Yes, I went to speak with your Devin… and I brought William with me."

Harry's jaw dropped. "You were unchaperoned at night with two men? Fanny, what were you thinking? If anyone saw… you'd be ruined. And I'd be blamed. You know I would. That was beyond reckless."

"Settle down, Harry," Fanny waved her free hand, poo-pooing Harry's outburst. "No one saw, and if someone had, the worst outcome would be that I had to marry William sooner. Come to think of it, I should misbehave more often to move the process along."

"Don't even think about it," Harry replied darkly. "I'd tell your father if I thought for a minute you'd get up to such nonsense."

"Harry, are you mad?" Fanny demanded, her expression hardening to anger. "What are you talking about?"

"You'd regret it if you and William didn't have the beautiful wedding you dreamed of," Harry pointed out. "You'll have the rest of your life to be his wife. Be patient for this part."

"Harry." Fanny laid a hand on her arm. "Harry, listen. The beautiful wedding is not nearly so important as the beautiful life William and I are going to make together. I was only joking about being improper with him, but not about wanting to hurry up the process. If I had fewer flowers and fewer flounces on my dress, would I be any less married afterward? Not a bit. I think the beautiful wedding is your dream, my dear. Your dream for me, since you've always known it wasn't likely to be in your future. But tell me honestly, Harry. When you imagine joining your life to Devin's, what do you see? Do you see yourself in a dress of royal white, with a huge bouquet of flowers in your hands and more woven into your hair?"

"I never imagined anything at all," Harry replied. "Not since I was a little girl, Fanny. I've long since stopped dreaming of my wedding day."

Fanny linked her arm through Harry's and started them moving forward again.

"Well, your day is coming, Harry," Fanny said. "Everyone who matters wants this for you. What are you imagining?"

"I can scarcely imagine marrying at all, let alone some sort of fancy ceremony. You're right, Fanny. I don't suppose I care very much what I wear or what flowers I carry. What matters is that Devin would be waiting for me there." She laughed and could hear the bitterness in it. "But even if I did want something elegant, what difference would it make? I can't afford any such thing. I can't even afford my own corset, for Heaven's sake."

Ahead of them, a middle-aged matron turned around and leveled Harry with an evil glare. Harry's face warmed in a way that had nothing to do with the sun.

"Well, that was embarrassing," Fanny quipped. "Harry, do keep control of yourself in public, will you?"

"Sorry," Harry mumbled. "But at any rate, the best I'll be expecting is a borrowed dress and a flower from the garden."

"And wouldn't it be sweet?" Fanny asked. "I could see doing very much the same... but without the borrowed dress. One of my own will do nicely."

Harry had to look at her cousin in a new light. *Maybe she's not as spoiled as I thought she was. Maybe my jealousy over her lifestyle made me see something that wasn't there.*

Ruminating, Harry tripped over her boot for the millionth time. Only Fanny's arm in hers kept her from tumbling face-first into the pavement.

"I should go back to bed," Harry growled, irritated by her clumsiness.

"No, you wouldn't like that," Fanny advised. "Come along, my dear. Hurry... but hurry carefully, would you?"

Harry allowed her cousin to steer her towards the bustling downtown area.

"Now then, you might be upset with me about this, but I'm going to say it anyway," Fanny continued as they closed in on their destination. "If you have the opportunity to spend time with Devin, do it. To hell with the consequences. If you're sacked, have him marry you. You'll be no worse off because he'll never ask you to find another situation and wait on some arbitrary date."

Harry nodded. There was sense in what her cousin was saying. It filtered into the back of her mind and lodged there, changing, rolling, metamorphosing without her awareness.

Fanny and Harry arrived, not at the ices shop she'd promised her father, but at a suffocatingly charming tearoom. Inside, a large and redheaded Irish lady with freckles and too much cleavage showing escorted them in silence to a private rear room. A round table sat on a polished wooden floor, and pink brocade draperies adorned small windows that only admitted a small beam of sunlight each.

Harry's excitement deflated when she found, not her beloved, but only his sister-in-law, her daughter and an unfamiliar dark-haired man. Katerina jumped to her feet and hurried over to Harry, taking her in a warm, motherly hug. Though only a few years older than Harry, something about the matron made her feel small and safe in a way she'd almost forgotten.

"I heard about what your uncle is trying to do," Katerina said quietly, for Harry's ears only. "I'm so sorry."

"He doesn't own me," Harry replied. "I'll not be held back by his dictates for long. I'm not sure quite how to handle all this, but..."

"But you're not giving up on Devin?" Katerina pulled back and scanned Harry's face with searching dark eyes.

"No," Harry said firmly. "Never."

"Very good." The Italian woman squeezed Harry's arms gently once more and then stepped back, half turning to indicate the stranger, who had risen from his seat and stood close beside them.

"Harriet, this is my husband, Christopher. Chris, Miss Harriet Fletcher. She… she's become quite important to your brother."

"So I gather," the man said in a fond voice. The look he leveled on Katerina blended tenderness with heat, and he laid a proprietary hand on the small of her back.

"And I'm Miss Fanny Fletcher," Fanny jumped in. "Harry's cousin. It's my father who started this nonsense, I'm sorry to say, but I intend to do everything in my power to rectify it."

"Goodness, where are my manners?" Katerina exclaimed. "I'm sorry, Miss Fletcher."

"Don't concern yourself over it," Fanny replied. "I understand. Harry is the focus now. If we all pull together, the course of true love might just prevail."

Harry regarded Katerina's husband, wondering how he would take such a sentimental and girly statement. He didn't react at all. Instead, the man seemed to be observing all of them closely, his expression unreadable, as though trying to make some kind of mental connections. Harry also noticed his hand, where it sat against Katerina's pale gold dress, had splotches of vivid color stained into the skin. *A working man's hands, just as Devin said.* She recalled how often ink had stained her beloved's fingers.

Realizing she was staring like an idiot, Harry stammered, "Sorry. I don't mean to stand here like a statue…"

"It's quite all right," Katerina reassured her. "I freeze up when the attention turns to me, as well."

Such a kindred spirit. I do like her.

"Let's take a seat, ladies," Katerina's husband suggested.

"Is Devin coming?" Fanny asked.

"He'll be here as soon as he can," Katerina assured her. "It's vital he continue his work."

Harry nodded. The thought that Devin was working, not only because it was his job, but in order to provide her a new life, warmed her right down to the soles of her aching feet.

They took their places at the table, and Katerina poured tea for everyone. "Might as well pass the time pleasantly," she said, arranging a few sweets on a small plate and placing them in front of her daughter.

"Thank you, Mummy," the girl said politely.

"It's good to see you again, Sophia," Fanny commented, drawing the child into the conversation.

"You too," she replied. "What's happening?"

"Well," Katerina said to her daughter, thinking as she spoke, if her faraway expression provided any indication, "Your Uncle Devin is quite in love with this lady." She indicated Harry by patting her shoulder. Harry blushed. "Her uncle doesn't want her to marry him, but none of us agreed, so we're trying to work out a way to make it all happen."

"It's like a fairy tale," Sophia replied.

She's right, Harry realized. *I never realized how uncomfortable living within a 'once upon a time' could be.* "Why is it," she asked, "that you are so willing to do all this for me? I mean, you don't know me particularly well. Why not encourage Devin to forget me, move on and find someone more appropriate?"

Three sets of eyes turned her direction, staring as though she'd sprouted an extra head.

"It's for Devin as much as you," Katerina reminded her. "If he loves you and you love him, you should be together. But also…" she broke off, pondering again. "Also, I know what it's like to have a meddling father interfere with a promising romance." She slipped her hand into her husband's, where it rested on the edge of the table. He stroked her wrist with his thumb. "If strangers hadn't stepped in and helped us, the outcome might have been much, much different." She shuddered.

There's more to this story, Harry thought, but now was not the time. "I appreciate your help. There's no way I could do this on my own."

"There's no way you'll ever have to," Fanny said. "You've done so much for me. It's the least I can do."

Tears stung Harry's eyes. She bit down hard on her lip to distract herself. "Thank you, Fanny."

Fanny patted Harry's hand.

Two voices, one male, one female, filtered through the door a moment before Devin entered the room. The owner, the red-haired woman Harry had noticed earlier, glared at him for a moment before shutting the door more sharply than was necessary, setting the teacups rattling on their saucers.

"Hello, all," he said, his voice light, but unnaturally so. His smile looked strained. "Hello, Harry." He approached and took her hand in his, gently kissing the soft skin on the back. Harry's whole body tingled, and she knew the faint blush she'd developed earlier had turned fiery.

"Stop mooning and take a seat," Christopher urged his brother.

Devin squeezed Harry's hand and circled the table, even as he commented, "I've had to watch you moon over your bride a time or two. Don't expect me to stop on your account." Then he addressed the room. "Looks as though I'm late to the meeting. What's been decided so far?"

"Nothing," Harry said.

At the same time, Fanny replied, "Everyone is in agreement that my father must not be allowed to win."

Devin looked from one woman to the other. "I agree," he said at last.

Harry bit her lip. So much was happening all around her, and she wasn't sure how to feel about any of it. *Overwhelmed, I suppose,* she decided. A thread of guilt wound its way through Harry. *They all want so badly to help me, but no one understands why I'm off-limits. If they did, would they all be fighting this hard to help me? If they knew the truth, would we be here now?* Unanswered questions tortured Harry, even while her friends plotted how to maintain contact between her and Devin without alerting Sir Fletcher, until such time as they could gather the needed materials to put her under her beloved's protection for good. *Devin... would you still want me if you knew?* She gazed at his beloved face. *Who am I trying to fool? Myself? I've been pretending all along. Uncle Malcolm is right, I don't deserve this, if for no other reason than my own dishonesty. I should tell him the truth. I should put a stop to this right now.*

Harry took a deep breath, opened her mouth to speak, and then the image of their shocked, horrified faces loomed up in her imagination, stealing her words before they could be uttered. She shut her lips again.

"Harry, is something wrong?" Devin asked.

Dear, sweet Devin. How much I love you. "I feel ill. Let's not do this right now, please?" Harry begged.

"Poor Harry," Fanny said, suddenly sympathetic. "All this is a bit much, isn't it? But don't you worry, love. All will be well."

"I'd like to go home and lie down," Harry said, hating the kindness in everyone's eyes. *Would you still look at me the same way if you knew?*

"Let me walk you home," Devin suggested.

Harry shook her head. "You mustn't. If he found out…and he will…"

"Then I'll take care of you, Harry. You know that," Devin urged.

"I'll be fine. It's broad daylight. Mrs. Bennett, can you please see Fanny home safely?" Her stomach had begun to churn, tightening down her voice to a squeak.

"Of course," Katerina said, resting a motherly hand on Harry's forehead while she peered into her eyes. "And I think you should probably go home and rest. Don't worry, Harry. All will be well. You'll see."

Unable to bear another moment, Harry stumbled out into the public part of the tea shop and down the street back to the hotel. Despite her desire not to cause a scene, tears trickled down her cheeks and great, gulping sobs tried to climb out of her throat.

Great fraud, she castigated herself. *Liar. Cheat. Even your own best friend doesn't know the truth about you, and yet they're all willing to go to such lengths to rescue you from injustice… an injustice that never happened.*

She shoved open the door to the hotel's main lobby and hurried past staring patrons, pounding up the stairs to the attic with a distinct lack of decorum. Gasping with suppressed sobs and the rapid climb, she threw herself across her bed, which groaned in protest of the sudden impact. Mercifully the second bed remained unoccupied, as her room-mate seemed to be attending to daily duties. Free at last to let loose of her misery, she released a torrent of furious weeping into her pillow.

"Mother, what do I do?" she asked the empty room. "Must I lie for-ever? What if the truth comes out? I'd be guilty of more than merely being what I am. Oh, why was I ever born?"

Uncle Malcolm's ugly words replayed in her head. "You don't de-serve an honorable suitor. No decent man would have you for any-thing other than a mistress."

Harry blinked away the tears clouding her eyes. Her gaze fixated on the window, and the view of the sea beyond, but her mind paid no attention to the wheeling gulls and rolling waves.

Mistress. Rising to her feet in a dreamlike state, she knelt before her steamer trunk and dug past a mountain of ill-fitting clothing to find her collection of books at the bottom. Withdrawing *Le Morte d'Arthur,* she returned to her bed and flipped through the pages. *I know what I have to do now.* Her stomach flopped at the thought, but at last a practical answer came clear. *If I'm brave enough to take hold of it, that is.*

Chapter 12

EEPLY asleep, Devin still fixated on Harry. Her face as he'd last seen her, stricken and sad, tortured his dreams. In his imagination, he took his beloved in his arms the way he'd longed to do at the tea shop. She felt so real, her warmth in his embrace, the scent of her washing over him, igniting his desire. The potent mingling of arousal and protectiveness he felt for her welled up until he thought he might burst with it. Knowing he was dreaming, he felt freer to indulge in the fantasy he scarcely dared entertain while awake. *It would be far too easy to take advantage, and that's the last thing I want.*

But in this dream moment, he allowed himself the luxury of unfastening her ill-fitting gown, drawing it down her arms and letting it pool on the floor. He imagined her tawny skin, bare and nearly glowing in the lamplight as her dark eyes turned to polished amber. Her innocent, kissable lips curled into a seductive smile. In his dream, she wore no corset, and only the most rudimentary of undergarments—a threadbare camisole with lacy straps and a pair of knee-length bloomers—to guard her most intimate places from his gaze, from his touch.

He drew in an unsteady breath, propping himself against the headboard as she knelt before him and slowly lowered one strap of her chemise, gradually baring one of the breasts he'd try so hard not to imagine. Not too large, but not too small, a dainty globe crowned with a pale brown peak.

"Beautiful," he murmured. "Now the other."

She seemed to know instinctively how to tease, revealing herself to him by inches. His sex swelled, tenting his nightshirt, and he realized dimly that he'd have to get his sheets cleaned in the morning. It all seemed worthwhile now, as he dreamed of his future, of claiming Harry for himself.

"Come here, love," he urged. "I want to touch you there."

She crawled forward, sensual as a cat, and straddled his lap. Aching to see his hands on her flesh, he grasped both breasts, weighing and gently shaping them. His thumbs traced her nipples, drawing a whimper from her.

"Do you like that?" he asked.

"Ahhh," she sighed, which he took to be an affirmative. Continuously stroking one erect nub, he lowered his face to the pillowy cushion of her breast and claimed the other with an authoritative lick. The already hard peak tightened further, reaching for more stimulation, which he was happy to provide. Nipping, sucking and licking her breast, Devin tutored his lady in the ways of sensual pleasure. Harry gasped and squirmed, but never tried to pull away. Her body was ready for loving, and he aimed to give it to her. *She'll be my wife as soon as I can manage it,* he told himself. *There's no harm in taking a taste in my dreams.*

Aggravated by the nightshirt that blocked them from skin to skin contact, he dragged the offending garment over his head and tossed it away, then tugged Harry's chemise from her body. Now she sat topless upon his naked frame, and a hint of fear registered in her eyes. Devin kept her gaze, staring deep into her soul as he pulled pin after pin from her dark hair. With an audible swish, the mass of shimmering brown silk cascaded around her slender bare shoulders, covering her breasts from his view. He ran his fingers up her arm, sweeping the hair to her back and sliding his fingers along her scalp, holding her in place so he could take her mouth in a deep, stunning kiss.

Harry opened eagerly this time, meeting his tongue with hers even as she captured his free hand and drew it back to her breasts.

She won't be this bold when the time comes, he realized. Though he found the dream enjoyable, he knew an innocent like Harry would likely feel awkward and uncomfortable when he began to touch her body in earnest. So, against that day, Devin enjoyed his dreamy caressing of his fantasy Harry's soft curves. Breasts gave way to ribs, the dip of a slender waist, the roundness of a womanly hip. Through his one-handed exploration, he kept Harry locked in a passionate kiss, one she eagerly returned. Drinking in her pleasured whimpers, Devin's arousal swelled and expanded to fill his entire being.

Please, morning, don't come too soon. I want to continue this dream as long as possible.

He opened the ties of her pantalets and eased the garment past her hips. She shifted to help him, and the soft white fabric pooled around her knees. Devin took a long look at her, taking in the symmetry of her curvy softness, until at last his eyes were drawn to her final secret, the dark curls at the apex of her thighs. He met her nervous gaze for a moment before reaching for her. He wanted to see his hand between her legs, to know her womanhood was his for the claiming. His fingers parted her plump lips, revealing juicy folds to his touch. *She's wet.* He grinned as he spread her moisture.

Harry whimpered, squirming against the intimate touch, but Devin would not be dissuaded. He sought through her most intimate places until he found his target. A hiss told him the knot of tissue under his finger was the seat of her sexual pleasure. With practiced care, he circled and stroked it, gauging the speed and pressure based on her whines and cries, and on the growing wetness that would soon ease his entry into her body.

Harry's hands landed on his shoulders and she clung to him for support as he pleasured her. Knowing she was approaching orgasm, he applied several firm strokes directly to her clitoris. Her body went rigid as a squeal of ecstasy tore itself from her lips.

Devin held her up with one hand on her hip while he worked her through the peak, and then rolled her beneath him. Her dark hair fell like a chocolate waterfall over his pillow. She moved, drawing her pantalets down from her knees and over her feet, leaving her completely naked and ready for his conquering. She extended her arms to him.

Devin knelt between her spread thighs, carefully bracing his weight. *I'm too big to lie on her. She's so petite.* While he'd been pleasuring his lady, he'd been able to ignore his own desperate arousal. But now, moments from completion, he knew he'd never last. Grasping one knee in each hand, he spread her wide. The tiny portal of her body beckoned. Devin took the invitation, covering her, though his weight remained braced on his arm. *This is the most vivid dream I've ever had.*

He positioned his sex and arched his hips.

Harry let out a protesting gasp and tried to wiggle away, but it was too late. The tip of Devin's erection remained planted inside her. One hard thrust embedded him to the hilt in the tightest, hottest, most deliciously clinging sweetness. He groaned, sweat popping out on his forehead.

This time, Harry didn't just whimper, she let out a screech, shifting hard to escape the sharpness of her deflowering.

The movement overwhelmed Devin and he went off like a shot, as though it was his first time as well as hers.

In his previous dreams about Harry, he'd awakened in a puddle of his own making, cold, spent and uncomfortable. This time full awareness dawned in a different sort of shock. "Oh my God!" Dark eyes really were looking back at him, wincing with discomfort. She looked as though she were in shock.

"Harry, what the devil are you doing?" he demanded. "Why are you here?" He levered himself off her and flopped on his back, arm over his eyes. "I can't believe this. I just can't believe it," he muttered. While his mind fought and sifted through mingled dream and memory, his body tingled with the aftermath of pleasure.

Beside him, Harry made a frantic grab for the bedclothes and yanked them over her trembling frame.

After a moment, a small, warm hand closed around his arm. Without thought, Devin hauled her up against him, cradling her naked body in his arms. He turned to his side, so he could envelop her completely, unsurprised to find her crying.

"Love, why?" he asked, more gently this time, as the shock began to fade. He stroked her bare back. "Why did you come here? Was this what you wanted?"

She nodded against his chest.

He tucked a finger under her chin and lifted her face. The moonlight shining through his bedroom window illuminated her tear-stained eyes. "No you didn't," he contradicted her. "You were looking for a slow courtship before your uncle interfered. What's going on, love? You know you don't need to trap me, right? I want to marry you. Yes, our plans are changing, but you're in no danger of losing me, I promise."

She mumbled something he couldn't hear.

Sighing, Devin tucked the covers over himself and his beloved and took her in his arms again.

"Harry, are you able to talk?" he asked.

She made a wry face, but he was glad to note her sobs had faded to the occasional sniffle and her eyes, though red, were dry.

"You know I love you, don't you?" he demanded.

"Yes," she admitted.

"Do you think I'm a roué, a seducer of innocent girls?"

"Of course not," she replied, looking startled by the implication.

"Then why did you treat me like one?" he demanded. "I wanted this all to be perfect for you, love. I know your life has been harder than it should have been. If you know I love you, then you know this wasn't necessary."

"It is," she insisted. "You... you're wonderful, Devin. I love you more than words can say. I hope that never changes." She rested her forehead on his chest. He scrunched her silky hair in his hands.

"I've committed to this, to us, Harry, and it's not a burden. I don't know if I've ever felt like this about anyone before."

"Devin," she started, and then her mouth opened and closed a few times. *She did this earlier today. Whatever her secret is, she must think it's terrible.*

At last, Harry finally seemed to steel herself enough to speak. "I can't marry you, Devin. I... no. It's not possible. I would only hurt you. But I can't let you go."

"Harry, why...?"

She laid her fingers over his lips, cutting off the flow of words. "Don't ask questions, my love, Please. I can't answer them. Trust me, there are things about me I can't bear for you to know. I'm... indecent. I don't want to harm you, so I can't be your wife. Devin, can't you..." she trailed off, her cheeks flaming.

"Can't I what, love? What are you asking me to do?"

She drew in a deep breath and released it. "Can you... be... my protector?"

He blinked. "Protector like... like a lover? Like you'd be my mistress?"

Harry nodded.

"No." Devin shook his head, the pillow rustling beneath his cheek. "Even if I were willing to put you in such position, which I'm not, you being a *decent* girl, I have a reputation to maintain as well."

"What do you mean?" her eyes widened. "I thought..."

"You thought I'd behave like the nobility? That I'd keep a discreet woman on the side while I went on with my life, eventually marrying someone 'fitting' and keeping two distinct existences?"

She nodded.

"Not a chance," he replied. "Listen, love. I'm nothing like that. I was raised to believe in love and marriage, to hate adultery. This abuse of your reputation... you'd become an outcast, don't you realize? Your cousin would never be allowed near you again. Neither would Katerina."

"I'd have you," she replied. "That would be enough for me."

"It shouldn't be," he insisted. "Don't sell yourself so cheaply."

"I have no choice," she forced out through gritted teeth. "I have no other options."

"Harry, I wish you could help me understand why our most recent plan... to marry as soon as possible... is no longer an option in your mind."

She gave him a stubborn look.

"Well then, let me explain something else. I can't keep a mistress. My position as a solicitor balances on a razor's edge every day. If any hint of scandal or bad behavior arises around my practice, I'd lose my license. As a servant of the law, I'm expected, no, required to remain above reproach."

A look of horror dawned on Harry's pretty face.

"That's why I wish you had talked to me, darling. What you're thinking... it can't work."

Her lip trembled. "Have I ruined everything?"

"No, love. Of course not. It's only... our plans have gone from nebulous to definite. I'll send a telegram to my father in the morning, requesting he contact a bishop we know to procure a special license. As soon as it's ready, we'll be married." *This isn't how I wanted to do this, but what choice do I have? I've ruined her. I won't abandon her too.* Of course, lying next to Harry, holding her naked body in his arms, she didn't seem ruined. *She seems like she's mine.* He kissed her forehead.

"I don't think this is right," she said softly.

"It's too late to worry about it now," he replied. "I love you, and we're getting married. The discussion is over."

He watched a silent battle play across her face and finally settle into relief. Her acceptance soothed a pounding discomfort in his chest he hadn't wanted to acknowledge. *She wants this. Whatever she's hiding, she thinks it prevents her from getting what she wants, but she truly does want us to be together.* As to her dark secret, he didn't pay it much mind. *No doubt it's far less serious than she fears. Nothing short of murder would dissuade me at this point.*

He'd thought she was probably concealing a sexual indiscretion, based on how ashamed she'd been, but her pained yelp and the sharp resistance a moment ago proved it was not true. *And would also not have been too serious to me. It's the woman I love, not her virginity.* Especially as her virginity was now gone, thanks to her plotting and his lack of awareness.

Sighing, Devin settled back down against the pillows and pulled his beloved close to him.

"Rest, darling. Sleep. Tomorrow, we'll work out how this is going to be handled. But we'll get through it together."

Harry sniffled, but her eyes were already closing.

Chapter 13

ORNING light filtered onto Harry's face, drawing her up from sleep into awareness. She opened her eyes to an unfamiliar room. *Why am I sleeping naked... and why does this bed feel so strange?* To her right, a window overlooked the long, low seashore and the softly rolling sea. To the right... Harry jumped back with a startled squawk, a moment before memories of the previous night filtered through.

Devin opened his eyes and she watched as morning light revealed a process from confusion to consternation to determination. *In a way, it's a relief for him to take charge. He's so strong and brave. It's nice to feel protected and cared for again. It's been so long.* One long, muscular arm snaked around her, drawing her against his solid frame.

The contrast of her feminine softness against his strength melted even more of the knotted fear inside her. *Tell him,* her conscience urged. *Tell him the truth. You know he won't abandon you. Not now.* It occurred to her with painful intensity that she might have subconsciously orchestrated this to trap him, just as he'd suggested, knowing the truth would have to come out eventually. *But then mightn't he resent you? Do you want a husband who looks at you with disappointment in his eyes?* And yet, Devin had been so fair-minded. Would he really blame her for a past she couldn't help? What had seemed impossible yesterday, when she lay mired in fear and despair, today seemed likely. *He loves me.* Somehow, her shy, bookish demeanor had been exactly what drew him to her. Her position, her lowered status, all of it, meant nothing to him. Their souls resonated together, and that, apparently, was all that mattered to Devin. *Tell him,* her conscience urged again.

But before she could steel herself to speak, his lips crushed the words back inside her, chasing them down as he drove his tongue into her mouth. Harry moaned at the forceful kiss. She grinned to herself. While she'd been ruminating on deep, dark thoughts, Devin had obviously been admiring her naked curves. *Well, girl, looks like you're about to be bedded again,* she thought with an internal sigh. *The first time was nice enough, though embarrassing... except the end.*

Though she'd expected some pain, the sharp sting had taken her breath away. She could still feel the ache. *But your maidenhead is gone, so it should be easier this time.* Sure enough, Devin's hand crept to her bare breast, thumbing the nipple to tingling hardness. *Now, this is nice, she decided.* The heat of arousal flared in her belly. She surrendered herself to Devin's kiss, to his touch. *Last night, he sucked them. I liked that too,* she recalled. *How strange that what seems so embarrassing to think about feels so good.* Devin's fingers closed around the aching bud, delivering a firm pinch that drove coherent thought clean out of her head. She whimpered. Devin drew back, staring at her with an expression that blended amusement and resignation.

"I can't resist you, love. Not anymore."

She nodded, her tongue frozen in her mouth.

"I hope you understand what you're getting into."

Still unable to speak, Harry reached out and stroked a strand of sleep-tousled hair from Devin's face. Her palm slid down his cheek, enjoying the sensation of stubble under her fingertips, before shyly tracing further. His neck, shoulder, and finally his chest found their way under her questing hand. He grasped her hand and pinned it to the bed beside her, tumbling her to her back and covering her body with his.

"I love you, Harry. Never doubt it," he murmured.

At last, she found her will to speak. "I love you too, Devin. I love you so much."

"You belong to me now." His voice a growl, he lowered his face and kissed the side of her neck, before delivering a stinging nip.

She gasped. "All to you. All of me belongs to you."

He laughed, a soft chuckle. "I know, and in case you've forgotten, I'll claim every inch."

She gulped. Between her thighs, moisture had surged, combining the aftermath of last night's intimacy with this morning's fresh arousal. But the thought of his large man-part pushing back inside still frightened her.

"Don't worry, Harry," he whispered, his lips so close to her ear. "Now that I know I'm not dreaming, I'll be gentle with you. Last night I was too rough. Naughty girl. If you'd just been patient, I could have taken you so slowly, you'd have only felt the tiniest sting." Then, his words seemed to register on his passion-befuddled brain. He lifted up again. "You're not too sore, are you?"

"I... I don't know," she stuttered, not sure how to be so matter-of-fact about her own body, her own sexual feelings.

"How do you feel inside?" he demanded.

Heat flared to painful intensity in her face and she closed her eyes as modesty fought a battle with the desire to answer.

"I don't know," she repeated.

Devin released her hand and pulled back, kneeling beside her tightly closed legs. "Don't be shy, darling. We're lovers now, and soon we'll be married. Open." He grasped her ankles and spread her, positioning himself in the aperture.

She wanted to beg him not to look. It seemed so wrong, so scandalous for him to gaze upon her intimate parts. Biting her lip, she submitted to the indignity, knowing Devin's experience would have to be her guide, since her knowledge came from rumors and gossip.

His hands slid up her inner thighs, pushing them just a bit wider. And then, as she'd expected, he touched the outer lips of her sex.

She inhaled sharply. The gentle caress seemed to be just what her body wanted. A jolt of heat that had nothing to do with embarrassment speared through her insides.

"That's it," he said in a gentle, approving tone, "I knew you'd be a passionate girl. I love it. Don't hold back from me, Harry."

The cool air touched her innermost folds, and she knew he'd opened her to his gaze. She swallowed hard and dared to peek at Devin's face. His expression as he regarded her most intimate secrets held nothing of triumph or conquest, only of tender love and determination. A sudden recollection of the previous night rose up in her mind, of a sensitive spot she'd scarcely known she possessed. When he'd touched it, her world had gone up in flames. *Will he touch it again?* She wanted him to. That fiery passion had drowned awareness, reducing her to a mindless rutting animal. *I want that.* A gentle thumb dragged over the spot.

"Ahhhh," she sighed. *How can anything feel so good?* Devin knew just how to touch her body. He circled the nub with his thumb, drawing gasps and sighs from her. Then a slight stretch added to the sensation as he slipped one finger deep into her well. He eased his finger in and out, never stopping his dangerous caressing of her clitoris, and the heat in her belly seemed to gather up into a coil, ever tightening as the peak she had experienced built again.

A little moan escaped her lips when he withdrew his one finger and returned with two. This time, she could feel the ache of her recent deflowering. And yet… *I want him to continue. I want this.* The realization caused her eyes, which she'd closed to focus on the sensations, to fly open. Suddenly beyond shame, she watched Devin's face as he pleasured her. Saw the fierce, intense focus in his eyes as he channeled all his love into his hands, spreading it through her untutored body. He seemed to be willing her to accept, to embrace this new aspect of their relationship.

Though the stretch inside her had taken on a hint of discomfort, it barely registered through the pleasure that raged hotter than a blast furnace in her core. She knew, on an instinctive level, that the pleasured peak she'd experienced the previous night was his goal. She locked her knees and arched her hips, reaching for it.

Pleasure exploded. Her body arched and twisted with the force of it. So strong was the climax, she scarcely noticed when Devin withdrew his penetrating fingers and shifted position. He steadied her with a hand on her flank and met her eyes.

Her breathing ragged, she drew him down to kiss her as he eased gently into her clenching passage. The sore flesh stung hard as he stretched it wide, but she offered no protest. Instead, she arched up to meet him, loving him more than she feared pain, and wanting to return a measure of the pleasure he'd shown her.

This time, after the previous night's release, he took longer to reach his completion. Her pleasure had waned, and she considered the sensation of his erection pushing into her body and then pulling back again. The uncomfortable stretching had eased, though soreness lingered. The growing ecstasy in his eyes, the tightness around his mouth, stilled her protest. Hesitantly she bent her knees and was rewarded with a soft tingle as the change in angle brought him in contact with a sensitive spot inside her. *Someday this will all be very nice*, she realized. *So both the English and the Indians were correct. It does hurt... at first. But it also feels good.*

"Argh, God! Harry," he groaned. Scalding liquid bathed the mouth of her womb.

I suppose... being bedded is... nice, she decided. *I don't dislike this at all... though I do hope the soreness fades quickly.*

She winced as Devin withdrew from her aching sex and settled her in for a long cuddle. Lying on his back, he pulled her to his side, her head on his shoulder. They drowsed in the lingering glow of spent passion.

* * *

Devin woke to the knowledge he would be late to work. Though no one checked up on the number of hours he spent in the office, lounging in bed was no way to make money. He rose from the bed with a quiet groan.

Harry muttered in her sleep and rolled to her other side.

The sight of her made him smile. *This isn't how I wanted to do this, but my Lord she feels amazing. Little minx. How I love her.*

She had certainly thrown a wrench in the gears of their courtship. *Well, to be fair, her uncle did that. She just panicked a little and made an ill-thought-out decision.* Now, looking at her sleeping peacefully in his bed, he couldn't bring himself to regret a thing. Deliberately defying Malcolm Fletcher while guarding his most deeply held secrets felt like trying to contain a waterspout in a cigar box, and the old man's hypocrisy was the cause of the spinning. *Decorum... propriety... manners... and whorehouses?* Having nailed down the source of Fletcher's extra income, Devin now wished he didn't know.

The law is vague, and I suppose owning shares in the company isn't strictly illegal, but for heaven's sake... fussing about my desire to marry Harry and then taking advantage of desperate girls. The knowledge sat uncomfortably in the pit of Devin's stomach, but since no laws were being broken, it was his job to keep the information confidential.

Shoving the distasteful ideas out of his head, he crossed the room, careful to avoid the squeaky floorboard in the middle, and washed up at his commode. *I should probably take a bath,* he thought, realizing his lovemaking with Harry had left him sweaty. Not to mention... he looked down at himself and sighed. No time for a proper bath, he washed their mingled juices from his sex and pulled on his clothing, before emptying out the washbasin and refilling it.

Leaning over, he kissed Harry on the cheek.

She stirred, dark eyes fluttering open.

"I have to go, my love," he told her.

"Mmmm," she hummed in a wordless protest.

Should I stay? After such a momentous night, she's probably feeling uncertain. I don't want her to be afraid. But no, her true security would come from their permanent, legal relationship. *She'll be fine. And I have to see to our future. She's my responsibility and I won't let her down.*

"I'm sorry. I have to. I have work to do, and I have a very important telegram to send."

She blinked, awareness dawning slowly.

"Promise me you'll stay inside. Don't go anywhere. If anyone should see you, there could be trouble."

"I will," she said, suddenly looking afraid. "I have nowhere to go, anyway."

"I love you, Harry. This will all be straightened out before you know it."

She nodded but the fear lingered in her eyes. Devin sighed. *There won't be any fixing it, I suppose, until the marriage contract is signed, executed and consummated.* He kissed her lips one last time and headed out into the street.

* * *

The sound of Fanny's nervous whispering drew Malcolm's attention away from the stack of reports he was scanning. More interested in the fact that the clubs in India in which he had heavily invested had turned record profits, he tried to tune out the girlish chatter.

Again the feminine sound cut through the silence, shattering his attention. With a sigh, Malcolm rose from his desk and stalked to the door, which stood slightly ajar. *Damned chits. I wish they would go outside.* He drew in a deep breath to roar at Fanny and Harry, only to draw up short.

Fanny stood in the parlor, of course, and her blond-headed fiancé held her closer than was really appropriate, one arm around her waist. Even in profile, he could see the worry in Fanny's face. What he could not see was Harriet. *Damn the wench, she's supposed to chaperone Fanny when young William comes around. If she went sneaking off to see Bennett... wait, that's exactly what she must have done.* He expelled his breath in a whoosh. *I'll have her job for this. Not even nine in the morning, and she's not here? What the devil can it mean?* It didn't mean anything good. Of that he was certain.

That Harriet was not with Fanny this early made him deeply suspicious. *Did she even sleep here at all?* Of course, she might be ill, she might be in bed. *Pray God that's it. She'll never be so grateful for a headache. I should ask Fanny what's going on...* but no, his daughter was loyal to the wench, and would undoubtedly lie to protect her.

Ringing for a manservant, he barked a terse, quiet order and settled back into his desk to wait.

* * *

The next time Harry opened her eyes, she felt no surprise at being alone, nor was she overly perturbed. Though the situation felt strange and a bit unsettling, she wasn't sad. *Maybe embarrassed,* she admitted privately as she stared unseeing out the bedroom window to the rose garden beyond. By the cold light of day, the plan to creep into Devin's bed like a modern-day Morgana seemed foolish beyond belief. *Impulsive, Harry. And unnecessary. You just robbed yourself of a beautiful wedding night.* Well, she amended, it could still be beautiful. Devin would see to it. But it could no longer be her first time. Gratitude welled up when she found herself alone. With so much to consider, having to see someone—anyone—didn't strike her as desirable. Finding something to eat, however, did. Her stomach rumbled and her throat stung with thirst.

Rising, she blushed to realize her state of nudity... not to mention the fluids leaking from her intimate places. A quick glance at the bed revealed what she had expected; a streaky mess of blood marred the white sheets, not in excessive amounts, but enough to be certain what had happened there. *I'll have to see if I can get it cleaned up. I'm ruined and it can't be fixed, but maybe the sheets don't have to be.*

Ruined. Such a strange word. As though she should crumble like an abandoned monument for being deflowered before her time. She didn't feel like a wreck. Despite the uncertainty, she actually felt better than she had in ages. *Devin loves me. Devin wants to marry me—will marry me.* That fact alone made her feel comfortable, secure and safe. As she wiped away the evidence of her naughtiness, she longed for a bath. Many aches radiated through her muscles and not only her internal places, where Devin had claimed her. Too many nights tossing and turning in a cheap and uncomfortable bed had left her hips and shoulders hurting. Her head ached from stress and crying, and her eyes felt burned.

It wasn't until she finished her ablutions that she realized she had only her clothing she'd worn with her. Though she'd donned clean garments for her clandestine nighttime plotting, they wouldn't stay clean forever. Particularly the pantalets. *I really did go off half-cocked, didn't I? Heavens. Whatever shall I do now? I can't go back to the hotel without alerting Uncle Malcolm, which would undoubtedly cause the scandal Devin is scrambling to prevent.* It occurred to her just how much trouble she'd caused for the man she loved, how much risk she'd put him in, and her heart sank. *Remember what mother used to tell you? Control your impulsiveness? Just how disgusted would she be with you right now, hussy?*

Of course, Harry remembered, if her mother had lived, someone like Devin would never have been considered beneath her. Their relationship could have progressed naturally, along prescribed patterns, and her damned uncle's opinion wouldn't have mattered. *Pure wishful thinking, miss. The whole powder keg was about to blow up right underneath you regardless. You're lucky you landed in as good a spot as you did.* The idle speculation irritated Harry even more. Pulling on her clothing—pantalets, chemise, and a hand-me-down day dress her cousin had discarded, she padded barefoot through the house, exploring. *Surely Devin won't mind, if this is to be my home as well.*

Across the hall from the bedroom, a small but functional kitchen yielded a loaf of bread so fresh, it must have been delivered that morning, a dish of creamy butter and a small pitcher of milk. Quickly rummaging through the cabinets, she found a tin of tea and a cup. The kettle already sat on the cookstove, so she lit the fire within and pumped water at the sink pump for her tea. *Easier to explore after breakfast.*

Her exertions the previous night and this morning had left her ravenous, and she devoured two thick slices of buttered bread while the kettle heated. A cup of steaming, milky tea dispersed some of her wilder ruminations and left her clearer in the head and better able to grasp her situation. *Yes, I made a horrible muddle of everything, but*

Devin doesn't seem overly perturbed by it, the dear man. He adapted quickly to the change in plans... and soon I'll be his bride.

The scenario pleased her, as it resembled one of her favorite salacious novels, but again she was struck by how uncomfortable living in a romance actually proved to be.

With a deep sigh, she rinsed her cup and plate and pushed her chair up to the small kitchen table before exploring the rest of the house. The sitting room she'd already seen, but she took a moment to peruse Devin's reading selections on the bookshelves lining the interior wall near the fireplace.

Eclectic, to say the least, she concluded, noting novels smashed in cheek-by-jowl with books of sermons and folios of poetry. Devin even had a full shelf dedicated to law books, though this proved less surprising than some of the novels she discovered. Leafing through one, she quickly returned it to the shelf. *Seems he likes a naughty read just as much as I do.* The thought pleased her, and though her snooping embarrassed her, she felt far from guilty for doing it.

Small house, Harry realized, when she arrived in the entry hall. *Now, what am I going to do? I suppose I could try to clean the sheets.*

She meandered back to the bedroom, where a small basket drew her eye. Inside, an assortment of men's clothing lay seemingly abandoned. Harry lifted a white cotton shirt and discovered a separated seam in the shoulder. A pair of trousers had a hole in the region of the left buttock, and a whole pile of socks needed darning. *Ah ha. Here's where my usefulness begins.* A sewing basket in the wardrobe provided needles and thread, and Harry opened the living room window to listen to the quiet conversation of the sea and the shrieking of gulls as she whiled away the hours repairing Devin's damaged clothing.

Chapter 14

"ANNY, I'm only going to ask you this once, and I expect the honest truth from you. Do you understand?"

Fanny looked at her father and for the first time in her life, feared him. She nodded, her lip between her teeth.

"Where is your accursed lady's maid?"

"Harry? Why I... I don't know," she answered honestly. "She didn't answer my ring this morning, and when I checked the maids' quarters, she wasn't there. All her clothing was there, but she was gone."

Her father's teeth ground so hard, she could hear it from the other side of the desk. "Where is she? Where did she go?" His hands clenched into purple fists.

"I swear, I don't know!" Fanny cried. "She didn't say a word to me. Last night, she said she was feeling ill and wanted to go to bed early. That's the last time I saw her."

"So help me, girl, if you're lying..."

"I'm not!" Fanny covered her face in her hands and gasped in several unsteady breaths.

"She must have gone to him," Malcolm muttered under his breath. "They're all conspiring against me, and you're part of it," he added, turning to his daughter. "Admit it."

"Yes." Fanny lifted her head defiantly. "Yes, I am. You're wrong about her, about Devin. They were made for each other."

"She's a cheap, lying whore," Malcolm snarled. "Do you really think a decent man of business like Bennett deserves that?"

"What utter nonsense!" Fanny laughed bitterly in her father's face. "Harry is a kind, intelligent, gentle creature and has done nothing to earn your scorn. I think you're right, she has gone to him. And I also think you should let her go. Stop fussing. She has what she wants now, and it's not your business anymore."

Malcolm fixed his youngest child with a narrow-eyed glare. "I'll see her in hell first." His quiet tone frightened Fanny far more than his blustering had. "And you'll be sorry for abetting her."

His open palm connected with her cheek before she could react, knocking her sideways. Grabbing a thick handful of long black hair, he dragged her over to the desk. Fanny shrieked and struggled helplessly in his grip. "Be still," he insisted. He tossed her down, so her belly knocked solidly against the wood. Her sobs turned to gasps. Stunned, she was unable to move as he seized a cane that rested against the side of the desk. It whistled as he swung it through the air and connected against her thighs with a solid thump. Oddly, it took a moment for the pain to register, but then a fire-bright agony bloomed. She yelped, but he wasn't finished. Another heavy blow, and then a third turned her buttocks to solid flame.

"Don't you *ever* defy me again, girl," he hissed. "Or today's thrashing will seem like a pleasant day at the beach. Now get out of my sight."

Weeping, clutching her aching bruises, she stumbled from the room. Though he had won this round, Fanny was more determined than ever that he should lose the war. *Both Harry and I will be far from him before he even knows what happened.*

* * *

Malcolm flopped down into his chair with a deep sigh, his anger ebbing away and being replaced with sorrow. *This whole damnable mess is beyond comprehension. What did I do to deserve it? Why couldn't she just behave? What the devil am I going to do with her now? Greedy chit.*

He lowered his forehead to his desk with an audible thump.

His own daughter's complicity made it worse. He'd hated being so hard on her. Of course, if he could explain, he knew she would comply, but he'd promised not to tell. *Makes me look like a villain, but no one understands. Ah, such struggles, being the head of the household.*

A knock at the door shook him from his unpleasant contemplations. "Come in," Malcolm barked.

The disreputable-looking figure who stepped into the room set the gears in the nobleman's head turning, and the absolute answer to everyone's problems suddenly sprang to life.

* * *

By the time Devin returned home after his day of work, dusk had nearly fallen. *I wonder how Harry passed her day alone in my cottage—our cottage,* he quickly amended, smiling at the thought of sharing his living space with his beloved.

Unlocking the door, he stepped over the threshold and into a scene of domestic tranquility. A cozy fire crackled on the hearth, dispelling the chill of the evening and the sea and casting a flickering orange light through the room. Harry, his Harry, perched on the settee, a basket of neatly folded clothing at her feet. The silver glint of a needle flashed in the firelight as her nimble fingers dragged white thread through gleaming cotton. A scent of stew wafted through the house, setting his stomach rumbling.

"Hello, my love," he said mildly, amazed by all he was seeing. "What are you working on there?"

Harry raised her head, amusement dancing in her pretty dark eyes. "Well, first I mended your clothing. Do you have any idea how many holey socks you had, love?"

"A fair guess," he admitted. Though the potent lure of dinner tempted him toward the kitchen, he forced himself to join Harry. "I was about to purchase new ones, since I don't precisely know how to fix them myself. When my mother comes to town, she helps me, but she's not due for another two weeks, and I was running out of clean pairs."

"Not anymore." Harry grinned, showing her straight white teeth framed by plump pink lips.

"You didn't have to mend my clothing," he told her, startled by her industry. *You shouldn't be. She's been working hard for a living since her adolescence. I suppose idleness would suit her far more poorly.*

"Yes I do," she replied. "If I'm to be your wife, Devin, that's exactly what I need to be doing." Her smile widened.

"Well, perhaps, but, Harry…" He paused to frame his words with care. "You were chafing in service, love. It bothered you. Why are you eager to darn my socks when you resented darning your cousin's?"

Harry blinked in surprise, her dark, delicate eyebrows drawing together. She inhaled slowly before speaking. "I suppose, because of what it means. If I mend Fanny's clothing, it means I'm a domestic, a servant. I don't mean to imply that service is a lesser thing. It's honest work. But other maidservants have the option of living a life as well. They fall in love, marry, and have families of their own if they desire. The problem with my service is that such things were denied me. I never minded the work itself. In fact, I'm rather good at it."

She drew the thread through the fabric again. "I would much prefer this to be my contribution to my family than to someone else's. Does that make sense?"

"It does," he replied. "I believe I understand now. Very well then. Do you think you might put the sewing aside for a bit? I have a powerful desire to taste whatever it is you've been cooking."

"Of course, my darling!" Harry exclaimed, tucking the needle into the shirt and dropping it on top of the basket. "I'm certain I'll need something to do tomorrow as well."

He offered his hand and she took it, allowing him to help her to their feet. Together they skirted the sofa and traversed the hallway to the kitchen. Devin seated himself at the table while Harry dished up a rich and fragrant stew. Here, so close to the cooking pot, he could detect a subtly unusual aroma to it. Something exotic that seemed to have blown in on a seafaring breeze.

"What did you make, love?" he asked.

"I found some lamb," she replied. "And I stewed it with herbs, spices and new vegetables from your garden."

"It smells like nothing I've tasted before," he replied. *How fortunate the neighbor brought by some excess meat the other day in exchange for my help in repairing her garden wall last spring.*

"I used some spices that are common in India. You had mustard seeds, cardamom and ginger in your cabinet there. Some turmeric, coriander and cumin would have been perfect, but I made do. I hope you enjoy it."

"I'm sure I will," he replied, trying to be kind, but cardamom and ginger on lamb struck him as a bit odd.

Still, when she set a deep bowl of her steaming concoction in front of him, he dug in with relish. *I'm hungry enough to eat the damned lamb raw, so anything should taste good at this point.* Fanny joined him with her own, much smaller portion.

The exotic spices burst in his mouth like rockets, not all at once in a dizzying confusion, but one after another, creating a choreographed display of flavors and sweet heat.

He chewed and swallowed. "This is delicious," he told her honestly. "I think I'm going to like having a wife."

"And I know I will like having a husband," she replied, "as long as it's you."

He made a face at her silly quip. "There had better be no other contenders," he commented.

She laid a hand over his. "I don't want any others," she replied.

Devin smiled before returning his attention to his bowl. Torn between wolfing down the repast like a starving beast and savoring every morsel, he concentrated his focus on the exotic stew, draining the bowl in record time and mopping up the gravy with a slice of bread.

At last, he sat back with a sigh, patting his satisfied belly. "You'll turn me into a fat country gentleman in no time."

She giggled.

"Well, my love, would you fancy a bath?"

"Oh, yes!" she replied. "I tried to wash up this morning, but I still feel ever so strange."

"And sore?" Devin suggested.

"Yes, a little," she admitted. "I found the necessary out back, but where do you keep your bathtub?"

Devin sighed. "One of the inconveniences I put up with in this little house. I don't have a proper bathroom. I have a supposedly portable tub, but I have to fill it with buckets of water."

"Buckets you have to heat up on your cookstove?" Harry guessed.

"Precisely," he admitted. "It's a nuisance, but at least it's good exercise."

"Well then, love," Harry suggested, gathering the dishes away from the table and moving them to the sink to be washed, "why don't you exercise your muscles with the tub while I tend to the water. Do you have any larger pots than this one?" She indicated the vessel in which she'd cooked the stew.

"I do," he replied. "It's in the tub. Hold on a moment."

It turned out that the corner beside the cook stove concealed a small pantry, with a wealth of cooking staples Harry hadn't imagined. Below the lowest shelf, which rested at about waist height, a tin slipper tub waited.

Devin withdrew a large stockpot and passed it to Harry, who began to work the pump at the sink, filling the heavy vessel. With a sigh, she heaved it on the stove.

"A pity it's too dark for sewing now," she commented. "This is going to take quite a long time."

"It is," he replied. "So in the meanwhile, let me tell you about my day." He dragged the tub to the middle of the kitchen, a move which necessitated relocating the table and chairs into a row along the far wall. "I must say, it's bizarre to be making documents for your uncle, even while ignoring his express orders concerning you."

"He doesn't own me," Harry muttered.

"I realize that, my love. So at any rate, I spent what was left of the morning working on his will. Incidentally, he's into some pretty shady business dealings, but never mind about that right now. At noon I sent a telegram to my father and one to the bishop, as I said, and then I returned to work. At teatime, I received both replies. The bishop will issue the license and my father will bring it. He and mother have decided, under the circumstances, that they will be rescheduling their visit for a week earlier—that's Monday, you know—so they can be of use to us."

Harry's face turned a dusky shade of purple at the thought of meeting his parents. In truth, he didn't much care for the idea that they would know his and Harry's private business either, but under the circumstances, he wasn't quite sure what else to do.

Harry hurried to the stove to test the water. The pot was so big, she could barely lift it, and Devin removed it from her hands, dumping the contents into the tub.

He pumped a potful of tepid water to balance the scalding heat before half-filling the pot and setting it back on the stove, so it could freshen the temperature later.

Devin retrieved a stack of white embroidered bath towels and some soap and set them in easy reach of the tub.

"Ladies first," he suggested.

Harry eyed the tub and bit her lip.

"What is it?" he asked.

"It's just… I've invaded your home and caused you no end of trouble. You should at least get the fresh bathwater."

He opened his mouth to protest, and then another idea occurred to him. Quickly he set to work removing Harry's dress. She let out a startled squawk and then fell silent, submitting to his unexpected ministrations without protest.

He had her naked in moments, but instead of handing her into the tub, he undressed himself next.

"What are you doing?" she demanded, her eyes tracing over his body as he stripped, but skating nervously away from the fullness tenting his drawers.

"Exacting repayment for my troubles," he replied. Harry made a nervous face. "Come on, love, I'm joking. All I want is to share this bath with you. That way, we both get the fresh hot water… and we also have another opportunity to be close."

"So soon?"

Interesting. There's desire mingled with the dismay. She'll be a passionate wife in no time. "Yes, Harry. I'll be happy to have you as often as you let me, both now and especially after we're married."

She bit her lip and met his eyes with a heart-melting expression of trust. "All right, Devin."

He stepped into the water, hissing as the heat stung his skin, and then held out his hand to Harry. She stepped in, but they quickly discovered the tub couldn't hold two comfortably. The only place for Harry was between Devin's thighs, and even that proved a tight fit.

"I can see that the addition of a woman into my life is going to require some practical changes," Devin commented as he dipped water in a small tin cup and poured it over Harry's hair.

"Oh?" she asked. Her word blended into a hum.

"Yes. I'll need a bigger bathtub." He wetted her hair again. "Because I can already see I'll want to bathe with you again soon. But a bigger bathtub won't fit in the pantry, and I probably won't be able to move it. So I'll probably need a dedicated bathing room." He lathered up soap in his hands and began scrubbing it into her hair. She moaned. *Sounds as though she likes that as well.*

"Devin," she mumbled through a mass of hair hanging over her face.

"Yes, love?"

"You've had a woman in your life before." She spoke the words as a statement, not a question.

"Yes," he replied simply.

"Many?" She lifted her hair up out of her eyes and turned to peek at him over her shoulder.

"A few," he replied. "Why do you want to know this, love?"

"I don't know," she replied. "Despite how strong our feelings are, we've had neither time nor privacy to develop a deep knowledge of each other. Surely, it's important for us to know things about each other, even if they're uncomfortable."

Devin could sense she was building up to something. *And she's quite right. There are things we need to know about each other. Maybe if I share a bit, she'll open up about this deep, dark secret that's torturing her.* Rinsing the soap from her hair, Devin urged her back, so her head rested on her shoulder.

"When I was at school, everyone indulged in a fair bit of shenanigans with loose women. It's tradition, you know. I tried it… twice. The first time was exciting, but I felt a bit dirty the next day, though maybe it was the hangover. Second time… no. I realized I didn't like that sort of one-night association. Over the years since then, I've made friendships with a few women who were willing to play on the shady side, discretely. To me, that worked better, though I always knew something was missing." Rubbing more soap on his hands, he smoothed the lather over Harry's slender neck and shoulders. "I don't think there's any reason for you to know more."

"I think you're right," she agreed. "The knowledge makes me want to pull someone's hair. Was… was the tea shop lady one?"

"Margaret?" He sighed. "Yes. How did you figure it out?"

"The look she gave me." Harry leaned back against Devin's shoulder and made an encouraging humming sound as his soapy hands traveled over her skin.

"Margaret and I have been friends for over a year. I realized my interest in her was waning just before your family came, and I haven't been with her in a while. After I met you, I didn't want her anymore. I realized I would have to endure unrequited arousal until I could finally marry you."

"And yet you pressed for a long courtship?" Harry sat up straight, as though startled by the idea.

"Does it surprise you, darling? It shouldn't. I only wanted what was best for you, love. I still do. Life led us along a strange path to get to this place, but your best interests, your happiness, your future. Those are still my priority. To me, this is what love means." His hands slid to her breasts and he teased the puckered sharpness of each nipple, drawing a gasp from his lady. "That and making the woman I love feel as much pleasure as possible. Do you like this, Harry? I know all this touching must seem strange to you."

"It doesn't," she gasped. "I knew… some things before last night."

"You did?" The information startled Devin greatly, stilling his hands on her flesh.

"I did," she admitted without embarrassment. "I don't know if India is an earthier place than England or if my mother was simply an unusual woman, but I will never forget the day we went for a walk and saw two mongooses rolling and playing in the field, and Mother explained how their play led to babies. She told me people do much the same thing, and it's enjoyable and nothing to be ashamed of, though the rules state only married people are allowed to enjoy it. I've also been to several Hindu temples. They have no qualms about depicting the act of copulation, sometimes in exotic ways, in their religious art. From this, I got the idea that the joining of two people was sacred."

"Ideally it should be," Devin agreed, stunned by Harry's open-minded attitude. "I'm surprised you weren't schooled when you got here, though, on the 'wrong' and 'dirty' ways men force themselves on women."

"I've seen that too," she admitted. "Remember the footman I told you about? I wasn't the first girl he tried to take advantage of. I was the luckiest though. Fanny found him trying to hold me down and chased him away."

Devin considered this information. Harry had grown up with nature and the naturalness of human mating. She'd been frightened, though not truly harmed, by an overzealous seducer. The pieces of the puzzle began to fall into place. She'd been nervous but willing when she crept into his bed. And each time they came together, her nerves faded, and her natural curiosity took control more and more.

He resumed his leisurely exploration of her body, and as he expected, she acquiesced easily to each touch, considering whether each one felt pleasurable to her. While he fully expected this bath to lead to more loving, he finally felt no need to rush. His pent-up passion had been spent the previous night and following morning, and now he felt little urgency, knowing his aching sex would be relieved inside his beloved's body soon enough... and for the rest of their lives.

He urged her to sit up, and then lean forward, and traced soap over the smoothness of her back, pressing deep where he felt knotted muscles. She whimpered and then sighed as each tender place relaxed beneath his ministrations.

"Worried, Harry?"

"Not much anymore," she replied softly. "I think everything will be all right now."

"It will," he agreed. "Soon everything will be perfect."

"I look forward to the day," she said with quiet intensity.

He rinsed the water from her shoulder and kissed her in the sensitive place where it met her neck. She shivered.

Sensing from the restless shifting of her hips that she was ready for more intense lovemaking, he urged her back against him and ran his hands down her torso. The confines of the tub interfered with his desire to touch her sex, though. "Darling, how daring do you feel?" he asked.

"What do you have in mind?" she asked, and a hint of maidenly nerves found its way into her voice.

"Nothing too threatening," he assured her as he grasped one ankle in each hand and lifted them out of the water, draping her knees over the edges of the tub and leaving her completely spread. "That's better."

As he expected, she froze at the strange move but offered no protest. He cupped her mound and pressed inward with questing fingers.

"I love to touch you here," he whispered. "You're so warm and wet. So eager." The folds seemed to swell as he caressed them, though the water of their bath washed her natural moisture away. "Never lose your eagerness, Harry. It's a blessing to us both." He found the blunt point of her clitoris, erect and ready for stimulation, and obliged. Harry's unnatural stillness relaxed into melting acceptance as he led her towards completion.

Harry wriggled and squirmed, her breath catching in airy cries. Her every move and sound swelled Devin's heart—and his sex. He wanted nothing more than for them to enjoy their intimacy together in equal measure.

With his free hand, he cupped her breasts and caressed her nipples. "Oh...oh..." she whimpered. "Oh, Devin..."

"Let it happen, love," he urged. "Let yourself enjoy it."

Her bottom rubbed against his erection, sending jolts of heat through him. *Soon, soon,* he reminded himself. *No rush. Pleasure your lady.*

Harry's breathing had grown harsh, shuddering sobs of pleasure escaping through her gritted teeth. *Good girl. That's it. Almost there.*

And then a quiet whimper escaped her. Though she only cried out softly, her body went rigid in his arms, trembling with the force of her ecstasy. It rode her hard, this ecstatic climax, shaking her from the core out. He could feel the power of her peak radiating through every place they touched.

She collapsed, spent, against his chest and he smiled.

"Devin?" Harry asked in a tiny, timid voice.

"Yes, love?" He ran his fingertips up and down her arms.

"Are you sure you don't mind... you know... all the noise and fuss?"

"Now you're shy, love?" He kissed her hair. "Not a bit. I think it's every man's dream to have a wife who rejected all other suitors but desperately wants to make love with him."

She turned, somehow managing to straddle him in the narrow confines of the tub.

She eyed him in the low light, her eyes coffee dark, but with a glimmer like distant stars. Her hands slid up to cup his face and she lowered her mouth to his.

Then she released his lips and began washing him the way he had her. Rivulets of warm water wetted his hair and she lathered and rinsed it. Devin had never had a lover wash his hair before, but her soft fingertips rubbing his scalp set his whole body tingling. She chased the tingles with sudsy fingers, tracing each line of his face, his ears, his throat.

She met his eyes with a questioning look, and he nodded, encouraging her to continue. Down his chest, arms and belly she washed him, each tender touch filled with love and the return of her desire. His had never waned, of course, and the stimulation quickly passed from pleasure to torture.

At last, Devin could take no more. He rose to his full height, leaving Harry kneeling at his feet.

She lifted her face, expression uncertain.

"You want to play, little girl? Play with this." He grasped her hand and urged her towards his straining erection.

Harry hesitated, then her fingers curled around his swollen length. Devin groaned. Her warm touch sent a jolt of heat through his belly. Carefully she washed every inch of his jutting erection and even smoothed soap over his aching testicles.

"Did I do it right?" she asked.

Sweet girl. Don't be nervous. "What do you want, love? Do you want to wash me or caress me?"

"Both," she admitted, and her blush darkened so much it became visible even at such a distance.

"Well, you've succeeded. Listen, Harry, if you want to make it back to the bed before I take you again, we'd better move now."

"What will happen otherwise?" she asked, slowing standing before him. Water sluiced off her naked skin, and in that moment, she reminded him of a mermaid.

"I might just have to bend you over the table and play stallion with you," he replied, his voice low with desire.

* * *

Harry stared up at her beloved as courage and curiosity warred with maidenly restraint. *Hell with it, Harita Fletcher. You're not a maiden anymore, so don't act like one. Prudishness will not get you what you want.*

Though the words refused to pass her lips, she stepped daintily out of the tub and ran one of the towels over her body. Devin's eyes followed her.

"I used to dream about you," she told him in a sultry, slow voice. "I dreamed I was a mermaid and you were a pirate..."

"Oh really? And what happened in those dreams? Did the pirate ravish the mermaid?"

"I don't know," she admitted. "I woke up before I could find out. What do you think happened?"

Devin stepped from the tub and roughly dried himself. "I think there would be much ravishing of mermaids."

"Do you really think so?" she teased, trying to sound scared.

"Oh yes." He advanced on her with a faux threatening step. She retreated toward the table. "Besides, this mermaid wants to be ravished, doesn't she?"

Harry swallowed hard. Devin's grasped her hips and whirled her around, pressing her forward onto the table.

"Let me see what the mermaid wants." Pinning Harry to the wooden surface, he ran a proprietary hand over her naked bottom. "Let's see what this tail is hiding."

Harry opened her legs and rose up on tiptoe.

"Someone's eager," he joked. He ran his fingers over her folds. "Poor mermaid. The sea washed away your salt. Let me wet you." Devin dropped to his knees behind Harry.

At the touch of his lips on her mound, she drew in a startled breath. "Devin?"

"Hush, little mermaid. I caught you... now you're mine to feast on."

He thumbed her folds open and shocked her senseless by taking a long, wet lick of her sex.

Within moments, Harry was squirming again, but this time Devin did not bring her to orgasm.

Instead, he rose up behind her.

Harry went still as she felt the slow stroking of his penis on her bottom. She bit her lip in anticipation. *Will it still hurt this time?* She no longer felt sore, but she could still feel the stretch of the last time he'd entered her

Harry bit her lip and tried to force her muscles to relax. Devin's erection homed in on the target, touching her clitoris for a shattering moment before sliding higher. And then he rammed home in a hard thrust that stole Harry's breath. No pain, and the lush wetness eased his passage into her depths. Her gasp turned to whimpers as he began to drive in, pull back and drive in again.

He really is ravishing me, she realized, *and I like it.* She rocked her hips in time to his thrusts, meeting him stroke for stroke.

"Devin... Devin, my love," she whimpered. "Ah... ah... ahhhhh." Pleasure peaked again. Harry dropped her forehead onto the table as Devin claimed her with powerful inward drives until his own climax overtook him, dragging a shout of pleasure from the depths of his being.

A moment later, he withdrew from her body and hoisted her into his arms, carrying her past the bathtub to the bedroom, where he tucked her under the blankets with him, and they slept.

Chapter 15

LL the weekend long, Harry and Devin romped like children, and not only in bed. His elderly neighbor, the only other person who had decided to inhabit the isolated stretch of shore away from the town, had gone visiting. Devin stopped by to check her house and weed her garden and Harry, who was going mad from being trapped inside the tiny cottage, tagged along to help. They walked on the beach together in the cool of the evening and watched the sun slip beneath the waves. They tended Devin's own garden and Harry requested several new plants for her cooking ventures.

"I haven't cooked much in ages," she said with a glowing smile. "I used to haunt the kitchen back in India, and Usha, the cook, made a pet of me. She taught me all her secrets since her own daughters were grown and gone. After coming to England, Fanny took all my attention. I'm surprised my cooking has turned out as well as it has. I expected to be rusty."

"It must be in your soul," Devin replied. "Look at the things you're passionate about: reading, cooking and sewing. Making your contribution to your own household. No wonder enforced service chafed at you, love. You were born to be a middle-class wife."

"I know," she replied, leaning forward to inhale the fragrance of a bright pink rose. "Even though we're not quite where we want to be yet, I already feel more at peace."

"Do you really think this little cottage will be enough for you in the long term?" Devin asked. "It's so small."

"It is small," Harry agreed. "Once we're married and I can move around more freely and go into town, I think it will be fine. It's a bit confining to stay in the house and garden all day long. But someday we'll either need to add on or relocate."

Devin frowned.

"Because once we have a baby…" she trailed off. *Oh dear. What if he doesn't want babies?*

"Right." He exhaled a deep breath. "Maybe my brother can help. He's good with his hands. I… I just love this place. I'm glad you suggested adding on."

Harry smiled but made no comment. *He's a sensible man and will work it out on his own. No need to nag.*

A moment later he embraced her from behind and laid a gentle kiss on the side of her neck. "My parents should arrive tomorrow afternoon, and I've spoken to the priest. We're all settled for a small wedding Tuesday morning. Does that suit you, darling?"

"Yes," she replied. "Sooner the better." But then a whole wealth of girlish worries crowded into her mind.

"You've gone stiff as a board, darling. What's wrong?" Devin asked.

"It's nothing."

"Most ironic words in the English language," Devin commented, "when spoken by a woman. Tell me… or do you want me to tease it out of you?" His fingers trailed over her belly.

Harry sighed. "I just… I have nothing to wear. Nothing proper for church anyway. No corset, and these bloomers… I've had to wash them out every day just to wear them. My dress… I'm quite tired of it." She shook her head, realizing how babyish her complaint sounded.

Devin kissed her cheek. "I completely forgot. All your clothes are back at the hotel, aren't they? Should I see if your cousin can send them?"

Harry shook her head. "She's probably furious with me for sneaking away. And besides, she doesn't take care of my clothes, I take care of hers."

"Harry, your cousin adores you. I suspect she's secretly cheering you on and would think nothing of helping you."

"Sorry, Devin. I can't ask her to do that. I just can't." The lesson had been too deeply ingrained in Harry over the years and she couldn't get her head around reversing the roles. *Please don't ask for more, my beloved. Please don't argue. This isn't about Fanny, it's me. And I don't even know how to explain.*

"Are you going to ask her to see our wedding?" Devin demanded.

Again, Harry shook her head. "What if her father follows her, tries to stop us? He's quite adamant."

This time, it seemed, she'd found an argument Devin could understand, as he sagged and let the issue drop.

"I'll see if Katerina can find you something to wear," he said simply, "including some undergarments."

"I would consider that a great blessing," Harry said softly, again cursing the impulsiveness that had led to this tangled mess of a situation. *And yet, despite it all, despite the risk to his reputation and career, Devin is still here, still loves me and still wants to marry me.* The warmth of her new reality illuminated every corner of her soul until she could practically feel herself shining bright as the glow worms playing among the roses.

She turned and wrapped her arms around her man. "I don't know what I did to deserve someone as wonderful as you," she told him, willing the love she felt to spill onto him. "It must have been in some other life because nothing I've done thus far has warranted such blessings. But from this day forward, I vow to love you with every fiber of my being. With every corner of my heart."

"Harry, I love you for who you are. You don't have to become my slave to earn it. I want the wide-eyed, spirited girl in her cousin's hand-me-down clothing. I want the intelligent, teasing, open-minded woman who captured my heart. I want you, Harry, only you. I love you."

What could she do but kiss him? And so she did, a lingering, tender embrace of pure affection. His own glow of love met hers, and the magic of their souls intertwining in a quiet, sea-scented garden lit up the night with an invisible light that brightened all the dark places.

Tell him, the little voice urged. *He loves you. Tell him the truth. He won't mind.*

But Devin swept his tongue into her mouth and the thought died. He hugged her close and then escorted her back into the cottage.

* * *

Harry hummed to herself as she scrubbed the sheets. It had taken forever to heat enough water for washing, but finding the tub outside, she'd been unable to resist the opportunity. Tonight they would rest on sheets scented with sun and sea. She shivered. *And tomorrow we'll be married.*

An echo of the warm and loving glow she'd experienced the previous night turned her lips upward. *I guess living in a fairy tale isn't so bad after all.*

Morning sun warmed her face as she rose from her spot beside the tub and wrung out the sodden bedlinens. A small line stretched from one corner of the house to a sturdy apple tree, and Harry spread out the sheet upon it. A gentle breeze set the fabric to dancing. Harry couldn't help dancing along with it, her long, dark hair swirling around her back, her skirt twisting high on her calves before settling back to her ankles.

I look like a lunatic, she thought without a hint of concern.

A cloud crossed over the sun, allowing the chill to bite into her flesh, and she shivered. A hard, hot grasp clamped down on her upper arm, arresting her movement.

"Got you!" a harsh voice snarled, and sudden terror froze Harry to the ground. Trembling like a startled doe, rooted to the earth, she stared in horror at her employer, whose unwelcome presence had ruined her afternoon. "I can't believe it," Fletcher growled. "You little slut. Have you no shame?"

No, Harry thought, *I feel no shame. How can I be ashamed to have earned Devin's love?* The idea that her relationship should be based on humiliation rather than pride caused a spark of anger to flare. It solidified her resolve and loosened her tongue. "Shame, Uncle? According to you, this is the best fate to which I can aspire. Is it not enough that you relegate me to a shadow life, to the life of a man's mistress? Must I be ashamed also?"

Confusion flitted across Fletcher's face but was quickly replaced with disgust. "Faugh, you're not of my line."

"Thank God," Harry muttered.

He shook her once, a hard, jarring shock of movement. "No more out of you! Just simmer down and let's go."

"Go?" Harry raised one eyebrow. "Just where do you think I need to be going?"

Fletcher dropped her arm and dragged his bowler hat off his head, raking his fingers through his hair. When he spoke, his tone was calm and low, the sort one would use with a startled child. "It's time for you to go home, Harriet. I should have guessed you'd never belong here. Now be a good girl and come with me."

"Go...home? But this is my home, here, in this house, with Devin. Where else would I want to be?"

He shook his head. "Listen, my gel, it's not right, what you're doing. If he understood what you are... what you're bringing to his bloodline, this fantasy would end anyway."

Tears burned in the corners of Harry's eyes. "I don't believe you," she hissed. "Devin loves me. He wouldn't care."

"And yet you haven't told him," Fletcher pointed out. "If you were so sure, wouldn't you have let him know by now?"

Harry hated that he was right. "What I have or haven't discussed with Devin is none of your business, *Sir* Fletcher."

"Ah, and there I disagree. It is the duty of all proper Englishmen to protect one another, particularly from whorish foreigners and their seducing ways, now come on."

"Bastard," she hissed. "You may go to hell. I'm not leaving."

"Sorry, my dear *Harita*," he replied, her name turning his already unpleasant tone to a sneer, "but I'm not offering options." Moving faster than she would have believed a man of his age was able, he grabbed her around the middle. "Come along quietly and don't make a scene."

Harry had no intention of following his instructions. "You have no right to call me that," she snarled. Planting her heels firmly in the ground, she began to struggle furiously, scratching at his hands and elbowing his ribs until she felt torn and bruised all over. He tightened his grip, restricting her breathing, and lifted her off her feet. Cursing her small stature, Harry kicked back, her boot heels digging into Fletcher's bony shins.

He squeezed harder

Now Harry felt as though she'd been tight-laced. Black spots swam before her eyes. She drew in a tortured breath, still fighting with everything she had, and screamed out desperately for help. Her last conscious thought was that she'd wasted her breath. No one would hear her scream. Then darkness closed in on her and stole her away.

* * *

With a sigh, Malcolm lowered Harry to the ground. *She has spirit. That will serve her well in her new life.* Hoisting the girl over his shoulder, he began to walk slowly towards the gate, carrying her out towards the road, where a rough cart waited to carry her to the life she was meant to live.

Chapter 16

ARRY came to slowly. Her first awareness was of a pounding headache. A moment later, sore ribs also bloomed to fiery life. She groaned. Her chest tightened as she realized her breathing was restricted, not with the tightness that had cut off her consciousness, but with a smothering sensation. Her eyes flew open, but a film of rough brownness obscured her vision. *What's happening?* Voices resounded near her, but in her panicked state, she couldn't take in what they were saying. *Calm down, Harry. Breathe. If you can see light through the holes in... whatever this is... you won't suffocate.* Drawing air into her lungs with slow deliberation, Harry focused on the voices.

"You understand my instructions?" a familiar voice demanded. *Malcolm Fletcher, that slimy eel. What's he plotting now?*

"Of course," replied a gravelly male. "Don't listen to any lying tales. Take the girl to Bombay and leave her with Slade. She'll fit in with her kind soon enough."

"Exactly. And have Slade send me a letter in a few months. I want to know she's doing all right."

A pause and then, "Don't give me that look. I care for the wench, even though she's outgrown her station. I don't want to see her harmed. She needs to go home, is all. She needs to be with her people, not ours. She's dangerous here."

"Yes, sir," the man replied. "Time to go, sir, or I'll miss the tide and the steamer will sail without me."

"We can't have that," Fletcher replied.

Harry heard a crunch, as if someone had jumped onto a gravel road, and then Fletcher's voice called from a distance, "Remember she lies. Don't listen and don't let her go. It's for the best."

"Yes, sir," replied the rough voice close beside her.

Harry stirred and whimpered.

"Quiet, you," the rough voice snarled. "Just be still. We'll be in South-wick soon, and then you'll be on your way home.

"This is my home!" Harry managed to protest, but it was no use. At last, she recognized what was happening. She had been wrapped in a burlap sack, which was tied at her ankles. A jolting movement and the hard, hay-smelling wood beneath her shoulders revealed she lay in a wagon. A wagon that would carry her like a pig to market. Carry her to Southwick and whatever fate awaited her thereafter.

* * *

"Hello!" a soft feminine call distracted Devin from his work. Lifting his head, he smiled to see his sister-in-law entering his tiny office, a bundle of fabric in her arms.

"Is that it?" he asked, rising.

"Yes, of course. Everything your lady will need for her special day… at least everything she will need to wear. I do hate the rush, though. I can't guarantee it will fit. My wedding dress didn't fit, and I disliked that, though I also had no choice. Where is she?"

"My house," Devin replied, lifting the short-sleeved confection of cream and pink vertical stripes and smiling. "Even if the fit isn't per-fect, this shade will look lovely on her skin."

"I know," Katerina smirked. "She and I match so closely in coloring, we could be sisters. Are you sure she's English?"

Devin began to nod, but then he frowned. "You know, I'm not sure. I don't know much about her background, except she's the daughter of

Fletcher's brother and his wife. I never heard if the wife was foreign, but I suppose it's possible."

"Maybe she's Irish," Katerina suspected. "She has a Celtic look about her."

"She does," Devin said, letting his mind drift to his beloved. "And yet, that's not exactly it either."

"Perhaps you should ask her," Katerina suggested.

Devin chuckled. "It's no wonder Chris loves you, sis. You're smart. Why didn't I think of that?"

Katerina smiled her shy smile but said nothing.

"You three will join us, won't you?" Devin asked. "I want you all there, especially you. Harry is going to need your help and support."

"Of course," Katerina agreed easily. "Will she need a special talk, since she has no mother?"

Devin's throat closed. He choked, revealing far more than he'd intended to her. She stared at him in alarm. "Um, no… that is, her mother was a progressive-minded woman and had her observe animals so she could explain."

"She's lucky then." Katerina accepted the explanation with no further questions, but her expression told him she didn't exactly believe it.

Grateful for her lack of comment, Devin gathered up the bundle of garments and set it on the edge of his desk. *Harry will be happy to see these things.*

* * *

Katerina couldn't quite credit what Devin was—and wasn't—saying. It seemed as though some goings-on had taken place between the couple.

Imagine if you and Chris had been in the same situation, rather than the reverse. How long would you have held out? Though she didn't even think the answer, she knew. So while she couldn't approve, she chose not to complain. *You want Harry for a sister, and being prudish won't help. If she and Devin have bitten the apple, then they have. I can't do a thing about it now, so best to let the marriage go forward unchecked.*

"I'm looking forward to seeing Mother and Father again," she commented.

"As am I," Devin replied eagerly. "After all, Father has the license."

She giggled. "That would be helpful."

"Indeed," Devin agreed. "Do you think they'll like her, Kat?"

"I do," she replied honestly. "Harry is just the kind of lost chick your mother likes to coddle. And now she'll have another chance at grandchildren since I've proved lacking."

"Kat," he exclaimed, startled. "You're no failure. You have Sophia after all."

"I know," she said, trying to play off her bitter comment as a joke, and then gave up. "I adore my daughter. We all do, of course, but I wanted a large family. Everyone wanted that, but nothing happened."

"One Sophia is worth a dozen more children," Devin pointed out. "I'm glad for her to be part of the family, and you."

"I'm glad to be part of it," she smiled, warmth welling up. Then she shivered. *Without the Bennetts, I wouldn't be here.* "I'm looking forward to tomorrow. A new Bennett is about to be christened."

* * *

The ride seemed to take forever, and all the while Harry remained concealed and half-smothered inside a hot burlap sack. The bumping and jostling of a rutted country road, and her own inability to brace herself with her arms restricted, left her feeling bruised and shaken. Eventually, she got her hands under herself enough to crouch, though she couldn't hold the position forever. She struggled and kicked at the twine knotted on the outside of the sack, but to no avail. Her boots prevented her from sliding her feet out, and she couldn't reach the laces to untie them. By the time they lurched to a halt, after what seemed like an hour, Harry felt exhausted and hysterical.

Boots crunched on the gravel again as her kidnapper approached.

"Please let me out," Harry begged. "I can scarcely breathe in here."

"Yer fine," the man replied. "Come on. A little longer and I'll turn you loose... once you can't get into any more trouble."

"I wasn't in any trouble before," she protested. "I just want to go home."

"Oh, you'll be going home all right." The big man grabbed her around the middle and flung her over his shoulder.

"Oof." The air exploded out of Harry's lungs, and her lunch almost went with it. Grimly she swallowed. Vomiting in this sack would only make a bad situation worse. Breathing slowly through her nose, she again tried to find purchase with her hands to prevent such terrible jostling, but it was no use. The sack slipped beneath her fingers.

She sensed they were heading downhill, and the crunching of gravel gave way to the swishing of grass and then the soft thud of sand. *Oh, God, we're going to the sea. Will he drown me?* Panicking she fought wildly again, kicking and trying to scratch, squirming, but to no avail.

The man slapped her hard on the rump. "Knock it off, dollymop," he snarled. "Don't make me drop you. You'll be just fine if you hold still."

His boots thudded solidly on something wooden and then she fell. Harry shrieked, but the solid impact of her bottom on planks cut off her cry.

"This is the last one, Cap'n," the voice said. "We can head out."

"What's this, Jones?" an equally rough voice demanded. "Since when do they come in sacks? You know the rules."

Harry desperately wondered what was happening.

"Sorry, sir," her kidnapper said. "This one came from Sir Fletcher himself. Says she's his mistress, a half-breed, only she's gone a bit daft from missing her home in India, so he wants us to bring her back there."

"Really?" The captain didn't sound too convinced. "Let's see what the wench has to say for herself."

Suddenly the rope fell away from Harry's ankles and she struggled out of the bag, and then sat back on the floor with a resounding thump. The hard planks beneath her bottom turned out to be the deck of a small steamship, smoke already belching from its smokestack. It rocked in the moorings, ready to set out to sea.

"Where are we?" she demanded. "What's going on? Why am I here?"

The captain, she saw, had dark hair under a dirty white cap, and appeared to be about forty, with crinkles around his eyes. Jones, older, crustier, his face craggy like the side of a boulder, closely resembled a mountain troll from one of Harry's fairy tales. The captain gave Jones a questioning glance. The man shrugged.

"Who are you?" The captain asked her.

"My name is Miss Fletcher," she replied, proud as a queen.

"Sir," Jones whispered sotto voce, "she's not to be trusted. At least, that's what Fletcher said."

"Same name." The captain considered.

"Of course!" Harry exclaimed. "He's not my 'protector'." Even the word brought a rush of color to her cheeks. "He's my uncle. He didn't like the man I chose to marry, so he's trying to punish me by sending me away to India."

"Mighty strange thing to do," the captain commented. "Both stories are strange. I don't think neither one is telling the truth."

"No, sir," agreed Jones, scratching his overly long gray hair. "She was staying in some man's house, bold as brass. I met her and Fletcher at the gate. I think she's someone's dollymop, but Old Man Fletcher didn't like sharing."

"Now that makes the most sense I've heard so far," the Captain replied. "But what should we do with her?"

"Let me go," Harry suggested. "I don't want any trouble. I told you, I'm to be married… tomorrow. Please. Just let me go home."

The two sailors looked at each other, questioning. Harry wanted to scream with the tension.

"Set sail," the captain ordered. "We're already almost a month late on this shipment, and I refuse to return without a full load."

"No!" Harry screamed. Lurching to her feet, she made a dash for the side of the vessel, only to be caught up in the captain's unbreakable grip.

"No you don't, my girl. Come along." He half carried, half dragged Harry into the lower deck of the steamship, opened a small white-washed door, and tossed her in.

She heard the key turn in the lock.

Frantic, Harry flung herself against the door. It vibrated but showed no signs of budging.

"Let me out!" she wailed, pounding with both fists. "Please, let me out. I want to go home."

Sobs choked her words and she slowly slid to the floor in a heap of skirts.

All I want is to go home.

* * *

By the time Devin stood outside his house, with his brother, sister-in-law, niece and parents in tow, excitement nearly had him bouncing on his toes like a child.

A heavy hand on his shoulder steadied him. "Easy, son. What's got you so worked up?"

"Don't tease, Father," Christopher admonished. "Have you forgotten how difficult it is to introduce your intended to your family?"

Devin inhaled deeply and turned to face them. *My family. My foundation.* His father, Adrian Bennett, stood ruggedly matured and strong, his dark hair laced with white at the temples. His hand rested on the back of a small but vivacious redhead of middle years. Her crow's feet showed when she smiled, but that didn't reduce her beauty.

"That's right, Adrian, love," she reminded her husband. "This is Devin's special moment. Don't tease."

They all regarded the door. *I'm glad they're ignoring the obvious, though it is as suffocating as an elephant in the parlor. She shouldn't be in my home alone, and she truly shouldn't be in my home alone with me. She's ruined, so they say, and it's my duty as a gentleman to marry her. Only, that's not why I'm doing it. I want to.* He'd known it for weeks, but the last two days had clinched it. *I never want to be parted from this woman as long as I live.*

"She's really very sweet," Katerina added, and Sophia nodded in enthusiastic agreement.

"Well then," Adrian blustered, clearly not ready to be finished teasing his youngest child, "let's meet this paragon. Don't stand on the stoop staring like a Bedlamite. Open the door."

Flustered, Devin whirled around and fitted the key into the lock, fumbling and nearly dropping it. At last, he managed to wrestle the normally obedient door open and stepped inside, only to trip over the threshold, something he'd never done before.

For his mother's sake, he suppressed a stream of vile curses as he flailed and finally caught his balance. "Harry," he called, hoping to hide his gaffe. "Harry, are you here? We're home. I'd like you to meet my parents."

Silence.

"I wonder where she could be. Perhaps the garden?" Traversing the parlor and kitchen quickly, he stepped outside into the cool of evening. "Harry?"

Again, no response. An unnatural stillness hung in the air, as though the sea were holding its breath. By the silvery light of a waning gibbous, Devin took in the yard at last, and his eyes widened. A thundering sounded in his ears and his breath sucked inward with a sound like sea waves over a submerged cave.

The bathtub sat filled with cold, filmy water. The sheets hung on the clothesline. No surprises there. But the gate, which he always kept locked when he was out, stood wide open. The ground covering heather he'd planted had been dug up, wildly uprooted in a haphazard jumble, before resolving into a pair of men's heavy boot prints... very heavy. The prints lay deeper on the earth than they had any right to, given how small they were. At the gate, a scrap of white drew his gaze. He approached and the tiny shape turned out to be a twist of fabric... *Just like the one Harry used to tie her hair up this morning...* "Oh, GOD! Chris, Father, come quick!"

* * *

Drawn up to his full height, Devin's head nearly brushed the upper doorframes of the hotel suite's interior doors. He normally slouched a little to appear less intimidating, but not today. Today he was going to use every weapon in his arsenal to create the greatest impression of size and strength he could muster. He threw open the door of the Fletchers' suite with such force that it slammed into the far wall with a resounding crash. When he stepped into the room, he brought his boots down hard on the wood at the edges of the decorative rug. Servants scattered like sheep, bleating senseless comments he made no attempt to comprehend. His quarry awaited on the other side of the prominent door in front of him, and nothing would stop him from taking the man apart. Behind him, the powerful figures of his father and brother flanked him. Though not as tall, both were muscular from years of work in the family factory. They formed an imposing entourage Devin didn't need but was grateful for anyway.

A small figure loomed up before him, and he nearly mowed her down, until the familiarity of her voice cut through his rage.

"Mr. Bennett?"

Black hair, blue eyes...pretty little face. Fanny moved stiffly, as though in pain, but she still placed herself fearlessly in his path. "Miss Fletcher."

"Where is she?" the girl demanded. "What have you done with my cousin?"

"Me?" He raised one russet eyebrow. "I did nothing. She came to me, so I kept her. Tomorrow was to be our wedding day. Isn't that what you wanted?"

Her eyes widened until they resembled blown glass marbles. "Y—yes, I mean... of course. I just... I didn't expect..." she stammered to a halt. "So she's with you then?"

"She was," he replied. "She was with me this morning. I brought my parents down from London early to witness our marriage. I was trying to figure out how to get you a discreet invitation. But when I arrived home from work, she was gone. Do you know where she is, Miss Fletcher?" Devin's tone was hard enough to pound nails, but even as he enunciated the words, he knew they were foolish. *Of course, she doesn't know. She's asking you where Harry is.*

"I have no idea," Fanny said. "She would never choose to leave you."

"I know," Devin agreed.

He stood face-to-face with the young woman and watched tension visibly creep up her back and into her neck. "Father," she whispered. "Oh dear."

"It's the only explanation that makes sense."

"It is," Fanny agreed. She stepped aside, symbolically conceding, and Devin surged forward.

He slammed the office door open with a powerful kick and stormed into the room. Fletcher's head shot up, and he regarded Devin with alarm, but a hint of triumph lingered around his hooded eyes.

"Where is she, you slimy bastard?" Devin demanded. "What have you done with my fiancée?"

Fletcher rose slowly to his feet, demonstrating his lack of fear in the face of the larger man's violent challenge. "I saved you from her."

Devin's breath caught. *Oh, God, he's killed her.* "What do you mean?" he forced out between his teeth. "Who said I wanted rescuing?"

"You needed it. There are things about her you don't know. I tried to warn you, but you never would listen. Trust me…"

"No!" Devin shouted. "I do not trust you. Not at all. Why should I? And how can you expect me to put faith in your nonsensical claims when you give me nothing at all to understand?"

"You know she has a secret," Fletcher pointed out. "Didn't you wonder what it was?"

Devin nodded. "I knew she'd tell me when she was ready, but I don't think there's anything she could say that would kill my love for her." He felt no shame, no embarrassment at admitting his deep feelings, not even with his teasing father and brother behind him, along with Fanny, who lurked at the edge of his peripheral vision. *That's why we're here.*

"She's a half breed," Fletcher enunciated slowly, as though talking to an idiot. "Her whore of a mother cuckolded my brother and tried to pass off her bastard whelp as his."

Devin blinked. "So? That's the dark secret? And what do you mean, half-breed? Half what?"

Fletcher rolled his eyes. "Half-Indian, idiot. Miranda allowed herself to be bedded by one of the servants, not once, but throughout her married life. Your beloved 'Harry' is an abomination, a hybrid of English and Indian that should never have been allowed to see the light of day. I couldn't bear to see her mongrel bloodline interject itself into good English stock such as your own, and today, I prevented it."

"What did you do?" Devin snarled. "If you've harmed her…"

"Of course not," Fletcher insisted. "I'm not evil. I merely sent her home, Bennett. At this moment, she's on a private steamship, probably chugging past France. In several weeks they'll dock in Alexandrea, cross Egypt to Suez, and then steam on to Bombay. She'll be back where she belongs by the end of August… in one of the special clubs I invest in. With her own wanton kind."

"Where she belongs," Devin pronounced, mocking the older man's sarcastic tone, even as rage flared hot and red as burning coal in his heart, "is with my mother and sister, preparing for her wedding tomorrow."

Fletcher blinked, clearly startled that his explanation had not produced a reaction of gratitude. "What? You can't mean…"

"I can. I would in no way blame the woman I love for sins committed by her parents. If what you say is true, and Harry is half Indian, then she is. She's still the same Harry and I still love her the same as always. Your snobbery and meddling robbed me of my bride, but you won't win, Fletcher."

Devin turned on his heel.

"Wait," Fletcher shouted. "What are you doing?"

Devin regarded the man over his shoulder. "I'm retrieving my woman. If it takes a year, I won't rest until she's safe with me."

"Have a care for your reputation, Bennett. If you marry a half-breed, you'll never practice law in England again."

Devin inhaled and then released his breath slowly. "Men work to provide for and protect their families, but family is more important than work. I'll clean stables before I allow Harry to be separated from me. To be harmed and used by your 'patrons'. Mark my words, Fletcher, I will get her back, damn the consequences."

He stalked out of the office. Behind him, he could hear Fanny's soft voice crying, "Father, how could you?"

"Silence, Fanny."

"I will not. You… you beast!"

In the hallway, he paused, placed one hand on the wall and leaned his head against it, examining the grain of the floorboards while he tried to calm his swirling thoughts.

"Son," Adrian laid a hand on Devin's shoulder, "how can I help?"

He shuddered, but no words would come.

"It's simple enough, Father," Christopher replied, stepping into the silence. "Devin will have to go after her as quickly as possible. I don't think we can stop the boat, but we can try to catch them. They'll need to refuel regularly. It's late, and I don't think any more steamers will be leaving today, besides which we would have to go to Southampton to book passage. It should be doable in the morning."

"Don't leave him alone," Adrian urged. "He's not in a frame of mind to make clearheaded decisions. He'll need help."

"I know."

"Come on, Devin." The two men took his arms and led him, stumbling towards the stairs. "Let's get you home. We have lots of work to do."

Although Devin knew they were right, his mind swirled, uselessly picturing Fletcher's business associates… men who made a living bringing British whores to India to work in his clubs. *And Harry is with them.*

Chapter 17

"**H**E did what?" Horrified, Katerina clapped her hand to her face.

"He's sent her away," Christopher explained, leaning wearily against the wall of Devin's parlor, just inside the front door. His wife approached him, and he wrapped his arms around her.

"No," Devin interrupted, "you don't understand. He's part-owner of several brothels in Bombay and across India. He's sent her to one of them." Pronouncing the words made him feel ill, and he had to swallow back bile several times to prevent himself from retching.

"Oh, dear Lord," Julia sank onto the sofa. "Oh, Devin, I'm so sorry. Whatever will you do?"

"The only thing I can do," he replied grimly. "I'm going after her. Maybe I can catch up with them, get her back before..." his throat closed in a gag. "But... but it doesn't matter." His voice broke. "I don't care, I..." Words failed, and he hid his face in his hands.

The sofa dipped beside him and something warm enfolded him. He uncovered swimming eyes to discover Katerina, her arms around him.

"I'm coming with you," she announced. "Harry will need a woman to help her."

Devin scrubbed at his nose, touched by her support.

"Kat –" Christopher began.

"No, I'm going," she insisted.

"What about Sophia?" he asked. "I don't think it would be a good idea to take her so far from home."

"We'll take her," Julia volunteered. "Or I will. If you're gone, son, your father will be busy. Chris, Kat, stay with Devin. Help him."

"Mother, we're talking about months. Maybe half a year if we have to go all the way to Bombay and search for her there."

Julia shrugged. "I trust Devin's judgment. If he says he loves this woman, that he will go to the ends of the earth to find her, how can I refuse to spend a few months with my granddaughter, which is something I would want to do anyway?"

"Bennetts support each other," Katerina added, addressing her husband with quiet intensity. "They supported us when we needed them. Now it's Devin's turn, and Harry's. I want to be there. I need to. There's no telling. "A tear slid down her cheek and she wiped it away impatiently. "If something terrible happens to her, she's going to need me... and need me to tell her we don't care... we accept her anyway..." Voice breaking, she forced out, "It's necessary."

Devin hugged Katerina gently. *No wonder I fell in love with her when I was seventeen.* While his whole heart now belonged to Harry, he still considered Kat a beloved family member and close friend.

Devin's distress coalesced into a clear, coherent thought, a prayer. *Lord, protect Harry. Keep her safe until I can find her and bring her home.*

* * *

Twenty-four hours later, the door to the cabin in which Harry had been confined swung open and stayed open. Up to that point, it had only been cracked enough to shove food and water—surprisingly good quality food and clean, fresh water—in for her.

The room itself, though spare, gleamed with polished wood and brass. Linens lay straight and smooth on the narrow bunk. The details registered slowly with Harry, subverted by her distress.

Her heart ached at her separation from the man she loved. She'd grieved when sleep had claimed her, that his arms did not encircle her. She grieved on waking to find herself alone, lying on the floor of a locked steamship cabin, and now far out to sea. She grieved every moment of lost conversation, until her eyes burned hot as coals and her chest screamed in protest of her endless sobbing. Now the clock on the low-lying bedside table read noon, and her hysteria gave way to numb exhaustion.

I missed my wedding. It would have happened by now. Should have.

Instead of becoming a bride, fate had decreed she would become a prisoner. *Is this Karma? Did I earn it by lying? By remaining silent when perhaps I should have spoken?* If so, the penalty seemed unduly harsh.

"By now we're skirting the coast of France," she realized aloud. Escape had become a ludicrous proposition. She spoke three languages, but English, Hindi and Marathi would be of no use until they reached their destination.

Even if I could evade the sailors and get to shore without drowning, I would be alone, half-dressed in improper and waterlogged clothing in an unknown place where I don't speak the language. Her own helplessness welled up in her heart, bringing with it utter despair; despair too deep even for fear.

Sprawled on the floor beside the open door, Harry gave way once again to bitter, painful sobs that tore themselves from her chest like wild, fang-laden beasts.

Her tears had long since deserted her, and yet she could no more stop herself from crying than she could turn the ship around and return to England.

"I should jump into the sea," she murmured listlessly, "and bring this nightmare to an end." But even suicide required more energy than she possessed. Instead, exhaustion seemed to reach out from the depths of her being and drag her into unconsciousness once again.

* * *

The luxury of a new train car meant nothing to Devin, nor did the soft conversation between his brother and sister-in-law. Though only just over an hour's ride, the time seemed to stretch out for years, each moment a misery of helpless terror as images of Harry, alone and frightened, tortured him.

He alternated between staring out the window without seeing the seaside scenery at all and pacing the narrow confines of the aisle.

"Try to be calm, Devin," Katerina told him in her soft, motherly voice, capturing his arm as he passed and urging him back into his seat. "We'll get her back just as quickly as we can, and you'll see, she'll be fine."

"She'd better be," he said darkly. "She'd just better be."

He examined his hands. Though he'd always been one to settle conflicts through diplomacy, and within the law, if someone harmed his beloved, he felt quite certain he would kill them.

* * *

Harry woke feeling miserable and thirsty. The cabin door remained open, so she rose, smoothed her hair halfheartedly with her hands, and stumbled into the corridor. A fresh sea breeze wafted down from the upper deck, blowing away the stuffy closeness of the cabin. The cool draft invigorated her slightly. Stiffening her spine, she moved forward, mounting noisy metal stairs in search of open sky, water, and above all, answers.

Harry blinked in surprise when she finally cleared the enclosure of the stairwell. Women crowded the deck, milling and chatting, their voices bubbling with excitement.

As she moved past them stiffly, her joints and muscles aching, heads turned her direction.

Not ready to make eye contact with anyone, Harry stared over the rail toward the horizon. *Gray-blue water as far as the eye can see. No land. No hope of escape, and little hope of rescue. Will Devin rescue me? Will he even try?* She bit her lip. Then her gaze turned toward the ship itself. Red paint had been expertly applied to the hull, deck and rails. It shone under a late afternoon sun. *How long did I sleep?* The black metal smokestack gleamed dully, a thick gray plume wafting from its fingerlike shape. Harry rubbed her forehead with her fingertips. The slanted sunlight hurt her eyes.

"Hello," a gentle voice spoke softly, drawing her attention without startling her. Harry turned and found herself face-to-face with a woman who seemed to be made of ice. White skin and white-blonde hair blended into one another, and a pale blue gown heightened the effect. Her corset had been cinched so tight, Harry's ribs ached in sympathy. Bright, sky-blue eyes and pale pink lips provided the only contrast of colors.

"Hello," Harry croaked.

"You sound thirsty, and you look like hell," the pale woman observed. "My name is Anastacia. Follow me, and I'll get you something to drink."

"Brilliant observations," Harry observed, letting a hint of irony drip into her tone, but she trotted after the woman anyway, and happily received a dipper of water from a barrel on the deck.

"So, do you have a name, or shall we invent one for you?" Anastacia asked.

Harry regarded her. *Witty, and she looks intelligent. Also kind,* she added, considering the drink that had made her begin to feel human again. *Maybe it's time to leave some of the past behind. Hiding what I am did me no good, and I'm sick to death of trying.* "My name is Harita," she said. *I never liked Harriet anyway.* "But most people call me Harry. Can you please tell me what's going on?"

"We're sailing to India!" A young woman with curly brown hair and a round, pretty face bounced up to Harry in a flurry of excitement.

"Yes, I know," Harry replied, and for a moment, despair threatened to overtake her again. "Why is everyone so happy about it?"

The ice woman's lips pursed even as her nearly-invisible eyebrows drew together. "Why would we not be? We're leaving London, getting an increase in pay and security, and we get to see the world. Sounds fantastic to me."

Harry gulped. *Oh, Lord. They don't know.* "Um, but don't you realize *why* we're going to India? They're taking us to work in..." she nearly choked on the word, and the heat in her face had nothing to do with the sunset.

"In brothels?" the cheerful girl suggested. "But of course. I mean, no one's going to take us all the way to India for free. Naturally, we'll have to earn our keep."

"But the pay is excellent," Anastacia added, "and we're all tired of England for various reasons. I, for one, hate the cold."

You look like you'd melt your first day in Bombay. Then the impact of their words sank in with Harry, and she stared from one to the other. "You're *willing* to do such a thing?"

"Harry," Anastacia said gently, "we're all in the Venus trade."

"Oh my Lord." *I'm surrounded by prostitutes. God in heaven, what next?*

"I take it you didn't get the same offer?" the brunette suggested.

Weakly, Harry leaned against the rail. She shook her head. "Not at all. I… I'm a good girl." *Please, God. I can still be a good girl, can't I? It was only Devin, and I love him so much.* "My employer… he tied me up…"

"In a sack," Anastacia finished for her. "Maria, go get her some more water. She looks about done in."

The brunette scampered off, returning with a cool drink and a sympathetic expression. "That's usually how it starts," she said. "You begin as a good girl in service, and then the master—or his son—wants special services. Next thing you know, he gets tired of you, and you're out on the street."

"If you're lucky," Anastacia added, "you don't end up *enceinte*, and you fall in with a reputable protector."

"That's not what happened at all," Harry insisted. She looked from one jaded face to another. "I'm sorry if that happened to either of you, but no. My employer… he's my uncle. He didn't like the man I wanted to marry…"

"I heard you say before that you're betrothed," Maria replied. "Is it really true?"

Harry nodded. "It really is, or it was, until my uncle turned up and snatched me, right out of my beloved's garden. Nearly squeezed the breath right out of me." Tears stung her eyes, though she would have sworn there wasn't another one left in her body. "I want to go home," she whispered.

"Are you really from India?" Maria asked, changing the subject rather than address the impossible wish.

Harry nodded.

"Don't you want to go back there?"

Harry heaved a sigh. "If circumstances were different. If Devin was with me, if we were married, then yes, I'd love to show him my home country, introduce him to people I know. But... not like this. Who would want to be stolen away from the man you love?"

"Love is a myth." Another blonde, heavier, curvier, and with a naturally pouty mouth sauntered over to the trio.

"That's not true, Eliza," Maria protested. "I still believe in love."

"You're a young fool," Eliza sneered. Then she turned to Harry. "Your man probably orchestrated the whole thing to get rid of you. That's what men do. They pretend to love you, and then they throw you away. Might as well get over hope, or you'll end up hurt."

Harry shook her head. "Devin would never do that. He loves me. This was supposed to be our wedding day." She choked but fought it down.

"I'm only trying to help you," the woman said, "but have it your way." She sauntered off with a seductive sway of her hips.

"Save it for the sailors, Eliza," Anastacia called after her. "We're not impressed. No one here wants to pay for your services anyway."

The woman stomped off.

Maria shook her head. "I don't like her."

"I don't either," Anastacia agreed. "I hope, wherever we end up, it won't be with her."

Harry stared balefully after the bitter stranger. *I hope she gives me a wide berth.*

* * *

"Tomorrow!" Devin cried, stunned. "No, you don't understand. I have to leave as quickly as possible. My…"

"It's fine," Christopher said, grabbing his brother's arm and dragging him away from the agent who sold passage on the steamship packet. This allowed the next customer to step forward.

Christopher plucked Devin's ticket from his fingers and tucked both it and his own into the breast pocket of his suit coat.

"I'm sorry," he said in a low voice, "but if you throw a fit, you'll only embarrass yourself and the boat won't leave one moment earlier than it was going to anyway. All is well, brother. We have staterooms side by side and we leave before noon."

"We'll never overtake them if they have a two-day lead."

"Then it's on to India," Christopher said, feigning cheer.

"She's alone with them, with no one to protect her," Devin snarled.

"I realize it," Christopher eyed his brother with a sympathetic expression, "but we can't do anything about it. Save your strength for the journey."

Devin made a face as he scanned the wooden box of a room. "Fine," he sighed. "Let's go back to the hotel and make sure we have everything ready."

"I agree," Christopher replied.

They stepped away from the booth and out into the weak light. The day had turned cloudy and dim, a pall hanging over the seashore. The screams of gulls resembled cries of fear or pain. The roar of the sea sounded like a hostile male voice. *Like Fletcher's voice, spouting his stupid nonsense. Why couldn't he have just left well enough alone?* Devin had slept badly the previous night, and tonight didn't look to be any better. *How will I ever rest knowing Harry is out there, alone and scared?*

"Come on, Devin, let's go," Christopher urged, and Devin realized he had taken root once again, staring off into the sea without seeing the steely gray water, the distant horizon, or even the spectacle of boats clustered close in and around the harbor.

"Sorry," he muttered, forcing his legs to start moving again.

Chapter 18

"THIS is where you'll be staying from now on," Jones said in his habitual growl. He indicated a large cabin in which rows of hammocks hung, stacked one above another. Harry regarded the room with trepidation. There would be no privacy here, of that she was certain. "There's a trunk on the wall yonder," he added, pointing at the far wall where, under a row of portholes, trunks crowded cheek by jowl on the varnished floor.

The last one in the corner stood slightly open, and Harry eyed it suspiciously. *I wonder if there's a reason it's the last one left.* "I have nothing to put in it." Her voice turned hard. "You see, when you're kidnapped and have no time to prepare, it's difficult to pack."

Jones shrugged. "Maybe you can buy something when we stop in Gibraltar. It won't be so very long."

Harry rolled her eyes. "How do you suggest I do so without money? No time to prepare, remember?" She planted her hands on her hips.

"I just got paid," he pointed out. "I could buy ye something... if ye make it worth me while." He stepped closer as he spoke, running his eyes suggestively over her frame.

The smell of his breath made Harry want to gag, and she eyed his ancient and craggy face with distaste. "I think not," she drawled. *As if I would ever consider such a thing.*

Offended, Jones let out a rude snort. "Well then, suit yerself. If ye have nothing to wear, on yer own head be it." He stomped out.

Harry shuddered with disgust and crossed to the corner where the open trunk awaited her inspection. Immediately she could see the latch was broken. *Good thing I have no valuables*, she thought, though the utter lack of supplies and possessions did bother her.

"Harry?" the gentle, childlike voice of Maria, the brown-haired woman Harry had met on deck, reached her ears, drawing her attention to the doorway.

"Yes?" she replied, giving the broken trunk a petulant nudge with the toe of her boot.

"I'm sorry, but you'll have to sleep here," she said, indicating a hammock near the door.

"Is that a bad thing?" Harry asked. *They all look the same to me.*

"It's nearest the chamber pot," Maria replied, indicating a large ceramic object near the door.

Harry frowned.

"But that's not the worst of it," Maria continued. "You're right below Eliza..."

"Oh, Lord!" Harry sighed. "Is she always so...charming?"

Maria nodded. "Just keep far away from her."

"I think I will," Harry agreed.

"You seem better," Maria commented, approaching Harry and giving her a sympathetic, sad smile. "I was worried about you."

"Thank you," Harry replied, patting the kindhearted girl on the arm and marveling at how normal she seemed. *I expected prostitutes to be like... well, like Eliza. Hard, sarcastic and rude. But she seems to be the aberration.* "I have to keep a clear head. No point wallowing in misery. Sooner or later, I will get away from this and go home. I might miss my opportunity if I give in to hysterics. Besides, I think I'm all cried out."

"Is it true what you said? Were you really about to be married?" Maria stared at her with wide, pleading eyes.

Harry nodded, but the thought of Devin belied her previous claim by bringing fresh tears to her eyes. "I don't think I can bear to talk about it now, but yes. Devin…" her voice broke. "Devin is real. I'm not covering up for some kind of shenanigans."

"Well, that's very unfortunate then," Maria said kindly. "I hope you do find your way back to him."

"I will," Harry replied. *I must.*

* * *

A vile retching sound drew Devin's attention away from the horizon to his poor sister-in-law, who once again bent over the rail of the ship. *Poor Katerina. She gets so seasick. It's a wonder she came along at all.* Christopher stood beside his wife, rubbing her back. He looked little better, though not green. Dark bruises ringed his eyes, showing he wasn't resting well. Devin sighed. *What a group. Not one among us is holding together.*

Though the hefty steamer on which they rode chugged away at a reasonable pace, despite weather, tide and wind, it still seemed too slow to a young man whose beloved had been stolen. As days passed into weeks, Devin began to understand what intercontinental travel actually meant. *My first adventure, and how I hate it. Are you out there, Harry? Are you all right, love?* He used all his powers of concentration, willing his thoughts across the water to her. *You can't be too far ahead of us, and I will find you. Stay strong and brave, love. I'm coming.*

* * *

Life aboard the steamer took on something of a routine, and Harry found it wasn't unduly terrifying. She suppressed thoughts about the future and focused on the moment, on getting through each day.

On the main, the girls, though hard and jaded, proved cautiously friendly, and when she refrained from judging or condemning them, they allowed themselves to converse with her, which broke up the monotony of the endless ocean. The small crew, while coarse and vulgar men, did not accost or attempt to force any of the girls, though some took advantage of the obvious offers. Harry felt no danger from them. Why would she? A few coins got them the company of a willing woman. She never offered, so they didn't notice her. Meals arrived at regular intervals, and on the main consisted of hot and tasty food.

Harry learned from her conversations and from eavesdropping that, with the exception of herself, all the thirty women on the small, private vessel had volunteered for this adventure. All were experienced ladies of the evening who, fed up with working the streets of London, had decided to find for themselves a new situation in another country. Maria and Anastacia became particular friends of Harry's, and she discovered that while Ana was nearly as jaded as Eliza, Maria retained a fresh-faced innocence, despite her chosen profession.

If it hadn't been for the bleak future, Harry might almost have enjoyed the trip. If, as she'd said, Devin had been at her side, her husband in truth, steaming down the Atlantic toward the Mediterranean would have seemed a grand adventure. But she could never let go of the anxiety at the back of her mind. What would happen to her when they reached Bombay? Would she be able to avoid being forced into prostitution? Would she be able to find her way back home to Devin? *Would he want me back even if I did?*

Eventually, they steamed into the shadow of the towering Rock of Gibraltar and docked, needing to take on fresh coal. The girls chatted eagerly as they climbed out onto the dock, plotting what they needed to use their hard-earned coins to buy.

"Remember, ladies," the captain called, "the ship leaves day after tomorrow. You're welcome to return to sleep, but please don't make us late if you decide to stay in town."

"No, sir," they chorused, giggling.

Harry eyed the harbor area with interest, looking for any sign of a benefit to her. *Maybe someone here can help me get home.* As always seems to be the case, the harbor area bristled with running, shouting sailors, stacks of cargo, swinging nets, and a general melee that made her head spin. *I remember when I did this before, going the other direction. What do I recall about Gibraltar that might be useful?* "It's been ten years since I was here," Harry told Ana and Maria, "but I remember a café down the way there that sold interesting food. Would you like to see if it's still there?" Her own stomach rumbled, but without money, she would have to return to the ship to eat.

"Yes, certainly," Ana replied, her ice-blue eyes shining under the brilliant Mediterranean sun. "Do you recall any shops for ladies? I suspect I'll be needing some sanitary towels soon."

"Me too," Maria agreed, shoving an errant curl back into her chignon.

Harry gulped. "I didn't even think of it."

"Don't fret," Maria assured her, patting her arm. "I'll pay for yours."

"Oh, I couldn't..." Harry began.

"Don't be silly," Ana interjected. "They're far from expensive."

Harry sighed. "I'll have to accept your charity," she replied with a frown. "I have no choice. But I will find a way to pay you back."

"That's right," Maria assured her. "It's not charity, it's a loan. Think of it that way, can you?"

"I'll try." Though accepting their offer grated on her sensibilities, enduring menstruation without supplies would be far worse.

They exited the harbor area and proceeded into a maze of narrow, crowded streets that formed the city. Shops of all types lured passersby with sweets, food, clothing and other tempting purchases.

"Something smells good," Maria commented.

"I think it's this pastry shop," Ana informed them, indicating a flat-fronted building with a service window under a shady awning. "Any idea what they're selling, Harry?"

Harry squinted at the sign, which unfortunately had been printed in flowing cursive. "It says *'Japonesa'*, I think." Both ladies stared at her. "I don't know," she protested. "I've been through here once and it was ten years ago. Want to find out?"

"Sounds like an excellent idea," Maria said, as always covering the awkwardness.

Again, the thought struck Harry that her friend seemed completely unlike any idea of a prostitute she'd ever had. Kind, gentle and a born peacemaker, she should have been the wife of a sweet and somewhat prosperous man. *Someone of Devin's class.*

Tall, stately and exotic, with her pale coloring and tilted blue eyes, Ana looked more like a princess than a lady of the evening. *How do so many fall? And why? I hesitate to ask, but... this confuses me.*

Lacking a coin to buy her own snack, she watched the girls examine the shop's fare and come away each clutching a plump, round pastry.

"Hmmmm," Maria hummed around a mouthful. "This one is filled with lemon cream. Delicious. Do try it, Harry!"

Harry accepted a bite of the sweet pastry and found it had been coated in a sugary glaze. "So good," she moaned around a mouthful of sweetness.

"Mine is filled with hazelnuts," Ana added. "You must take a bite."

Acknowledging wryly what her friends were up to, Harry nonetheless accepted enough tastes of each pastry to feel she hadn't missed out on anything.

"You two are absolutely lovely," she said, quirking one eyebrow at them. "I know what you're doing. Thank you."

"It's just..." Maria began. "It's just we know you've been through a hard time, and you probably have more hard days ahead. I don't want you to feel so unhappy. I know you'll find your way home somehow, Harry, but in the meanwhile, I don't want you to get your spirits down."

"You're a sweetheart," Harry told her seriously. She heaved a deep sigh. "I really don't know what to do though."

"You'll figure it out when the time comes," Ana said. "Just keep your wits about you. You're smart, Harry. That will help you think clearly."

Harry nodded. "I feel a bit fuzzy these days, but I'll try. I... this is all so frightening."

"I'm sure it is," Maria said, soothing her friend with a warm hug. "I'm nervous, and I know what I'm getting into."

"Come on, you two. Let's not loiter in the street," Ana suggested. "It's getting hot. What do you say we find the shop we need quickly, and then look for some shade?"

"This is only the beginning of hot," Harry warned them. "The heat in India makes this look like a pleasant spring day."

"We'll simply have to adjust," Maria said cheerfully. Together they trotted along the narrow, winding streets past rows of buildings from which all manner of goods could be purchased. They passed a low, white building with columns and a cannon out front, and then Maria stopped with a squeal.

"What?" Harry demanded.

The girl pointed. "What is *that?*"

Harry regarded a low stone wall before them. "It's a monkey," she said matter-of-factly.

"Monkey?" Ana sounded revolted. "What's it doing running loose through the town?"

"Oh, you'll find monkeys all over Gibraltar, even in town. They're native here," Harry explained. "But what's the problem? Don't you like monkeys? I think they're charming."

Ana shuddered. "I went to a menagerie once. There were monkeys. One threw unspeakable things at me."

Harry fought to suppress her laugh. "Well, monkeys are a bit like curious bees. For the most part, if you don't bother them, they won't bother you."

At that moment, the little tan primate rose up on its hind legs and waddled toward them. Ana shrieked and ran away from it. Maria tried to do the same, but somehow got tangled in her skirts. A loud sound of ripping fabric revealed the damage. Startled by their overwrought reactions, the monkey bolted for cover and disappeared.

"What happened?" Harry asked.

"I stepped on my skirt," Maria sulked, pressing one hand to her chest. "It tore."

"Let me see," Harry suggested. Kneeling in the street, she examined the hem. "It's a bad tear," she informed her friend.

"Damn it!" Maria hissed. All around them, crowding tourists scowled at the young woman. "Now all my skirts have holes in them. How I wish I'd paid attention to my mother's sewing lessons when I was a child."

"I can fix it," Harry offered. "I sew quite well. Do you have a needle and thread?"

"Of course not," Maria snapped. "I can't sew, remember?" Then she shook herself. "Sorry, Harry. That was rude of me."

"Don't worry about it for a moment," Harry replied. "You were startled and upset. I didn't take it personally. Well, if we can find a shop with a few sewing supplies, I'll be happy to fix, not only this skirt, but anything else you might want repaired. It would be a nice way to repay your generosity for…" she regarded the crowd of people still staring at them. "For what you offered to buy for me. Come on, let's see where Ana's run off to."

* * *

That night, the ship's cabin had very few girls sleeping in it. Only two others snored quietly in their hammocks as Harry lay awake, staring at a water stain on the ceiling. It bothered her to the very core of her being that her friends, both of them, had found other places to stay for the night. *They'll come back with money… but I don't like it.* Images of the sweet loving she'd shared with Devin welled up in her mind. *How can anyone, man or woman, trade such intimacy for a few coins?* The idea made no sense to her, though she knew the practice was common enough. *I'll never do that. I'll starve first.* Closing her eyes, she willed sleep to come.

* * *

Harry crept down the same street of Gibraltar, this time alone. *I can do this. This island is owned by Britain. If I can find someone official—a police officer, or some kind of diplomat. Even a nobleman—perhaps they'll help me. At the very least they can get word to Devin.* She glanced over her shoulder. The portholes of the ship seemed to stare at her, daring her to try to escape their gaze. *Begone, steamer. I don't want you. I don't want any of this.*

Trying not to attract any attention, Harry forced herself to walk slowly toward the town.

Where did I see that official-looking building with the cannons? I imagine it would be a good place to start. The people of Gibraltar are technically English citizens, so they should be willing to help. Her heart seemed to want to leap from her chest and flop on the street like a fish.

I can do this. I can find help... demand it. No one has the right to kidnap a British citizen with the intention of forcing her into the Venus trade. I won't stand for it. She passed the pastry shop. At this early hour, no one had yet begun to gather, but the enticing scent of sweet, fried dough wafted into the street. *Just a little farther.* She fought the urge to run. Enough people milled around, and she didn't want to risk the attention of idlers, whose loyalty she couldn't trust. *No telling who might side with the captain, with his crew. They're regulars here. Can't trust anyone.* For a moment, doubt assailed her. *What if they're all on his side? I'm sure any soldier has found comfort with one of the passing girls at one time or another. Maybe even the mayor.* She shuddered. *No, no matter what, kidnapping is a crime. They have to help me.*

She could see the government building in the distance. Two of the small local primates screeched and chased each other around the columns. *Almost there.*

"Gotcha." Powerful arms swept Harry right off her feet.

Harry screamed and kicked the air. "No, put me down. No!"

He swatted her behind playfully. "Nothing to look at, folks," The captain's voice addressed the bystanders. "This little tart was trying to slip out of her contract."

"No, he's lying," Harry shrieked, lifting her body up from his back and trying to make eye contact. All the milling ladies and gentlemen looked away. "I've signed no contract and I'm no tart. I'm being kidnapped. Please, someone. Please help me."

They turned back to their business as one.

"At least can someone please send word to my fiancé? Devin Bennett, solicitor at law, Brighton, England. Please..."

No one responded, not even to meet her eyes. Harry kicked and struggled, but to no avail. Inexorably the Captain carried her back, unconcerned with the abuse and blows raining down on him, until they stood in the doorway of the same sparsely furnished cabin where her nightmare sea voyage had begun.

He dropped her on her feet. Harry faced him, seething and crying at the same time, rage and tears clouding her vision. "Why?" she demanded. "Why won't you just let me go? I don't want to be here. I'm not a lady of the evening. I signed no contract and I won't do this. Please, just leave me here and I'll find a way to get back to England." *Back to Devin.*

The captain regarded her with a considering look on his face. At last, he shook his head. "Sorry. I get paid to deliver the full complement of thirty girls. I barely turn a profit on this venture as it is. I can't afford to lose a single one of you."

"But... but..." Harry spluttered, not knowing what to say next.

"Listen, when you get to Bombay, talk to Slade. He's the owner. He's one of the fairest businessmen I've ever met. Maybe you and he can strike some kind of bargain. Or once the paperwork is approved in Alexandria, you can run off into the desert and die. Once I sign off on my cargo, I don't much care. But I *will* have thirty girls in Alexandria."

Harry slumped to the floor.

"Chin up, miss," he added. Then his craggy face turned stern and his sea gray eyes narrowed. "In repayment of this little escape attempt, you'll be spending the rest of your shore leave locked up. And if you want to have the opportunity to get out in Malta, you'll give me your word right now that you won't try anything like this again. Swear it, Miss Fletcher, or I'll keep you locked up till Alexandria."

Harry tilted her head back, tears running into her hairline, mingling with sweat and turning her already tangled hair to knots. Strangled sobs fought their way up from her heart to fill her throat and choke her.

"Swear it, Miss Fletcher."

Harry covered her face with her hands. "I swear," she whimpered.

The sound of the lock clicking proved inaudible over her bone-shaking sobs.

* * *

The sight of Gibraltar on the horizon brought a shout of hope to Devin's heart, but he kept it inside. *We made good time. What if they're still there?* In his cabin below decks, a small treasure trove of hope awaited his reconnection with his beloved. Marriage license, wedding dress, and a thin gold band he couldn't wait to place on her finger.

The sun barely skimmed the horizon, lying on the water in brilliant shades of red and gold. *I wonder if she's enjoying this sunset.* He hoped she was. *Find something to smile about, Harry. And know I'll find you the soonest I ever can.*

As their large, commercial steam paddler approached the docks, a much smaller vessel chugged past, out into the Mediterranean.

* * *

After being so successfully routed, Harry sank into a deep depression. The sea had lost its charms for her and only seemed like a final, permanent solution. Rather than be tempted by the lure of the rolling waves, Harry lay, listless and unresponsive, in her hammock.

"Harry," Ana said, gently touching her arm. "Harry, I brought you some food."

Harry made a soft and inarticulate sound but said nothing.

"Please, Harry, you need to eat."

Guilt welled up, merging with melancholy to blacken Harry's mood further. "I'm sorry, Ana. I don't have any appetite. Nothing sounds appealing, and besides, what's the use?"

"Harita Fletcher!" The beautiful woman exclaimed. "How on earth can you lie there and give up? You had one setback. One! I thought you had strength, girl. Here you are, unravished and as safe as if you were home in your own bed. How dare you give up?"

"They're too strong for me." Aggravated, Harry sat up, carefully positioning herself so the unstable hammock didn't pitch her to the floor. "How can I escape? When I get to India, they'll own me, and I won't be able to do a thing about it."

"Stop it!" Ana snapped. "Just listen to yourself, Harry. Yes, men are stronger. That's a given. That's why women have to be smarter. Always remember your body is your own, your will is your own. Even if someone overpowers you, it is still your own. Your worth comes from your heart, from your mind, and your strength of character. You can find your way back home, someday, somehow, but only if you don't give up."

"But find my way home as what?" Harry demanded. "Will Devin still love me if I'm forced to do... that?" Will he still accept me?"

"If he loves you, yes," Ana replied. "If not, he was never worthy of you to begin with. I think, from what you've said of him, should the worst come to be, he would grieve, but he would not love you one iota less than before. It is your spirit he loves. Endure, Harry, and never stop fighting. It may be that what you fear never comes to pass, but if it does, remain steadfast and don't let it destroy you."

Her strong, bitter words cut deep into Harry's heart. Truly, she wanted to believe Devin would love her no matter what, would love her in spite of any violence done against her heart or her virtue, but she didn't know. Their relationship had been too short, too fraught with troubles, for her to be certain. *So then she's not telling me to save myself for him, but for me. And with such force. She sounds so fierce, like this is personal for her.* "Ana, what happened to you?" Harry asked.

"You mean how did I become a whore?"

Harry frowned at the ugly word but nodded. "Yes."

"Like you, I was engaged to be married. I loved my fiancé very much. He's Russian, a friend of my mother's family," Ana began, studying her hands with an intense gaze.

Is, not was. So he didn't die. Something went terribly wrong. Is this how my story will go too? I loved a man, and something went terribly wrong...

Ana continued. "He was called home to St. Petersburg to see to his father. It was to be a six-month separation, while I continued preparing for our wedding. Two months later, a friend of his stopped by and asked to talk to me privately. He said something had happened to Dmitri. His eyes looked red and he was shaking. It was all a ruse. The moment we were alone, he forced himself on me, the bastard." Her voice trembled. "That day my innocence was stolen."

"What happened?" Harry asked, wide-eyed and appalled by her friend's misfortune.

"What do you think? I told my parents, but they blamed me, said I should have known better than to let a man get me alone and isolated. They turned me out. My…" This time her blue eyes began to swim with tears. "My intended found out… I suppose his friend boasted to him, and he abandoned me too. I had no home, no friends, and no recourse. I know they say a lady would rather starve, but honestly, Harry, have you ever been that hungry?"

Harry shook her head. "Never."

"So… a man—not even a gentleman, a sailor—offered me hot food and a warm bed in exchange for a favor, and I was desperate, so I agreed. One turned into another, and then another, and now it's what I do." She swallowed and it seemed the tears disappeared into her belly, feeding her bitterness. "It's what I do, but it's not what I am. Do you understand?"

Harry nodded. "You are a smart, pragmatic woman with a strong will. You are a good friend. I understand the difference."

Ana nodded. "I thought you would. I hope you don't have to make the decision I did, Harry, but if you do, you're still you, no matter what. They can claim your body by force, or lure you with irresistible offers, but they can't destroy your will unless you let them. Now you get out of this bed and live, girl."

Harry rose to her feet. Ana towered over her, but she still accepted the fierce hug.

"Ana?"

"Yes?"

"Someday, somehow, you'll find a way out of this and be all right."

A shudder ran through the taller woman's frame, and her voice, when she spoke, was far from steady. "Thank you, Harry. Sometimes it's easy to forget. Yes, someday I will reclaim my life, and this will all be a dark and distant memory."

They stepped back from each other just as Maria bustled into the room. "I must say, Harry, I'm a bit disappointed in you," the little woman piped. "You promised to fix the hole in my skirt. I bought needles and thread—a whole set, so you could fix all my clothes like you said you would—and you never did. Now I have only rags to wear."

Harry straightened her spine. *I have a way to earn money without degradation. I have friends who stand by me even when I forget to stand for myself, and I have a goal. Why in all of God's blue oceans am I moping around?* "I'm sorry I got sidetracked," Harry said to her friend. "It was bad of me. Bring me everything you have that needs mending, and I'll have you set to rights in no time.

* * *

Devin stood by the rail, staring out at the rock of Gibraltar as it slowly disappeared beyond the horizon. They had missed Harry's boat by a day. No more. It should have been cause for rejoicing. But then, as the tug was maneuvering the bulky paddle steamer out of the harbor, it had brought them too close to a submerged rock, opening a substantial hole in the hull. The result had been a hasty trip to shore on rescue boats and a week in dry dock.

To pass the time, he'd questioned people all over the island about whether they'd seen anyone resembling Harry. To his surprise, she'd captured quite a bit of attention making a spectacle of herself, claiming to be kidnapped. The consensus seemed to be that she was a whore trying to escape from a signed contract, but the fact that she'd given his name and address, had begged them to send a message told him a great deal. *My Harry, my mighty little warrior, is still fighting. She hasn't given up.*

Devin lifted his eyes to the night sky above him. A lone star twinkled, and he made a wish in a softly-voiced undertone. "Don't give up. I'm coming, love. No matter what happens, I will always come for you.

Chapter 19

ATERINA sighed with pleasure, curled into her favorite place in the world; her husband's powerful arms. Feelings of love welled up within her as he finished their loving with a tender kiss. *It's been too long.*

Their cabin on the commercial steamer that would take them on the first leg of their journey also felt like a hug, she decided, with its warm wood walls, functional carpet, and wide, luxurious bed, perfect for cuddling with someone special.

And how blessed I am to have someone special here in my embrace. She traced Christopher's beloved face with her eyes and fingertips. The warm gray eyes that had captured her from the first day they met. The strong jaw lightly dusted with rough, brown stubble. The soft lips she never could stop kissing. She drew his head down again.

"Satisfied, love?" he asked, his eyes shining. With her free hand, she trailed fingertips up and down his back.

"For the moment," she replied, teasing him. Then she released a slow breath. "How did so much time go by? I love being close to you."

He touched his lips to her forehead. "You weren't in the mood, love. Far be it for me to push you."

"I wish you had," she admitted. "Sometimes, with Sophia, your work, and travel and all… I just forget to make time for us. It's a shame and I regret it."

"Katerina, love," he said, "I don't think that's really it, is it? I mean, work is the same as always, and Sophia isn't so hard to care for now that she's big and has lessons with her governess much of the day. What's really been holding my sweet wife back?"

She bit her lip. "I suppose… that miscarriage bothered me more than I let on."

Christopher nodded. "I know, darling. That's what I thought."

She closed her eyes, and when she opened them to lock gazes with him again, her vision had lost some of its sharpness. "What if that's it, love? What if Sophia is our only child forever? I so wanted to give you a large family. Sons to inherit the business… But in all these six years since she was born, I only conceived once, and then…"

"Hush, darling," he interrupted her. "If the Lord blesses us with more children, I'll be glad of it. Sophia is so much like you, she's adorable, and so more daughters—or sons—would be fantastic. But, Kat, you two are enough on your own. My ladies, my wife and daughter. How greedy would I be to act dissatisfied? Love, even if we'd never had Sophia, you alone would be enough for me. I love you. Little darling, have you forgotten I love you? How did that happen?"

"I could never forget," Katerina protested.

"You did," he insisted. "I know it strikes to the core of your womanhood when you want to conceive and it doesn't happen, or when it does, but then it unexpectedly ends. Don't forget in the midst of it all that your husband loves you. You, Katerina, not only your womb. I think I may have been the one who let you down, if you've forgotten my love for you."

"Chris, I know you love me. I thank God for you every day…"

"And when was the last time I said so?" he asked.

She shrugged. "I don't need to hear it every day…"

"Yes you do," he insisted. "Twice would be better. When you wake in the morning and before you go to sleep at night. More as needed. Well, I won't let it happen again. You, my dear, will have all the love you can handle, all the time. And all the loving too."

His hand slid down her body, tracing each curve. "My Lord, you're beautiful. Look at you, darling, lying here freshly bedded, nipples pink, legs open. I could take you again, right now.

Joy welled up in Katerina. She had worried, between Christopher celebrating his thirtieth birthday and her own lingering melancholy over the recent loss of a baby she'd desperately wanted, that their explosive passion was fading. Not so, it seemed.

Two blunt fingers slipped into her warm wetness and pressed deep, teasing her with the promise of pleasure. She gasped.

"Hmmmm, so wet and hot. I think you're ready for more, aren't you, Kat?" He used his fingers to imitate what he wanted to do to her.

"Yeeeees," she wailed.

In one fluid movement, he rolled to his back, perching her on top of him. His fingers slid up the scarred and uneven skin, feeling the crisscrossing injuries that had spurred them to marriage in the first place. Now, after seven years, she no longer hated for him to touch them. She rose, her long dark curls sweeping his thighs, and guided him back into her.

She sighed as he stretched her wide again. *This is so much better than I deserve, she thought, b*ut she no longer voiced such insecurities aloud. "I'm so thankful for you, my love," she murmured as their lovemaking recommenced in earnest.

* * *

"There you go, good as new," Harry announced, handing a pile of clothing to Maria.

The girl dropped the bundle into the trunk and held up the skirt. "Amazing. I can't even see the tear. What did you do?"

"Trade secret," Harry said with a smirk.

"I'll look lovely in these." Delighted, Maria whirled around the cabin, letting the skirt flare out with her movement, and nearly entangling the hammocks.

"Easy," Ana urged with a laugh, stepping out of the way. "Harry, do you think you could do some of mine next? I have ever so many holes. One of the bad parts of working the streets is that you have to wear everything all at once, and then everything gets ripped or dirty together."

Harry shook her head. *Anastacia Alexandrovna Thomas should be dressed in silk and attending the queen, not opening her legs in some dirty London alley.* Her story broke Harry's heart and at the same time inspired her.

"Show me what you have, and I'll fix it," Harry insisted. "Maybe in Malta we can find some lovely soaps and wash ourselves and our clothes up extra special."

"Why bother?" Maria asked. "The sailors don't care, and once we get to Alexandria, we'll be trekking across the desert. It will be ages before anyone cares how we smell."

"We care, don't we?" Harry asked. "I mean, don't you feel better overall when you know you look and smell your best?"

"She has a point," Anastacia concurred. "We should at least have pride enough to care for ourselves for our own sake, regardless of clients."

"That's right," Harry agreed. "Now, show me, Ana, what you want repaired."

* * *

Devin found his brother leaning against the ship's rail. Unsurprisingly, the mechanically-minded Christopher was studying the smokestack, not the horizon. He seemed to sense his brother approaching, because he said, "When Kat and I first got married, Father and I had a conversation about how steamships were being developed. Now I'm on one. Seems surreal."

"It does," Devin agreed. "I wish we had a happier occasion to travel."

"As do I." Christopher turned his attention away from the metal contraption and its smoky output and turned to his brother. "We'll find her, Devin. Somehow, we will find her."

"I know," Devin agreed. "I won't stop until she's safe with me again. I love her, Chris."

Christopher nodded. "A long time ago, Katerina went away from me, and I didn't know if I would get her back. It was a terrible time. If something had happened to her..." He shook his head.

"I remember that. It was terrible. Kat and Sophia at the same time. I'm so glad your family pulled through."

"Yours will too," Chris replied. "Keep the faith."

"I know," Devin insisted. "I said I am."

"You did say, but I want to be sure you believe it."

Devin closed his eyes. *Brothers know too much.*

Neither one dared to say what both were thinking... that every day Harry remained in captivity, the greater the chance she would be subjected to some kind of assault. Devin took comfort in his brother's assurances and tried not to think about what they could not help.

* * *

Days aboard ship turned into weeks. Nearly a month had passed since their departure from England. Day after day the burning summer sun beat down on the deck of the little vessel. There was no escape from the heat. Below decks, the stuffy cabin grew even more unbearable, crammed with thirty female bodies. The sailors stank, their sooty skin and garments crusted with drying sweat, until the girls refused them even if they did manage to dig up a spare coin.

"Thank goodness for steam power," Harry commented, regarding the belching, dirty smokestack.

"Why is that?" Maria wanted to know.

"Because," Ana explained, "there's no wind." She leaned on the rail. "No wind on a sailboat is a serious problem. We could be stuck for days or even weeks."

"With the steam paddles to move us forward, we won't be becalmed," Harry added. "It will get us off the water sooner, though I hate to tell you, the heat in India won't be any better."

"You two know so much," Maria complained. "I never got to learn. School wasn't an option for my family."

"Knowledge is the cure for ignorance," Ana pointed out. "Can you read, Maria? If so, the world of knowledge lies in books, just waiting for you to discover it."

"Yes," the little brunette said. "Not well, and I can't admit to enjoying it much, but I can do it."

"Oh, I love to read," Harry exclaimed. "I'm an absolute bluestocking." She giggled. "Well, I have to admit, my favorite books aren't so very erudite. I like the naughty ones." She winked at her companions and all three laughed.

Interesting conversation notwithstanding, the sea seemed suddenly determined to hurry the little steamer along. A hot, stale wind blew up from behind them, almost pushing them into Malta, where Harry was able to use the coins she'd gotten repairing clothing for the ladies to purchase, as she'd hoped, soaps scented with exotic tropical flowers, and soon the ladies and their garments smelled as enticing as they looked. The crew grumbled at the sight of freshly laundered fabric hanging to dry on lines rigged between one rail and another, but they soon found themselves scrambling to amass some money to take advantage of the luscious prostitutes in their midst. Harry had to laugh when they came to her, begging to borrow the soap.

The last day of the first leg of their journey, with the coast of Egypt in sight, the captain took Harry aside.

"Our contact will be meeting us in Alexandria in two days. Normally, I let the girls explore the city. It's quite colorful, but I will need your word once again that you won't run off."

Harry eyed him thoughtfully.

"If you run, you won't get far. The city is under Ottoman control and while a few speak English or French, the majority are Arabic. They won't shelter a runaway woman, and even if you tried, no one would understand you. Your best bet is to stick with the group."

Still, Harry remained silent, regarding the man with narrowed eyes. He hadn't caused the situation, but he had exacerbated it by refusing to listen, to consider a woman's words. "I won't run," she told him at last. "I'm not stupid, you know. I grew up in Bombay, and I have every intention of ferreting out my father's friends, who are influential military people, and telling them what happened. How I was minding my own business—a respectable woman on the verge of marriage—when I was kidnapped by an ill-intentioned man and brought to you bound in a sack.

"Instead of seeing that I clearly wasn't a willing professional, you kept me anyway. Why? Money and deadlines. I understand you're a man of business, but you also abetted a crime. Most likely, nothing will happen to you. The world is set up against women and their rights, for the benefit of the men who exploit them. I can't do anything about that. But I can tell my story, and I will. No one should have to go through what I did.

Harry gulped and continued her tirade. "No one should be taken from her home and told she'll be joining the Venus trade. That's a choice a woman must make for herself. Even if she so chooses, there's usually some exploitation behind it, in a world where a woman need only set one toe over the line, even from desperation, to be changed from angel to whore forever. I know you don't care. You make a living on that exploitation, and despite what you told me, it must be profitable. I also know you don't care about my opinion, but you have it, nonetheless. I hope someday you consider it."

"Are you finished?" the captain asked.

"Quite," Harry agreed.

"The rules are the same as in any port. Sleep here if you'd like. Or go ashore. But don't miss the deadline or you won't like what happens to you."

"I understand," Harry replied.

He turned to leave, and then regarded her over his shoulder. "Good luck, Miss Fletcher," he told her, and then quickly disappeared. She could hear his boots clattering on the metal staircase.

Harry blinked. The look he'd given her had held a hint of… respect? She shook her head. "And they say women are hard to understand."

* * *

A cold and sneaky wind from the Atlantic crept past Gibraltar one night in early August 1856. Around the boot of Italy, it met up with a draft of hot air from Morocco. Sensing the intruder, the African wind determined to chase it away, but the Atlantic air would not be dissuaded. A quarrel broke out, and then an altercation, and two days later, a violent storm began to lash the sea. Swirling wind and choppy surf threatened to capsize boats and made a mess of coastal towns for miles around.

The storm chased a steam paddler into the port at Malta with only a few hours to spare. The captain took one look at the still, ominous sky, tinted green and with a sharp black edge on the far horizon, and ordered crew and passengers ashore, urging them to take shelter as far from the ocean as possible.

Following the crowd inland, two men escorted a weak and wobbly woman through narrow streets, past brick buildings with thick, white mortar, and shops whose windows had been nailed shut, and at last, found refuge in a small inn nestled between two shops. The freestanding, two-story structure was fronted by a low wall made only of decorative metal spindles beneath a stone lintel that matched the building. Bright red shutters made the tan and white structure cheerful, but to the travelers, cheer seemed less important than the stout, sturdy construction of the place.

As Devin registered their visit with the owners, Christopher escorted his wife down a hallway tiled in glorious blue and white mosaic flowers and into an interior bedroom where a rather narrow bed awaited, dressed in simple but spotless white sheets.

"Are you going to be all right, darling?" he asked her, smoothing sweaty hair back from her face.

Katerina nodded. "I always forget how sea travel makes me ill... until it's too late."

"I've never seen you this bad. Our last three trips to Italy, you weren't this sick. I'm rather alarmed."

"Be at ease, my love," she insisted. "It was the choppy surf. Now that I'm on land again, I'll be fine."

Christopher refrained from mentioning just how much sailing they had yet to do. Another ten days or so to Alexandria, and on the other side, a further month from Suez to Bombay. *I hope she grows accustomed. I don't know how much more sickness she can sustain. It was a mistake to bring her. She's too fragile for this. The trip to Italy is bad enough. This is four times the distance.*

He smoothed her hair again and kissed her forehead. "Rest, love. I need to check up on my brother."

Katerina nodded, but he could see she was already nearly asleep. He ran his fingers over her cheek and left the room, closing the door behind him.

Devin waited in the hallway. "We're all set," he informed his brother, "and the price is only mildly exploitative. They say this building has been around over fifty years and has weathered hundreds of storms and even a few rare cyclones. They're not expecting this to be a cyclone, by the way."

"I'm not sure I trust any of that," Christopher commented. He leaned against the wall and rubbed his aching forehead with one hand. "That sky looked terrible… and have you ever experienced a stillness so ominous?"

"I haven't," Devin agreed. "Cyclone or not, it's sure to be nasty. I'm glad we made it ashore in time."

"As am I. I think poor Kat would not have taken well to a storm at sea. She's already sick enough."

"Is she all right?" Devin asked, his face showing concern at his sister-in-law's predicament.

"I hope so," Christopher replied. "I can scarcely remember her being this ill. Not even en route to Italy. Poor love. Maybe a few days on land will do her some good."

Devin made a face. "I wish I knew what to say. I don't want you to think I'm putting Harry above Katerina. It isn't like that."

"It's a damned impossible mess is what it is," Christopher replied, "but no offense taken. I'd be frantic if something happened to my wife. Seasickness is a nuisance, and she's a bit weak, but it's not all that dangerous overall. She'll recover, but if something happened to Harry, she'd be the first leading the charge, green or not."

"You're right about that." Devin grinned, though Christopher noticed his eyes remained pinched with worry. "She's such a funny lady, your wife," Devin added.

"How so?"

"She sees herself as this meek little mouse," Devin explained. "She's so retiring, and yet she does these incredible, brave things."

Christopher nodded, love for his wife welling up within him. "She's as shy as she claims to be. She really would prefer to live in her narrow, safe life: home, a few friends and family, our little world. But her past makes her passionate about abuse. If someone she cares for, particularly a woman or child, is suffering, she feels compelled to speak. You can't imagine how proud I am of her."

"I don't have to imagine it," Devin said dryly. "I can see it all over your face. Don't think I've missed those satisfied grins you wear all the time."

Christopher smirked. "Just wait until you're married. You'll see."

"I'd like nothing better." The bleakness on his brother's face pierced Christopher with awareness of how insensitive his comment had been.

"Sorry."

Devin shrugged. "I can't fault your happiness. After all, you two are here to help me, to help Harry. Go ahead and be happy."

"I'll try not to be obnoxious about it," Christopher said. *Good thing Kat is asleep and can't hear this. She'd be so embarrassed.*

"You're always obnoxious about it," Devin replied. "Better get some sleep if you can. I think it's going to be damned noisy around here shortly."

"No doubt," Christopher agreed, thinking of the coming storm. "You're welcome to join us if you'd like."

"I'll keep that in mind," Devin said, but Christopher could see in his face that he had no such intention. *Maybe the storm will help him vent some of the wildness he must be feeling. I hope it does. I don't like to see him this pent up.* But there was nothing to say on the subject, so Christopher returned to his room, tossed aside his clothing, and cuddled up with his wife, grateful their ordeal had ended seven years ago and thankful for the peace of a happy marriage.

* * *

The two quarreling winds brought their fight ashore near the harbor, knocking the boats about in their moorings, opening hulls and crushing smokestacks. They splintered the pilings in their rage and gouged huge clawing scratches in the beach.

Pebbles kicked up in their swirling maelstrom flew far ashore, shattering windows and smashing flowerboxes. Dirt fell to the streets, only to be picked up again and flung against the buildings.

Trees bowed before the force of the battle, but their penitence did not save them from being torn out of the ground and flung far, to the terror of those inside the buildings. Rain drummed hard on the flat roofs, but it was the wind that most frightened the tiny humans inside.

In a rented room in the center of the island, a tall, slender woman cowered in her bed, whimpering, cradled in the arms of a dark-haired and muscular man, who tenderly stroked her hair and murmured soothing words in her ear.

Next door to them, a second man, taller and younger, his dark hair burnished with bronze, leaned against the wall, staring out the window at the angry black sky. The roiling clouds matched the churning anguish in his soul. Fury as black as the storm, as violent as the wind tore through Devin's heart. Somewhere far away from him, his woman, the keeper of his heart, was suffering and in danger. Perhaps being assaulted. Perhaps being forced to sell her body for someone else's riches. He'd pushed the dark images away for so long, but today they would not be suppressed.

He had wondered, in the past, how men could love or even marry women with such a past. Today, for the first time, he understood. *A woman is not her virginity. She's not her history or her choices. They shape her, but she is herself. What I love about Harry goes so far beyond her pretty face and curvy little body. Beyond her sweet lips and tender eyes. I love her so much. Her intelligence and humility. The naughty sparkle in her eyes and her irrepressible sense of humor. Her loyalty. Even her impulsiveness. If some other man has touched her...*

Anger flared hot and bright as the lightning that lit up a cowering palm tree in the courtyard. He wanted to roar louder than the thunder. Yet oddly, what cut into Devin's guts most was not the thought of someone poaching on his claim, but the pain Harry would endure as what she had saved and tenderly bestowed on him was claimed by force by another, or by others.

Throat burning, Devin reached out with his consciousness, searching the vast cosmos, fearless in the face of the storm, seeking the one he loved. He could have sworn he could feel at a far distance, almost to the edge of his reach, a tiny, flickering spark, dim but undiminished, shining like a beacon. In his mind, he pictured sending his strength, his love, his presence. Whether it was his imagination, he wasn't sure, but it seemed the spark burned a bit brighter before a loud clap of thunder shattered the connection.

Devin blinked at the sight of a large branch... no, it was a tree trunk! It barreled toward the window in which he stood.

Jumping aside, Devin backed into the corner of the room, away from the window, as a whole damned palm tree smashed through the glass and ended up lying on the bed, calm as any infant tucked in for a restful night. Cursing, Devin skirted the invader. Driving rain blew through the opening, soaking him to the skin.

He hammered on Chris and Katerina's door, not sure if they'd hear a quiet knock over the roaring wind.

Chris opened the door.

"I think we'd better retire to the hallway," he suggested. "There's debris and the windows aren't holding."

Christopher nodded and a few moments later, they all huddled against the interior wall, Katerina squeezed between the two men.

"I'm frightened," she murmured.

"I've got you, love," Chris murmured loud enough for Devin to hear. He patted her arm.

"It can't last forever," Devin added.

They hunkered down to weather the storm.

Chapter 20

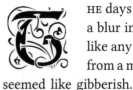HE days it took to cross Egypt would always remain as a blur in Harry's mind. The port of Alexandria looked like any other port. Busy, noisy and smelly with sailors from a myriad of nations shouting at each other in what seemed like gibberish.

They spent two days in the city, exploring the markets where the scent of spices evoked memories of a childhood that seemed like a faraway dream.

On the morning of the third day, a ratty-looking man wearing a headdress in a houndstooth pattern chattered at the captain from under a ragged mustache that twitched when he spoke. Protruding front teeth completed the ratlike appearance. Harry did not like the look of him at all. He signed for the cargo: thirty professional girls delivered as promised, and handed a bag of coins to the captain, who dismissed them with a wave and stalked back to his boat.

The rat-man escorted Harry and her companions to the station and loaded them onto a train. It smelled of those same spices, and Harry spent the hours lost in a dream of her mother's arms and the hot Indian countryside, the big house with white columns and the scent of cumin, cardamom and sweat that lingered in all the hallways.

Though Egypt couldn't be more different from India, from language to culture to religion, the scents managed to fling Harry ten years into her history. Terrible memories blended with poignant ones, completely drowning her awareness. While her friends chatted and watched the exotic scene outside the windows, Harry could only look inward and backward. She didn't see the camels, didn't hear Maria exclaiming about them. She didn't see the desert, even when Ana waxed poetic about its endless, stretching vastness, and then quoted Percy Shelley. "Round the decay/of that colossal wreck, boundless and bare/ the lone and level sands stretch far away."

Still, the images replayed on the insides of Harry's eyelids.

Standing on a stool in the kitchen as Usha toasted spices in hot oil and added onion. Standing in the garden watching hummingbirds flit in and out of colorful hibiscus flowers. Drinking a cool, fruity lassi. Following Kumar around the house, pestering him with questions. *Kumar. If there's anyone in India who truly cares about me… it's that man.* An idea began to form in the back of Harry's mind, though it refused to gel properly into a thought. *Ah well. I have nothing but time to ponder it.*

* * *

Devin stared in dismay at the wreckage that had once been the port of Malta. While not truly destroyed, the docks and cranes had suffered significant damage and the islanders were desperate for help from any willing, able-bodied men. They'd taken one look at Christopher's work-bulky muscles and Devin's impressive height and begged on bended knee. *No reason to refuse. The captain has dedicated his entire crew.* He sighed. *I hope the work can be completed quickly.*

* * *

"Get away from me," Harry snapped at the little rat-faced agent. He regarded her with wide brown eyes and took another step in her direction. She scarcely dared take her eyes off him to seek an escape route.

How did I get here? Waking from a nap to find herself alone in the rented room in Cairo, where they awaited horse-drawn wagons to drive them to Suez and the last leg of their journey, she'd been in search of the necessary when this desert rat had somehow managed to corner her in a dead-end corridor.

The look in his eyes made Harry want to vomit. "I know you speak English. You spoke to the captain readily enough, so I know you understand. Get away from me!"

He chuckled. "Fussy for a whore." He advanced another step.

Harry's back touched the wall, effectively ending her retreat. Heart pounding, she took mental inventory. *Nothing on my person or near me that can be used as a weapon. I'm out of luck. Oh, God.* "It was a mistake. I'm not a whore."

"Just a good girl in a bad situation?" he asked, stepping closer, his smelly robe swirling around thin and birdlike legs.

"That's right," Harry agreed.

He shook his head. "Liar. Only a slut goes out dressed so immodestly."

She blinked, considering her garment, which covered her from neck to toes. *I wonder what he means. Is it because I lack a corset? Is it because it fits my body instead of hanging loosely?* "What constitutes modesty varies by culture," she commented, trying to maintain reason in the face of growing panic. She gulped as his final step brought his feet between hers and his body plastered against her frame. *He's so skinny. Maybe I can knock him off balance.* Even as she concocted the desperate idea, she knew it was foolish, as the man's thinness clearly consisted of wiry, corded muscle. Harry prayed for a miracle.

His hand closed around the softness of her breast. His loathsome touch broke her restraint and she screeched, shoving wildly at his shoulders.

"Fight, bitch," he said with a laugh. "Only makes victory more enjoyable."

"No!" Harry screamed, kicking at him with her scuffed boots.

In one quick movement, he whirled her around and pinned her to the rough stone wall, crushing her upper body with his while a soft swishing sound and general fumbling in the vicinity of his belt tightened her distress to absolute terror.

"Ahmed, really," a familiar, serene voice cut through Harry's terror. "Do you really want to fight for it when you have willing women all around?"

Ahmed ceased fumbling with his garments and seemed to consider Ana's question. "You offering?"

"Are you paying?" she asked.

"I can pay," the ratty little man replied in a lascivious voice.

"Then let Harry go. She hasn't the first clue how to please a man. Come with me."

The crushing pressure on Harry's back eased and she drew in several rapid and unsteady breaths.

"Go back to the room and lock the door," Ana said in a low voice over her shoulder. "Don't come out alone again."

Once the hallway cleared, Harry bolted back to the room and cranked the key in the lock. Sinking onto the bed, she buried her face in her hands, gratitude for Ana's rescue mingling with her lingering distress and a feeling of intense guilt. *She saved me, but at what cost?* The thought made Harry nauseous, and she swallowed hard against a rising up of bile. Flinging herself down on the narrow cot, she laid an arm across her eyes and shuddered. *I thought perhaps I could be philosophical about rape... but there's no way. It's a horror that should be eliminated from the face of the earth.* Knowing women all over, including Ana herself, had suffered the very fate Harry had just escaped brought helpless tears to her eyes. *Keeping women defenseless and ignorant only makes it easier for unscrupulous men to prey on them.* "I hate this. I hate it."

Shaking with fury, bitter tears rained down, scorching Harry's hands and spotting her dress.

Then a new and even more horrifying idea occurred to her. *What if the captain was wrong and Slade won't consider? What if I'm forced to do... that?* Not one rape but many, over and over, forced to lie under different men at the whim of an employer she'd never requested. She'd tried so hard to ignore the thought, but it loomed like a ghost in her mind, dark and terrifying, and a scream of helpless agony welled up, only to be choked off by the sobs clogging her throat. *There is no way this will end well.* Trembling and weeping, Harry stretched out on the bed, her mind finally going mercifully blank.

* * *

Devin hefted a chunk that was once part of a damaged crane and tossed it on top of a pile of wood fit only for burning. Sighing and wiping sweat from his forehead, he plucked a splinter out of his palm. His blisters had blisters. Some remained swollen and filled with fluid. Others had burst to raw, oozing lesions that seemed disinclined to heal. *Christopher, with his work-calloused hands, has no blisters. My only callous is on my middle finger, where my pen rests.* He regarded the throbbing mess ruefully. *I'll have the hands of a working man before we get underway. Damnation, how long can it take? We've been a week already.*

His grumpy thoughts were interrupted by the arrival of his brother, whistling and looking very much in his element as he approached and inspected the crane. "I say, gentlemen, your base is too narrow. This thing should have twice the stance or it will tip over."

"What do you know about it?" A short man with deep mahogany skin and lighter, almost golden hair snapped.

"Nothing much," Christopher said with a short laugh. "I've only built a whole cotton mill full of machinery, including looms, dyeing vats and three cranes. So never mind. I'll just wander off."

The man's hostile look turned thoughtful. "Three?"

Christopher nodded. "For lifting bales of raw cotton from train cars and loading finished fabric in."

"Men, widen the stance of this crane," the bossy fellow shouted. Smirking, Christopher approached his brother.

"You're in a good mood," Devin said gloomily, still staring at his hands. "Of course, the way the bedsprings in your room were squeaking half the night, I can imagine why. Don't you ever get tired?"

Christopher's smug look turned downright devilish. "Would you?"

Devin snorted. "Glad someone's enjoying himself. All right, back to work. I don't know how much longer I can stand to remain stuck on shore while Harry's out there in God knows what kind of danger."

Christopher's grin faded. "All right." He hurried back to the pile of shattered boards still waiting to be cleared away from the edge of the newly repaired dock. "You know," he called, "there's not much left. We might be able to get away tomorrow. Let's talk to the captain."

"Finally, some good news," Devin muttered. He grabbed another hunk of wood and yelped as a fresh splinter punctured deeply into one of his blisters. "I could use some."

* * *

"Has anyone got an extra sanitary towel?" Ana asked, clearly unembarrassed. "Looks like this will not be my week to earn some extra coins."

Laughter greeted her ribald comments, even as Harry's cheeks burned. *Have I ever been so bold?* She couldn't remember a time. Even with Fanny, she would not have been quite as blunt.

"Not me," Maria replied. "I ran out last week. Barely made it."

"I'm out too," another voice called from across the cabin. The cabin they shared on this leg of the journey had a similar configuration to the one in which they'd set off from England, but instead of hammocks, this one had stacks of rigid and uncomfortable bunks. Very little open space remained, but they shared one steamer trunk for every three girls. *At least ours has a lock.* Choosing a set of bunks with Maria and Ana definitely improved upon sleeping so close to Eliza, whose loathing for Harry had not diminished in all the weeks they'd been away.

The speaker, Caroline, continued, brushing burnished curls with a mother of pearl brush she'd bought in Alexandria. "These sour old men wouldn't know one end of a woman from another and couldn't care less about us, but a lack of sanitation is a serious problem, even with Harry here to soak out the stains. Do you think they'll have anything to purchase at our next refueling stop?"

"Women bleed the world around," Ana reminded her. "They'll have something. Too bad it'll be two days. What a mess."

"You can have one of mine," Harry offered. "Any day now, I'll need it, but if we stop, I can get some more." Then Harry groaned internally as Eliza sauntered up to her.

"Why is it you're not out?" The brassy tart taunted, eyes sparkling with mischief. "Everyone is out. Every girl on this board has bled since our departure. Why not you?"

"Who knows?" Harry tried to sound insouciant. "I suppose it just hasn't started yet."

"Maybe it hasn't… and maybe it won't. How long has it been, little sister?"

"I don't know," Harry replied, wondering what Eliza was suggesting. "What difference does it make?"

"So innocent." Eliza shook her head. "Or are you? No woman's time in the forty days since we met… and who knows how long before that. Add occasional nausea, and what does that tell us?"

"That I've been kidnapped, thrown on a boat and forced to endure a stressful and frightening situation that as yet has not been resolved," Harry snapped.

"No one believes that," Eliza replied with an ugly laugh. "You're a liar, Harita Fletcher. You're no more innocent than the rest of us. You're increasing."

"I am not," Harry shot back, "and I don't know why you dislike me so much, but I wish you would just go away."

"Why should I? You trapped yourself, girl. All those disgusted, judgmental looks. Did you spread your legs for your imagined fiancé, or are you really just a whore like the rest of us?"

"Stop it!" Harry shouted, accidentally drawing everyone's attention to their conflict. "Devin is real. He loves me and the rest is none of your business."

"What's wrong with you, Eliza?" Maria demanded, jumping to Harry's defense. "Why don't you just leave her alone?"

"Can't you see it, Maria? Has she put a spell on you or are you just that gullible? She's judging us all, looking down that pert little nose of hers at all the 'dirty whores', but she's no better. Once her brat is born, she'll have no choice but to earn her keep on her back. You won't be so high and mighty then, will you?"

The unfounded accusations ignited a flurry of furious, whirling thoughts in Harry's mind and she struggled in vain against the tears.

"You're wrong," Maria said. "Harry is my friend. I chose this life, but I for one hope she doesn't have to."

She's a liar and you'll be sorry." Having delivered her parting shot, Eliza flounced away.

Harry regarded her friend, eyes swimming, lip trembling. "I swear I would never judge you, Maria. Before, I didn't understand, I..."

"Hush." Maria laid a gentle finger on Harry's lips. "Hush now. I never thought you did. This is a hard life, for all it's so common, and I wouldn't wish it on anyone. But, Harry, could it be true... what she said?"

Harry shook her head, wanting to deny it, but honesty compelled her to admit, "I don't know. I love Devin so much... I suppose it's possible." Her face flamed.

Maria's expression darkened. "Damned 'gentlemen' and their love."

"No," Harry protested. "It wasn't like that. Devin didn't seduce me. He tried ever so hard to behave honorably. I missed our wedding by a day. If our plan had come to fruition this..." her belly clenched with nerves. "No one would have known. But, Maria, now what am I going to do?"

"I don't know," the girl replied. "I wish I did. Maybe it will still prove to be nothing. I think, under such upsetting circumstances, being late or even missing a month wouldn't be unheard of."

Harry pondered, and realized with a sinking feeling that something did indeed feel different. Different in a way she could never recall having experienced before. She sucked in a deep breath. *This complicates everything.* Shoving the thought away, she focused on Maria, who had continued speaking. "You're from Bombay, aren't you?"

Harry nodded.

"Is there anyone you can contact? A friend or relative? Someone who could help you?"

Harry considered. "Maybe. My parents' friends were so shallow and stuffy. They would consider me contaminated. If I'm also…" she trailed off and shook the thought away vigorously. "I might have someone who can help me, if I can find him… He'd be very disappointed, I think."

"I hope you can find him, disappointed or not, for your sake," Maria commented. "Who is it?"

Harry regarded her friend and then glanced around the room. "Can you keep a secret?"

Maria raised one dark eyebrow.

"I'm serious. If anyone found out, they'd hate me more than Eliza does now."

The second eyebrow joined the first. "That must be some secret."

Harry nodded. "I can try to find my father. My natural father. His name is Kumar Mangal and he was a servant in my mother's household."

Maria's jaw dropped. She opened her mouth and closed it in a rapid flapping motion that reminded Harry of a fish. At last, she gave a little cough and said, "Well then, that would be a good thing." Then Maria swallowed down her surprise and said, "Don't worry, I won't say a word. Now let's get that towel for Ana before she ruins her dress."

"I can fix it," Harry reminded her, but hoisted herself to her feet anyway and hurried to her trunk. *At least I can make myself useful… take my mind off everything.* Her belly lurched, reminding her that forgetting was a costly luxury she wouldn't be able to afford for long.

* * *

The port of Alexandria loomed on the horizon like a beacon. *I've never been this far from home. Not even close. Egypt, land of pyramids and desert, camels and traveler's tales.* He imagined visiting the ancient sites of Egypt, with his intrepid Harry by his side, with Chris and Kat, making a holiday adventure. *It could be fun. She's well-read. I'm sure she knows all kinds of things about Egypt. The pyramids by day, and mad, tropical passion at night.* The thought brought a tight smile to his lips. *I hope she still retains her adventurous side after this ordeal.* Trying to hold onto that morsel of hope, Devin focused his attention on the horizon. Finally, after losing two weeks, they were approaching the brief overland connection before heading to their final destination. *Almost halfway there.* The vastness of the world momentarily dawned on Devin, making him feel like an ant. Then he blinked away the sensation and focused on his goal: *Bombay and Harry. On to Alexandria and finally embarking on the Eastern portion of our journey.*

Chapter 21

"ELL, I have to say, this part of Bombay looks a great deal like everything else we've seen. Maybe a bit… domeier, but nothing more," Maria said, regarding buildings with white columns, rows of homes and businesses and shops, shops everywhere. Pouring rain obscured the view somewhat, and they crowded under umbrellas. "How disappointing. A city is a city the world around."

"It is," Harry agreed as they hurried along a slick and muddy street linking the harbor to the town. "When I first arrived in London I was surprised by the cold, but little else. I mean, there are parts of India that are like nothing you've ever seen, but this British, commercial part of Bombay—which is familiar, as I used to live near here—is quite ubiquitous."

They passed through surprisingly wide streets between three-story buildings with awnings, among a crowd of milling pedestrians, umbrellas in hand to block out a late-season rainstorm. Stone and plaster in gold and white had been accented with red roofs and colorful shutters, some brilliant and fresh, others faded from exposure to the elements. Palm trees dipped and waved as though in welcome, driven by a gusty wind that skimmed the town to make its way to them and dampen them with driven raindrops.

"Well, there is one thing that's different," Ana mumbled through a hand clapped over her nose. "What the devil is that smell? It's worse than the Thames in summer."

Harry took a deep sniff. Even though her now-undeniable pregnancy had sensitized her nose, the scent did not offend her. "It's the smell of Bombay," she replied. "I can detect cumin and cardamom strongly, and there's a scent of jasmine." She sighed. "It smells like home to me."

"It smells like armpits and human waste," Eliza drawled, holding a handkerchief over her face.

"Well, it's hot here," Harry explained. "London smells, too. Anywhere does when many people crowd into a small space."

"What can you tell us about this place?" Maria asked, peering through the rain at their new home. "Why do people want to come here?"

Harry thought back to the lessons she'd learned from her mother, as well as from locals she'd known in her childhood. "Bombay is built on a series of islands," she began. "It's excellent for shipping because the harbor is so deep. Unfortunately, there are many bogs filled with mosquitoes and disease, so do be careful of insects." Her words produced violent shudders among her companions. "It was owned by the Portuguese in the 1600s, and they called it *bom baya* or good bay, which is where the name Bombay comes from. They gave it to the English in a dowry. The English, Dutch, British and Mughals—who are the Indians in power—squabbled over each other's ships and caused each other a great deal of trouble in the past, but it's much more peaceable now."

"Pirates?" Maria asked, eyes wide.

"If any are still living," Harry replied, "they'd be too old to do much more than tell stories about their glory days. Trade and industry are king now, have been for decades. It's why my family came here—military, you know, to protect the interests of the Empire."

"It's why we're here too," Eliza pointed out in her sneering voice. "The captains of industry make all that lovely money, and we can help them spend it."

"Hurry, ladies," their guide said. One of the stuffy sailors from their last leg of the journey, he now guided them to their final destination, the club where one Jonathan Slade reigned over a network of dens of iniquity in which alcohol, gambling and loose women could be purchased by those whose income sufficed for such expensive indulgences. "If you're interested in local history, the most recent developments are a series of causeways between the islands. The swamps are slowly being pushed back and the land made useful for building. I don't doubt we'll get the mosquitos under control soon."

"When you get a chance," Harry added, "be sure to visit Elephant Island. There's a gorgeous Hindu shrine there."

"Pagan trash," Eliza muttered, drawing an ugly scowl from the sailor.

Harry found it interesting that their quest led them to a humble-looking two-story building right in the center of the commercial district. Unlike the surrounding businesses, which had hung shingles above the door advertising their purpose, the club did not announce its presence. It stood between a newspaper office and a towering four-story hotel. Unlike its neighbors, it had no balconies. The row of windows along the upper and lower floors was guarded by faded green shutters that barely contrasted with the golden-colored façade.

As they entered the club, the girls fell silent and their complaints stilled. An echoing, two-story space opened up to the roof, with a balcony all around, ringed with closed doors painted in bright colors. The ground floor consisted of a single huge mosaic in blue and white tiles. Tables, chairs, gaming apparatus and various pieces of furniture designed for idle chatting stood in comfortable clusters.

"Uh…" Maria let out a short squeak and then shut her mouth with a snap.

"Wow," Harry said, staring wide-eyed at the lush accommodations.

"Not bad," Ana added, regarding the opulence with a critical eye.

"You're right, it's not bad," a gravelly male voice cut into their awe. "It's only the most extravagant, desirable club in town. Not just anyone is allowed to partake of our establishment. Only those who can afford to pay and pay well. You were selected because you are the best, and you need to think of yourselves as the best. We offer premium contracts and fair practices because we believe that happy girls have happy clients. If you want to enjoy the benefits of your position, be sure to uphold your end of the bargain."

Harry regarded the man with curiosity as he stalked towards them, boots clicking on the tiles. *So this must be Slade, the owner.* Her heart threatened to hammer through her ribs at the sight of the man who held her ultimate fate in his hands. He looked like her imaginary idea of a pirate, with dark wavy hair flowing around his shoulders, a loose white shirt, open at the neck, and skin-tight breeches tucked into black boots.

He met the eyes of each of the girls in turn, taking in their nods, until his gaze fell on Ana. His smooth delivery faltered, and he too fell silent for a moment, apparently rendered dumb by her beauty. Then he visibly shook himself and continued his speech. "I hope all of you carefully read the contract you signed, or had it explained to you, because there will be no deviation from the terms. In case you've forgotten, the deal is this: you will provide to the house a monthly share of your profits equal to half the average a girl earns in a month. The more you work, the greater your share will be, but that will remain up to you to determine. I understand indisposition, but so should you, so plan accordingly. In addition, as the contract clearly states, for the first year, a fee will be collected each month to cover the cost of your transport. If anyone has a problem with this, please speak to me privately. In the meanwhile, you will have three days to acclimate yourselves to your new environment. However, should you wish to begin working earlier, you may feel free to do so. After this, I will bring you to Cali. She will assign you to your locations. Requests are considered, though not guaranteed; however, if you have a friend you want to be assigned with, that is likely to be honored. Any questions?"

Again, his eyes lingered on Ana, but she remained silent, regarding him with a cool, unreadable expression.

"Um, Mr. Slade?" Harry spoke up, hands and voice trembling, "may I please speak with you in private?"

* * *

"What the devil is going on now?" Devin demanded, pacing the red-tiled hallway of their Cairo hotel.

"Settle down, little brother," Christopher said grimly.

"I will not," Devin growled. "They told us in Alexandria that the horse carts leave every few days. Why would it be a week or more?"

Christopher heaved a huge sigh. "I'm sorry. The usual driver is ill. They're searching for a replacement, but it's not easy work. The path across the desert can be treacherous for men and beasts." He lowered his voice. "I know you want to hurry to get Harry back..."

"You're damned right I do. We're already a month behind schedule, between all the delays and the storm." He leaned against the arching wall and rested his head on the white plaster. "I'm sorry. I know you're doing your best. I don't mean to blame you."

"Of course not. But risking our lives, and Katerina's life, in the trackless desert won't save Harry. Only calm, clear thinking will do that."

Devin shook his head. "She's got to be nearly there by now. Every day we delay..."

"I know." Christopher laid a hand on his shoulder. "I'll tell you what. You go ahead and flail. I'll take care of the thinking."

Devin swallowed down a roar of frustration. "Am I being stupid?"

"Yes, but if you weren't, under the circumstances, I'd worry about you. You're acting like a man who loves his woman, and there's nothing wrong with that."

Devin rubbed his aching forehead. "How's Katerina doing?"

"A little better," Christopher replied. "She always gets seasick, but I've never known her to have problems with the train. It's unfortunate she fell ill just now, and she feels terrible about it."

Devin frowned. "I hope she recovers. We have enough trouble. I don't want to have the guilt of putting your wife into a precarious situation to add to it."

"As I recall," Christopher retorted dryly, "she put herself into a precarious situation and wouldn't take no for an answer." He grinned at the thought of his wife. Devin could actually see images of Katerina playing behind his brother's eyelids. *They're so happy together. Their life is damn near perfect. It's so unfair. When do I get to settle in with the woman I love and be happy?*

* * *

"Well, you're right." Slade dropped the sheaf of papers on the desk and regarded Harry with an uncertain expression. "There are twenty-nine contracts and not one says Harita Fletcher or Harriet Fletcher or anything remotely similar. So you're saying my investor had you kidnapped and sent here?"

"Yes, sir," Harry told him. *Please believe me. Please let this matter.* "I'm not a working girl, or at least not in this way. I was a lady's maid and companion, nothing more. I… I can't do that. I won't." She stuttered to a stop, biting her lip.

"I'm not in the business of forcing unwilling girls," Slade commented. "There's really no need. Plenty of women volunteer, so I can afford to be choosy."

"You see," Harry said. "I'd not be an asset to the business. I promise, if you let me go, I won't cause any trouble… well, I might trouble you for a sheet of paper and a pen …"

"Not so fast, girl." Slade narrowed his eyes. "It's not that simple. There's much more at stake here than a misunderstanding. Hundreds of pounds have gone into bringing you here."

"I didn't ask to be brought here," Harry protested. "I was on the verge of marriage. This is the last place I want to be." She fought to regain control of her emotions, but the tide was rising in her.

Slade, damn him, seemed cool and calm as he met her parry with a simple shrug and dropped into the seat behind his desk.

"So is that how it works then?" Harry demanded. "All your talk of contracts, but one simple misunderstanding and we're at an impasse?"

"I don't know what to suggest, Miss Fletcher," Slade said, leaning back in his desk chair and putting his feet up on the wood. "Clearly, I have no interest in unwilling girls, and no need for them, but I still have investors to answer to. My business doesn't run without sponsors, and they like reports and numbers. They like to know how their money is being spent and what expenses cut into the profits. The money spent getting you here will need to be accounted for."

"But I don't want to be here," Harry reminded him. *Please, God, let me think of a solution. Help me. I can't just succumb...* "I didn't ask to be snatched from my fiancé's home in a sack and dragged to the docks. I tried to get off the ship in England. I tried to get away in Gibraltar. I did everything I could."

"I appreciate the frustration that must have caused you..."

"Do you?" Harry snapped, her voice growing louder and shriller with every word. "Can you truly grasp how frightening, demoralizing and humiliating it is to be kidnapped, thrown into a boat full of prostitutes, dragged away from my home, nearly raped and now being told I must repay a debt I never wanted to incur? A debt I would have given anything to prevent? If you say such a thing, you're a fool!"

Slade exploded from the chair and circled the desk, grabbing Harry by the arm and shaking her once, a hard snap that momentarily cut off her tirade. "Now listen here, Miss. I do wish you hadn't been brought in this way, but I will not be spoken to in such a fashion, do you hear me?"

The details of the man, from the fragrance of cologne and sweat lingering around his body, to the stubble on his chin, to a ragged spot in his clothing seemed to loom large in her vision. Her thoughts rolled in her head... rolled, and then clicked into place. *Lord, let him listen.*

"You have a hole in your shirt."

His face crunched down into a befuddled scowl. "What?"

"Right here." Harry touched the little opening in his left sleeve with her fingertip.

"Are you mad? What difference does that make?"

She raised her eyes to his, finding warm brown depths that nearly matched her own. *He's like me,* she realized. *All right, no need to be afraid.* "I have an idea. I think I know how we can both get what we want."

* * *

"And he agreed, just like that?" Wide-eyed, Maria pressed both hands over her heart and flopped back on her bed.

Harry took a moment to admire the simple yet luxurious furnishings in the small, private bedrooms the girls would inhabit. *Nice of Slade to provide rooms for sleeping that are separate from the 'working' areas.* This small dormitory, with two sets of bunk beds, stood in a separate wing of the building from the public areas. Simple but wonderfully soft bedding covered comfortable mattresses. Beautiful colored rugs adorned the floor, providing the only note of strong color in a room otherwise cool and white.

Maria and Ana had requested to stay together, regardless of location, and had requested Harry as well, and apparently, that meant they were staying in the main club. The other girls had been moved around the city and into the surrounding areas to take up residence as needed. All but one. From a perch on the top bunk of the second bed, Eliza glared at them with a baleful expression, then leaned back on her bed, hands behind her head, and made a great show of studying the smoothly plastered ceiling.

"I couldn't believe it," Harry replied, ignoring her nemesis and returning to the conversation at hand. "When I pointed out how much ready-made garments cost, how much he could save by hiring me to repair and maintain the clothing and make new garments myself, he looked thoughtful. Then he actually took off his shirt and had me fix the hole right then and there. I think it was a test." She blushed to recall the sight of his naked, muscular chest. "So I have a month to prove that having me work as the on-site seamstress and garment expert is a benefit equal to... other work, and he'll give me the same contract he gave you all. One year of service to pay off the passage and I'm free and clear."

"That's fantastic, Harry!" Maria exclaimed, and Ana, from the lower bunk below where Eliza lay frowning, nodded eagerly.

"There's a reason we agreed to this," she said, "or at least why I did. I can't speak for anyone else, but the professionalism and fairness of the contract impressed me. It's rare for a business owner to give so much thought to the needs and rights of working girls like us, so I'm not surprised he took your suggestion into consideration. And you're not wrong. You'll save the business a fortune, and probably provide better quality clothing than anything he can buy ready-made from a shop. Certainly, it will fit better."

"That's my plan," Harry replied. "I need to be as useful as possible for this to work, and I'm so grateful. I still can't believe it."

"Did you tell him about…?" Maria trailed off, indicating the vicinity of Harry's belly. While to her, the slight outward curve felt like a beacon illuminating her pregnancy, she knew it wasn't visible at the moment.

"Not yet," she admitted. "Why borrow trouble? First, I want to prove myself so valuable he won't be able to object much. Besides, it can't be the first time someone's become *enceinte* in this line of work. I'm amazed it doesn't happen all the time."

"That's because we take steps to prevent it, idiot," Eliza snapped from the bunk. "You're pregnant because you weren't careful."

"Shut up, you." Ana pushed up on the mattress to annoy Eliza before turning to Harry. "Not that it matters now, but there are several techniques to reduce the risk, none of which is absolutely foolproof."

Maria sighed and turned to look out the window, and Harry could see her lower lip trembling. "What's wrong?" she asked, laying her hand over her friend's where it rested on the white cotton sheet.

"It's not idiotic not to know. I didn't know either." She dug her teeth into her trembling lip to still it and turned wide eyes on Harry. "I was in service, like you. But unlike you, I didn't meet someone kind. I tried so hard to mind my own business, but when the master took a liking to me, there was no escaping him."

"Oh, Lord," Harry groaned. "What happened, love?"

"What do you think?" Maria asked, bitter and upset. "He forced himself on me. I was a good girl, but ignorant as a sheep in the meadow. I understood the mechanics but had no idea how to protect myself. I fell pregnant almost immediately, and when the mistress found out… she turned me out. No reference, no severance pay. I was alone in London, in a delicate condition. I tried to find employment, but no one would have me. I think I might have starved… or jumped off a bridge, but I didn't want my babe to suffer, so I did what I had to do to protect him." She choked. "It was horrible on the streets, but it's amazing what a person can become used to." A sniffle and a suppressed sob interrupted her narrative.

"Did you find a family for your baby?" Harry asked gently.

Maria shook her head. "He was stillborn. All that work, all that…" she swallowed hard, "and he never drew his first breath. If Slade's man hadn't turned up with a contract… well, the river looked better and better every day. I'm so glad I met you two. You gave me a reason to live again."

This makes horrible sense. I always knew she was too good for this life. Harry dragged Maria off the mattress and into a tight hug. "Someday, you'll find something better. You just wait and see."

Eliza laughed bitterly. "Once a whore, always a whore," she sneered. "Don't give her false hope. You'll make it worse. This life will wear us out, grind us under, and take us too young. That's what always happens."

"That's not true," Harry snapped, irritated beyond words by Eliza's constant harping. "This is what you do, it's not what you are."

"Not unless you decide to make it so," Ana added. "I don't. This is a means to an end, nothing more. And here we are in a new, vast country where no one knows us. In time we'll be able to save money and make our way to a better life. That's what I aim to do. If you want to wallow in this life until it finally kills you, be my guest, but I won't choose that fate."

"If you think you have any more choices than a worm on a hook, you're mad." Eliza rolled her eyes.

"Then I choose madness," Ana replied, her stern gaze fixed on the mattress above her. "Better madness with hope than your version of reality."

Unable to find a suitable reply, Eliza fell silent, for which Harry felt a great deal of gratitude.

Chapter 22

"EAT pies? Ale? Blancmange?" Ana shook her head. "I thought this place was supposed to be luxurious," she complained in a carrying voice.

Slade regarded the gorgeous icy blond from his seat on one of the comfortable sofas, where he sat with his feet up on an end table, scribbling in a large folio with a stub of a pencil. "If milady objects to the accommodations," he drawled in a faux starchy voice, "she can seek employment elsewhere."

"I can't do that, and you know it," Ana shot back. "We have a contract, remember? I was only suggesting that it might be a good idea to consider a more interesting menu."

"Because you know so much about food? Are you volunteering to cook for us, Miss Thomas?" he asked.

"Not at all," she replied. "I don't know a saucepan from a salt cellar."

"Then I respectfully suggest you shut up," he said.

From her seat in a little-used and semi-private alcove near the dining area, Harry smiled down at the chemise she was repairing. The banter between those two had been growing in frequency and intensity in the last four weeks. *They like each other. I hope they can find their way to admit it.*

"Right," Ana said. "I don't know about cooking, so I'll shut up, because obviously, I don't know anything about luxury either. I mean, after all, my mother is only a cousin to the royal family of Russia. I only spent a quarter of my childhood in the royal palace. My father is only one of the richest businessmen in England. I know nothing of wealth or opulence, so I'll shut up." Her lips curved upward in a saucy smile.

Harry watched Slade out of the corner of her eye. His face had taken on a riveted expression. *He always looks like that when she smiles.*

"You're royal?" Doubt dripped from his tone.

"Only a distant connection," she replied airily. "Not actually royal myself, but I've seen things. Listen, Mr. Slade, if you want people to feel luxurious, the presentation needs to be seamless. This place has some of the trappings of wealth, but the seams are showing. You have to think like a wealthy person, and it's all in the details."

Harry looked from Ana to Slade and dared to comment, "That's not going to be natural for him, Ana. He's clearly a self-made man. The details of wealth are far from his everyday experience."

"What do you know about it?" He snapped in her direction, clearly angry at having his conversation with Ana interrupted.

She met his eyes with her own matching ones. "I recognize what I see," she replied. "I know what it is to be two things, and therefore nothing, or am I wrong?"

He regarded her with eyebrows drawn together and then sucked in a sharp breath. "I see it, now that you've mentioned it, yes. But enough about that. I'm trying to understand what Miss Thomas is suggesting. All this talk of seams should be your purview."

She smiled and returned her gaze to her sewing.

"Well, let's have it then, Miss Thomas. What do you suggest? How can I make rich men feel at home, so they spend more money? And why do you care?"

Ana sauntered over and plunked herself beside him on the sofa. "Do you think I want to do this forever, sir?

He gave her a look that spoke volumes, demonstrating he'd never considered such an idea before. Harry watched unabashedly. "What do you have in mind then?"

"Russian food," she said proudly.

He looked askance at the lovely woman. "In heaven's name, why?"

She laughed, a deep and throaty sound. "Because it's different. Everyone expects French food at a fancy place, but no one expects the exotic. Indian won't do... you can buy it on any street corner. Britain and Russia are at war, though no one wants to admit it, and that makes someone of Russian descent—such as myself—tantalizing. I can personally attest to that. Finally, Russian food features many preserved items and root vegetables, which makes it more practical than French, which relies on freshness."

The dazed expression on Slade's face clearly had nothing to do with Ana's beauty. He looked as though he'd been hit by a train. At last, his mouth stopped flopping open and he spoke. "You present an interesting idea." He ran a lingering gaze over Ana's face and body. "How do you feel about continuing this discussion... in private?"

She returned his heated stare with a cool one. "That depends. To talk? Certainly. If you have anything else in mind, you'll have to explain how it will be credited to my account."

Harry saw one corner of Slade's mouth lift, carving a dimple into his cheek. "You drive a hard bargain, Miss Thomas."

"I do," she agreed.

A second dimple joined the first. Slade rose and extended a hand, and Ana accepted it. They did not release each other as they exited the room.

Harry snickered.

"What's so funny?" Maria asked, slipping into a chair near her friend.

"Ana's playing Slade like a fiddle," Harry explained. "I suspect she will have a change of position soon."

Maria frowned, eyebrows drawn together in obvious confusion.

"Slade's taken a liking to her," Harry explained. "I have a feeling if he begins to see her as his, he won't want her working with anyone else."

Maria's frown deepened. "Some people have all the luck," she muttered.

Luck? What on earth? "I don't know what you mean. Ana is practically a princess. Becoming the mistress of a club owner in India is a step down, not up, compared to where she could be."

"But it's better than where she was," Maria protested, sounding as melancholy as Harry had ever seen her. "No one will ever see fit to change my stars."

"Don't think like that," Harry urged, reaching out to clasp her friend's hand.

"Wake up, Harry," Maria snapped. "Ana is a diamond—beautiful and hard. Everywhere she goes, people desire to possess her. She uses it to her advantage, and it gives her great power. Even you have a skill, which makes you valuable. I'm nothing. I'm weak and soft and uneducated. This fancy whorehouse is the best future I can expect."

"It's not," Harry said. "Try not to despair, Maria." But her kind words fell on deaf ears. Maria rose stiffly and stalked from the room.

* * *

"How long to Bombay, Captain?" Devin asked a grizzled man with hairy mutton chops adorning full, red cheeks.

"I'd say ten days, give or take," the man drawled in a thick Scottish accent. "I've never seen such unfavorable weather. Our screws are near worn out from all the churnin'."

Devin ground his teeth. *Don't I know it? Every hour has felt like a year.* "Thank you, sir. I'm eager to reach our destination."

The man chuckled. "No jest, son. Ye act like yer meeting yer bride."

"I am," Devin replied simply, and walked away, leaving the man's jaws flapping.

"Devin?" Christopher met his brother near the rail. Though a hazy drizzle dampened their hair and clothing, the hot air kept any chill at bay, and the moisture actually felt refreshing. Uncaring of ugly looks, Katerina stood cradled in her husband's embrace, her head on his shoulder. The high humidity had her curly hair escaping its chignon and springing wild and free around her face—her very green and nauseous-looking face.

"Yes, Chris?"

"I hate to say this, now that we've come this far, but are you sure this girl is worth it?"

Devin snarled.

"I'm sorry, but you have to understand. I'm concerned for my wife. She's unwell, and I barely know your girl. Let's be honest, *you* barely know her. How can you know she even needs to be rescued? Maybe returning to India is just what she wanted."

Devin shook his head, but Katerina spoke first. "No." She turned in her husband's arms and sent him a penetrating stare. "Of course Harry is worth this effort," she said firmly. "Harry loves Devin, loves him so much it frightens her. Remember how she couldn't believe anyone would help him be with her? She's not playing games."

"How do you know, though?" Christopher insisted.

"I know what I saw, love," she said, no less determined. "I know what it feels like to love someone you think you don't deserve. I saw in Harry what I felt when we were courting. Put your mind at ease, my darling. If my love means anything to you, if we have anything good together, Devin and Harry will be just fine."

Christopher's lips twisted. He'd been routed, Devin saw. He could argue no further without calling into question his love for his wife. "You know how much your love means to me," he murmured into her ear. The wind carried the words to Devin. "You're my everything. My whole world. But I care about my brother and I want to be sure he'll be happy. It was only a question."

She looked up into his eyes. "A question that has been answered. Be easy, my darling. They'll make a fine couple. I only worry about poor Harry. I hope she's not been harmed."

The odds were against Katerina's wish, but he prayed with everything he had for them to be true anyway.

* * *

Returning from the telegraph office, a strange mixture of feelings churned Harry's guts to nausea. Sending a message to Devin, she couldn't help wondering if he would care. *Maybe Eliza is right. Maybe Maria is, and he wasn't as serious as I wanted to believe.* A new and horrifying scenario presented itself in her mind. She had offered herself to him, and being male, he had accepted. Being a gentleman, upon taking her virginity, he'd offered marriage and made the best of it. But what if he saw her disappearance as a reprieve. *What if he's glad I'm gone?* "No," she whispered to herself. "He told me he loves me. I have to have faith in that. I have to."

She ran her hand over the side of her belly, where the flesh now curved outward. "Don't worry, little darling," she whispered. "Your father will help us. I know he will."

Trying not to let go of hope, Harry pushed her way through the big double doors of the club and into the bustling madness of thirty minutes to opening. "Harry, there you are!" Ana exclaimed, grabbing her arm and dragging her forward. "My best silk gown has a rip in the bodice. How long will it take you to fix it?"

Harry sighed. "Silk is hard, Ana. The stitches always show. I'll fix it, but probably not in time for tonight. Don't worry, though. Remember I said I was making you something special? Well, look on your bed. There's a blue silk sari. I think you'll like it, and it will suit your coloring very well."

"Harry, you're an angel," the blonde gushed, "I can't wait to see it."

"How did your silk dress get torn?" Harry asked.

Ana blushed, the pale skin of her cheeks turning a becoming pink, and she mumbled something unintelligible.

"What was that?" Harry pressed, teasing her friend.

"Uh, um… Slade tore it."

Harry laughed. "I'll charge him extra for it."

Ana giggled and sailed out before Harry could come up with the next volley of repartee. Shrugging, she crossed the central room, skirting the carved columns and turning left past the dining area, where tufted leather chairs surrounded small round tables. A door, cleverly concealed in a mural painted on the far wall, opened into a hallway along which the girls' dormitories lay on both sides. She ducked into her room to find Ana crowing over the dramatic, ethnic-looking garb. Harry collected her wicker basket, waved to her friend and traipsed out the door.

A quick knock on all the doors yielded a basket full of sewing. Feeling lonely and a bit forlorn after her unpleasant surmises, she made her way back to the public portion of the club and tucked herself into an alcove where she could observe the action without being obtrusive. A white cap covering her hair and the loose dress concealing her expanding figure gave her the air of a matron. The flickering light sent strange shadows dancing over her face. *In a room full of beautiful women, that makes me invisible.*

She wove the needle through cotton, silk and satin, repairing torn bloomers, drooping hems and burst seams. One dress needed alteration to be passed from a larger girl to a smaller one. Another needed to be let out.

In the club, the evening had begun. A quiet hum of male conversation and the dense scent of sweaty bodies wafted through the room. A pianoforte tinkled in the corner. *Devin said his sister-in-law played well, but I never got a chance to hear her.* So many things she'd never done. Normal things. She'd never met Devin's parents. Never seen the family home, or the factory he admired but didn't want to work in. *Our relationship was in its infancy. What if he did forget? What if he did assume I wanted to go?* Harry blinked furiously to dispel the burn in the corners of her eyes.

Added heat amplified the burn as she recalled how she'd foolishly spent her last coin on a second telegram, one she sent to Devin's parents, in case his went astray. She'd been so short of funds, she'd only been able to provide two words: *Bombay, Slade.* She hoped it would make sense. *I hope someone will care.* This life, poised on the edge of prostitution, still bothered her, and she had no desire to raise their baby in it.

A tickle, soft and gentle, bubbled through her insides, drawing a smile to her lips. *We'll figure out something, little baby. Don't worry. Momma will take care of you.*

A rustle, a thud and a sigh drew Harry's attention to the table nearest her alcove, where Maria had just taken a seat.

"Are you all right?" she asked her friend. "I do hope you're not still angry at me."

Maria turned in profile, keeping her eyes on the room while she talked to Harry. "I was never angry at you. I was angry at fate, and you got in the way. I'm sorry."

"I quite understand," Harry replied. "So what brings you this direction? At this time, you're usually circulating."

"He's watching me," Maria replied, her scowl deepening.

"Who is?" Harry asked, scanning the room.

Her eyes landed on the culprit just as Maria spoke. "I don't know who he is, but that fellow with the blond hair, over in the right-hand corner, with two soldiers. Do you see him?"

"I see," Harry confirmed, squinting to make out the man's features at such a distance. "You don't know him? Why is he staring? What does he want?"

"I have no idea," Maria replied. "He's come every night for a week, but he never approaches me. He just sits and stares."

"Maybe he's shy," Harry suggested.

"Maybe he's broke," Maria shot back. "Humph," she snorted. "I'll go find out." The girl flounced from her seat and sailed across the room, sliding into the one empty chair left at the table. Harry strained her ears to eavesdrop on the conversation.

"What's wrong with you, sir? Can't keep your eyes to yourself?" she demanded.

"Is it wrong to look?" he replied. "If so, I apologize." His voice sounded gentle and curious.

Harry focused harder, trying to understand what this fellow had done to provoke Maria, who was normally so placid and kind.

"It's eerie," she replied. "You're here, I'm working, but you never ask for a turn. You've been staring for days and you've made no requests. What do you want from me?"

Even at this distance, Harry could see his cheeks darken. "A moment of your time."

"Time is money," Maria snapped, quoting Benjamin Franklin. *I wonder where she picked up that quotation.* "And my time costs more than most. Are you willing to pay?"

"Huh…" he choked and cleared his throat. "How much?"

She leaned in and whispered to him, which caused him to choke harder. Taking a sip of the brandy in front of him, he croaked, "That's a lot of money."

"I'm well worth it," Maria boasted, fluttering her shoulders.

The man's voice turned intense. "You certainly are. Priceless, I'd say. Well, it's a bit of a stretch, but I'll have a go."

As Maria led her conquest past the table, Harry could see the anger, disgust, disappointment and fear blending with the triumph on her pretty, round face.

* * *

Standing on the docks in Bombay's harbor, Devin and Christopher surveyed the scene. The bustling port, from which a scent of spices, overripe fruit and massed, milling humanity, wafted over them, both resembled other ports and, ironically, made them aware they'd arrived on the other side of the world.

Katerina also regarded Bombay in silence, though Devin suspected in her case it was because she still felt ill. Her green face provided a telling clue.

"Well, now what? Christopher demanded.

"Uh, we find Harry," Devin replied, his eyes riveted to the skyline of Bombay. Somewhere in all that vastness, the woman he loved waited, in who knows what kind of situation, for him to rescue her.

"Well, yes," Christopher replied in irritated amusement. "But how? Have you given a thought to how you're going to find one woman in this entire city?"

In truth, he hadn't. Focused on speed, first to catch up and then to minimize the time she spent in Bombay with her captors, he had

not given a second thought to what he would do on his arrival. "I…
uh, I don't know," he admitted. He could have sworn Harry's essence,
that spark of her soul that so drew him, shone bright and clear on the
edge of his perception, but of her location, even her direction, he had
no idea.

Katerina made an unpleasant sound and swallowed hard. "I suggest
we begin by finding a hotel. You might also send a telegram to your
parents."

"Too right, love," Christopher agreed. "Perhaps the telegraph operator can give us a clue where to begin."

Devin considered the awkwardness of the conversation. *Good thing
it's no one I know.*

Christopher flagged down a uniformed soldier loitering against a
wall that edged the harbor. "Excuse me, where could some weary travelers find a hotel?"

The man regarded them with jaded eyes until his gaze fell on Katerina. Apparently, her angelic beauty and obvious distress touched him,
because he not only named the hotel, he gave them detailed directions,
twice, before pointing them on their way.

It appeared Bombay, with its exotic and intense aromas, did not
please Katerina's stomach any better than the steamer had. She gagged
and gulped, leaning on her husband for support.

What an auspicious start, Devin thought.

* * *

When Maria returned to the public room an hour later, she looked
more confused than ever. Harry had never seen such an expression on
her friend's face before. "What happened?" she hissed from her alcove.

"Nothing," Maria replied, still blinking. "He paid for his hour and…
and…"

"And," Harry insisted.

"And he talked to me."

Harry grinned.

"What's he doing?" Maria demanded.

"He's treating you with respect, like a lady," Harry replied.

"But I'm not a lady," Maria protested.

Harry's smile grew wider. "To him you are."

* * *

"How is Katerina doing?" Devin asked as he and Christopher strode into the street. Devin wrinkled his nose at the sight of a ragged beggar, his white hair standing out in a wild halo around his brown and bony face. A stench rose from the man and his grin revealed only three teeth.

He gabbled at the brothers in an incomprehensible language and Christopher handed him a coin.

"Namaste," the beggar said, pressing his hands together.

With a curt nod, they edged past and Devin pointed the direction the hotel's clerk had given them for the telegraph office.

"Katerina is miserable." Christopher's face twisted with worry. "I may need to find her a physician."

"For seasickness?" Devin asked.

"She's sick on land and sea," Christopher replied, "and she never adjusted, the way she always did en route to or from Italy. I'm alarmed at her condition."

Devin winced. *I hope this voyage doesn't do her any lasting harm.*

* * *

"I can't think about this," Maria protested. "Talk to me, Harry."

I would rather talk about your potential suitor, but I'm sure that will come in time. "About what?"

"How did your errands go? We missed you at lunch. Aren't you hungry?"

"So many topics," Harry replied with a laugh. "I had lunch in town." She licked her lips at the memory.

"What did you have?" Maria asked, though Harry knew she didn't appreciate Indian food. Her reactions so far to what little she'd tasted had been far from positive. *She must be desperate.*

"It's called Masale Bhat. It's a combination of seasoned rice, potato and cauliflower. I ate a lot of it as a child."

"You're born to it," Maria said.

"It's true," Harry replied, not pointing out that many Westerners had adapted to the taste, and some even grew to love it. *She wants a distraction, not an argument. Besides, one likes what one likes.*

Maria made a face, and Harry continued. "I sent a telegram to Devin and his parents, but I have no idea if they will receive them or care."

"Now who's being gloomy?" Maria demanded. "All this time you've been steadfast in your belief that Devin loves you and will find some way to save you. Now you don't know if he cares. What happened?"

"I put things together in my mind," Harry replied. "What could he really do? It's such a long way and the passage is expensive and arduous. What can I honestly expect? We courted only a short time."

Maria acknowledged the truth in Harry's words with a rueful press of her lips. "Any news from your father?"

Harry shrugged. "Ironically, it's difficult to find an Indian in India. There are so many of them that they go largely unnoticed. I'll need to keep looking."

"Excuse me," a mustachioed gentleman approached, seating himself at the table with Maria and covering her hand with his. "Are you working?" His gaze slid to Harry and then away, dismissing her.

"Yes, I am," Maria replied, feigning enthusiasm. She allowed the man to lead her away.

Harry frowned. The blond man who had her friend so flustered was also scowling. Making a rapid decision, Harry rose, leaving her sewing in the alcove, and approached him. This time he sat alone, his friends having left to pursue their own adventures.

"Who are you?" he asked, staring at Harry's mob cab in revulsion.

"I'm a friend of Maria's," she replied. "You're not angry with her, I hope."

"I don't see what business it is of yours," he snapped.

"In this place, loyalty and friendship are all we have. Maria has suffered enough from this life, and she hates it, so if you have some perverse intentions toward her, stay away. I'm much tougher than I look, and I will make *your* life a misery if you add to hers."

I have no such intentions," he replied, his voice insistent, his eyes sincere. "I find her interesting is all."

"Well," Harry said, "if you enjoy her company and hate her profession, you need to ask yourself whether you're willing to do anything about it. If not, don't raise false hopes in her."

His affront melted into consideration. "I need to think about this."

"Please do," Harry urged. "Maria is a wonderful person trapped in a nightmare. A worthy man will find a way to understand." With that parting shot, Harry returned to her work. *It would be lovely if this man, or someone like him, took her away to a better life.* Harry was certain Ana and Slade would become business and life partners before long as well. Though she felt glad for her friends, her own sorrow over Devin, over the loss of the man she loved—a loss she'd finally accepted—made her want to weep. *At least I have you, my little angel.* She splayed her hand on her belly. *You will always be my reminder that I was once loved.* Tears clogged her throat and spilled over onto her cheeks, so she gathered up her sewing basket and retreated to her room.

* * *

"I sent the telegram," Devin announced as he approached his brother.

Christopher had saved him a seat, as promised, in a new, faddish restaurant called Lionel's, which the two had spotted from the street while seeking their hotel. In front of Devin's brother, a plate of chicken and a large bowl of rice sent wafts of tasty spices toward the door, drawing the younger man like a beacon. His stomach growled, as he'd been out and about since early morning, with only a cup of tea to sustain him. A single discordant note interrupted the pleasant tablescape beneath a white fluted column. All around them a crowd of English and Indian diners scraped plates with strips of flatbread and sighed with contentment. But only one guest sat at the Bennett table. Katerina, it seemed, had declined to join them... *again.*

Devin shook his head. "I suppose Father will be home by now. I let the clerk know where to find us, in case of a reply." Devin sank into the chair and helped himself to the leg and thigh of the spiced bird along with a healthy scoop of rice.

"Good," Christopher replied, though his attention was on neither the food nor the conversation. "I still can't believe the office was closed yesterday."

"Well, his replacement told me the regular operator was ill with a malaria attack."

"Did he have any information about Harry?" Chris asked listlessly, poking at his rice with a bit of bread, but not taking a bite.

"Sadly, no." Devin sighed. "Apparently he's not a frequenter of houses of ill repute—or so he says—but he told me stolen white women don't end up in Bombay plying the Venus trade to white men. There's too much risk of exposure. His best bet was that she'd been sold to slave traders in the interior." Pronouncing the words made Devin's stomach knot and rendered the juicy meat on his plate inedible.

Christopher's jaw set. "I'm sorry."

"I think our quest might have to take a different tack," Devin suggested.

With a head shake, Christopher dismissed the notion. "I'm sorry, but no. Not yet. I won't let Katerina go anywhere else until she's been seen by a physician. She's worse again today, couldn't even get out of bed."

"Chris…!"

"No, Devin. Harry matters, but my wife matters also. I won't risk her."

"I'll go alone then." Devin pushed his plate away and crossed his arms over his chest.

"Go where? You don't even know what direction to head," Christopher pointed out. "She might be in the city. You only have the opinion of a single telegraph clerk to go on. A few days, Devin. Keep seeking information. Once I find out what's happening to my wife, we'll choose a plan of action. Please?"

Devin considered. Though he wanted to go scattering himself in all directions, he knew his brother was right. If he went the wrong way, Harry would be no better off than if he'd waited, and perhaps a bit worse. "All right. Tomorrow, you search for a physician and I'll ask around and see what other information I can gather."

Christopher reached across the table and clasped his brother's shoulder. "We'll find her."

Devin squeezed his eyes shut.

Chapter 23

EVIN yawned as he stalked down the tile floor of the hotel in search of his brother, coffee, and someone to do his clear thinking for him. A night of poor and restless sleep had not improved his demeanor in the slightest, and he had developed an ache in his jaw. In short, he felt like hell.

Christopher had taken a chair in the adjoining restaurant, alongside a long bar plastered in creamy white that was only manned in the evening. Several small wrought-iron tables with matching chairs provided convenient if somewhat less than comfortable seating, scattered across a floor of plain dark-red tiles. A sideboard along the wall opposite the bar held much-needed sustenance.

Chris held a steaming mug of coffee in one hand and a slip of paper in the other. His face contorted in a puzzled expression.

"Good morning," Devin mumbled, approaching the sideboard and helping himself to a cup of tea. He settled at the table with a sigh. *Wake up first. Food can wait.* "What do you have there?"

"It's a telegram from Father," Christopher replied. He set the paper on the table and took a gulp of his own beverage. "He's glad we arrived safely. Sophia is having a grand time being spoiled by Mother and..." He trailed off.

"And what?" Devin felt far too tired and grumpy for dramatic delivery.

"And he received a telegram from Harry."

The cup slipped from Devin's fingers. A hasty grab prevented it smashing to the floor, but hot tea spilled everywhere, scorching his fingers and lap and staining his trousers. He barely noticed the discomfort. "What?"

"Yes, see for yourself. Father didn't know what to make of the message." Christopher slid the telegram across the table and Devin grabbed it, setting his cup down so he could grip the missive in both hands.

"*Bombay. Slade.* What does that mean?" Devin asked, perplexed.

"Drink your tea and wake up," Christopher snapped, clearly just as out-of-sorts as his brother. "She wanted to let us know that she was here in Bombay, which is, I'm sure you'll agree, the most important piece of information we can get. As for Slade, that's harder. I'm sure it's a name. Perhaps related to the establishment she's been taken to?"

"That's good information too," Devin said, his foggy brain grasping its significance at last. "A name and a city. Well done, Harry. She's so smart."

"Yes, she certainly is," a soft female voice broke through their conversation. Katerina, her mouth pinched and her face pale, crept into the room and tiptoed to the sideboard. She moved as though she feared making too much noise, lest she upset a sleeping giant. Then she took hold of a plate and, shuddering at the coffee, began loading up fried eggs, bacon, sausage, toast and jam enough to feed an army.

"Easy, love," Christopher commented. "That's a lot of food and your poor stomach..."

"I can't help it," she replied in a desperate whisper. "I'm starving. If I become ill, then I do. But I have to eat this all right now."

"Let her listen to her body," Devin advised. "I think she might know what she needs, even if it seems strange."

Christopher shrugged. "Do what you need to do, love. I don't like to see you feeling so poorly."

"I know. I'm sorry to worry you." She sat and stuffed a large bite of toast into her mouth.

"Darling, I worry about you because I love you. I hate to see you suffering. We're finding a physician today."

"Oh, please," she mumbled around her mouthful, then swallowed and added, "there's no need for that. I'll be all right in no time, you'll see."

Christopher didn't respond, but his face showed he had not altered his determination one iota.

Devin watched the interplay with interest. *So this is what marriage is like.*

* * *

An hour later, Katerina, exhausted by the ordeal of eating breakfast, had gone back to bed, and Christopher and Devin returned to the docks. Ruthlessly suppressing the full implications of their quest from his mind, Devin reasoned that the best place to ask for directions about houses of prostitution was one full of sailors, and so they'd begun their search in this place.

A seedy-looking fellow with wild whiskers around his chin but no mustache examined filthy fingernails and said, "If you want a quick tup, I recommend that place over there." He pointed to a dirty shack just beyond the harbor. "Cheap."

"We were recommended to seek out a man named Slade."

Watery blue eyes met each of theirs in turn. "High-kick. Well, I see yer dressed for the role. Slade's girls are expensive. Can't afford 'em meself. But I s'pose fer you two... Only question is, which one. Slade has about a dozen spots around the country, at least six here in Bombay. I don't rightly know where they all are, but I know there's one about four blocks thataway." He pointed a gnarled finger with swollen knuckles off to the west. "Ye'll have to ask in the neighborhood. I don't know the exact spot."

"Thank you, friend," Devin said, handing the man a coin. The dirty sailor cackled and pocketed it, his eyes straying to his own favorite establishment. He trotted off.

"Well, shall we?" Devin suggested.

"Indeed," Christopher agreed.

* * *

They found the club readily enough. The plain, two-story building stood out from its neighbors as the only one on the street lacking a shingle. A quick peek through the window revealed the kind of decadence they'd expected, but the door was locked. A brisk knock brought a frowsy-looking woman with smeared cosmetics and an obvious hangover.

"We open at six," she said, eyeing the brothers greedily. "Ask for Bessie."

"Actually," Christopher corrected, "we're looking for Mr. Slade. Is he available?"

The woman's face fell, which aged her a good ten years. "Slade stops in once a month to check up on things. His day ain't until next week."

"Any idea where we can find him? It's quite urgent," Devin said.

Bessie shrugged. "There are five clubs in town. He circulates." She rattled off the other four addresses and shut the door.

Chris and Devin regarded each other in speaking silence. From all of India to all of Bombay to one of four locations. *We're homing in, darling.* Devin sent the thought out into the cosmos. *We will find you.*

* * *

"Hullo, Harry," Ana chirped. "What have you got there?"

"A note from my father," Harry replied. "I finally managed to track him down. He's living outside Thane but wants to know if he should come to visit. What should I say?" The baby stirred within her and she pressed her hand to the spot. "I hate for him to see me like this."

"It's a fact of your life now, Harry," Ana pointed out. "Don't forget your baby is his grandchild. But to answer your question, can he actually do anything to help you?"

Harry furrowed her brow. "I don't know. Our relationship has never been acknowledged. To the world, he's my father's former employee. His letter says he's farming now, so I doubt he's particularly well-to-do. He has a family. I would hate to upset them…"

"What a difficult situation," Ana said. "I wish I had a good answer for you. What can you do if he can't help?"

"Keep doing what I'm doing, I suppose," Harry replied. "You know Slade best of all of us. Do you think he'll sack me when he finds out about...?" she touched her belly again.

Ana laughed. "Not a chance. He was showing me the books and he couldn't stop gushing about how much money he's saved because of you. If you need to stay, he will find a way to accept you and your baby."

Harry closed her eyes in relief. While a whorehouse, no matter how fancy, was not the most wholesome place to raise a child, anything was better than starving on the streets.

* * *

"Slade's not in," the burly man behind the bar said. "He's been called away but should be back tomorrow. "Would you like to leave a message?"

"Yes," Devin replied. He pondered how to describe the situation in brief and then gave up. "Tell him I'll be here tomorrow at ten for an urgent meeting."

"Who should I say you are?" The tapster asked.

"My name is Devin Bennett."

The man scrawled a note on a scrap of paper.

"Devin," Christopher called from a nearby table, where he'd taken a seat.

Devin raised his eyebrows at his brother.

"Since we're here anyway, let's have a drink. We can toast to fruitless ventures," he added, referencing their failure to find a physician.

"I can drink to that," Devin agreed. "But won't your wife be upset if you linger in a place like this?"

"I doubt it," Christopher replied. "She knows she can trust me. It's just a drink."

Devin requested two brandies and joined his brother. The potent liquor helped Devin relax. *I'll find some answers tomorrow.*

* * *

"I suppose I'll tell him not to come," Harry decided at last. "I'd likely harm him without helping myself."

Ana squeezed her shoulder.

"Are you working, Miss?" A silver-haired gentleman with an expensive, silver-tipped white cane asked Ana. She readily agreed and they departed, leaving Harry alone in her usual alcove.

Though certain she had made the right decision, it still left her with a hollow feeling. *We're on our own, my little one,* she thought. Focusing on the pile of silk in front of her, she began piecing seams together to create a provocative gown for Eliza.

* * *

Devin swirled his brandy around in his glass, regarding the eddies in the amber liquid as his mind swirled in pools of unanswerable questions. Lifting his head, he scanned the room. At a nearby table, a pretty, round-faced brunette in a revealing dress sat with a blond man, their heads together in intense conversation. His hand covered hers and she froze and then slowly relaxed, allowing the touch.

A stunning woman who looked like ice brought to life emerged from a hallway, smirking. Her thumb touched each of her fingertips as though she were counting. Two men played cards and smoked cigars. Christopher grimaced at the acrid stench. A woman in a mob cap and loose dress sat sewing in an alcove.

As he watched, she rose, hefted her basket onto her hip and headed toward the far wall. As she turned, sunset light illuminated her face.

Devin's jaw dropped and his breath caught on a gasp.

He bolted from his seat, heedless of his brother's startled questions, and ran after her.

"Wait," he called, but the woman seemed not to notice. She pressed on the wall, opening a hidden door, and disappeared.

* * *

Harry traversed the private hallway to the rear door of the club. Beyond, in the alley, a pail awaited rubbish, and she had too many scraps and snips of strings in the bottom of her basket. They were driving her mad clinging to the silk. Dumping the scraps into the bin, she turned to reenter the club. *I need energy, life, the illusion of company. I don't want to be alone tonight.* Though she'd rejected an offer of help from her father, and paid lip service to Devin not needing her anymore, in her heart, lonely desperation ached like a wound.

She longed for a strong draught of something: fun, liquor, anything that could take her mind to another place, but nothing would substitute for the love she'd had. The best she could hope for was empty distraction. With a sigh, she turned her attention back to the door, intending to return to the public room and her sewing.

* * *

Once the door closed, it completely disappeared into the mural on the wall. Devin scrabbled over it, trying to discover the catch.

"Can I help you, sir?" A voice that sounded both provocative and disdainful cut through his wild focus.

He glanced sideways to reveal a lushly curvaceous blond, who was regarding him with a hungry expression. "Can you show me how to open this?" he asked, pushing against the mural.

"Customers are not allowed back there," she replied. "That is our private space. If you're looking for female company, I'll be happy to show you the entertainment rooms." She ran her hand down his arm. "My name is Eliza by the way."

He shook her off. "I'm not a customer, not really. I saw someone come in here. Someone I have to talk to. Please help me."

"Who do you think you saw?" the woman dropped her faux enticing act. He glanced again and the chill in her blue eyes seemed to burn into him.

"My intended," he replied. "Miss Fletcher. She was sewing…"

The woman's jaw dropped. "Are you joking?"

"Why would I joke? Please, help me find her. I've been so worried."

"So you're real, are you, Devin?"

"How do you..."

"She cries your name in her sleep. She talks about you until we're all sick of it. I thought you were some excuse she made." Eliza tortured him with a long, considering look, as though debating some heavy question. Then she reached out and pressed the center of a flower. The wall swung open.

"Thank you," Devin called from halfway down the hall.

Open doors revealed several rooms with bunks in various states of disarray. At the far end, another aperture stood ajar, revealing a dark and dirty alley beyond. Hearing banging noises from outside, Devin proceeded in that direction. *I hope I didn't make a mistake.* How embarrassing to have followed the sewing woman so far. *She'll probably slap my face.* Convinced he was seeing things, he nearly turned back, but some quiet voice in his heart whispered to continue. *A slapped face is a small price to pay to know for sure.*

He exited the building. That woman in the mob cab was returning, her basket propped on her hip. The silvery moonlight illuminated her face, revealing what he'd scarcely dared hope.

"Harry..."

* * *

At the sound of a familiar male voice breathing her name, Harry's head shot up. Her jaw went slack and every muscle in her body seemed to lose strength as the basket slipped from her fingers. She stood frozen like a block of ice in the sweltering Indian heat, staring at the mirage that had suddenly stolen her sanity by taking the form of her lost beloved and speaking in his voice.

"Harry." He took a step forward, and then another, until they stood toe to toe, and still she didn't move. Couldn't. Her body refused to respond. Her blank, buzzing mind offered no suggestions for thought or movement. She stood still as a bas-relief carving in a Hindu temple and stared.

His face creased in doubt and long, strong fingers reached out, ripping off the mob cap and taking half her hairpins with it. The silky locks dropped around her back and a sultry breeze ran teasing fingers through the strands. She shivered.

In a breath, Devin gathered her in his arms, lowering his head to claim her mouth. At his touch, a whimper escaped her. His heat melted her into a puddle of mindless joy. She threw her arms around his chest and opened to his passionate ravaging.

For months she'd suppressed tears, fought them off when she could and truncated them when she couldn't. All this time, she'd tried to be brave and strong, to pretend life didn't terrify her and that motherhood was within her ability to cope, even without her beloved. She'd lied through her teeth, to herself and everyone else, until she'd almost believed it. But now, in a dirty alleyway behind the whorehouse, she felt her strength crumble to dust. "Devin. Oh, my darling," she wept against his lips, her words tumbling out with a flood of tears.

"I'm here, Harry. I found you. Oh, God, I found you." He kissed her while she cried, smearing the salt of her tears between them. Slowly he moved her until the wall of the club compressed her back and he had her pinned between his powerful chest and the rough brick.

Passion, fear, disbelief, pain, loneliness and loss, she passed all to her beloved, letting him take the burden from her, letting him support her while she wept. Heat rose with their wild embrace, until her body shook with unexpressed need. Though she spoke no word, he seemed to understand her desire. His hand closed on her breast. She arched her body, pressing full length against him and grinding her soft flesh into his hand. Desperate to be certain he was real, she paid no mind to the setting. Devin filled her awareness, blotting out the alley, the dustbin, even the moon. Only the wall anchored her to reality, and even that only by a thread.

The thread snapped as he lowered the bodice of her dress. The simple garment hung low on her arms and crisscrossed over her breasts. High necklines made the Indian heat unbearable, and working in a house of ill repute, even the seamstress could afford to look a little wanton. Tonight, the indecent design led to a greater benefit. Devin had no trouble baring her breasts in the moonlight. He stooped and pressed a reverent kiss to each nipple. Harry sobbed and clasped his head to her, urging him to turn his tender caresses to the intense stimulation she craved. He complied, sucking hard on one aching tip while he chafed the other between his fingertips.

Harry's head fell back against the wall as she offered herself to her beloved without fear or reservation.

Devin rose and crushed her to him, claiming her lips in another eager kiss. She reached for the fastenings of his trousers, fumbling until the fabric succumbed to her fingers, allowing her to slide her hand inside and take hold of him.

"Now, Devin," she insisted. "I need you now."

"Yes, love. Right now." He lifted her skirt. *Thank goodness not too many petticoats.* Harry wanted nothing coming between her and complete unity with her man. He tried to untie her pantalets, but the string knotted, and he finally ripped the fabric apart in frustration.

Harry moaned, aroused by his wildness. Two fingers slid under Harry's skirt and into her well, and she cried out in a combination of pleasure and shock. The stretch felt uncomfortably intense after so many months without, but she made no protest.

Devin slid his trousers to his ankles, but the difference in their heights became a problem. His probing sex thrust into her bunched skirts about at the level of her navel, nowhere near where she ached for him.

In one quick, decisive movement, Devin wrapped one arm under Harry's bottom and lifted her. Rough brick bit into her bare back as she wrapped her legs around his waist, her arms around his neck. Her weight supported, Devin was able to find the right angle and push deep into her body.

A long wail of pleasure ripped itself from Harry's throat as every inch of Devin's love claimed her. She rocked her hips as best she could while he pounded hard into her.

"My darling, my darling, ahhhhh!" The peak of ecstasy clamped her body down, embracing her beloved with wanton sweetness that brought him to roaring completion in an instant.

They panted, sucking air into laboring lungs as their hearts pounded.

"Are you real?" she whispered as he slowly lowered her to the ground. "Are you really here?"

"Yes, love," he murmured between kisses on her lips, cheeks, eyes and jaw. "I finally found you, Harry."

"What… why…" still words fought her. "How are you here?" she managed to pronounce at last.

"I came after you," he whispered, his voice raspy, "the very next day. I tried to catch you in Gibraltar, and then in Egypt. I've been searching Bombay for days."

"All this time? All this way?" She could scarcely imagine it.

"What did you think I would do? Let you go? Not a chance. I love you, Harry." Her forehead fell against his shoulder. Devin let her skirts drop back into place and adjusted his trousers. Finally, he smoothed her bodice back into place to restore her modesty. "Come with me."

Harry reached for his hand, but instead, he tucked her into the curve of his shoulder, close to his body.

"Where are we going?" she asked.

"To my hotel. We need privacy, and I don't think this… place offers much."

"You're right," she agreed as they emerged from the alley into the street. If people stared or gave disapproving looks, they never saw it.

* * *

Still stunned to have gone looking for answers and instead finding his beloved, Devin hurried her back to the hotel. *I have to touch every inch of her to be sure she's real.* Dusk had fallen to true night while they'd loitered in the alley, and now darkness seemed to pursue the couple, hurrying them from street to street. Devin realized, to his shock, that the hotel where they'd been staying was situated only about three blocks from Harry's place of business. Shaking his head at the ironies of life, he hurried her through the lobby and up the stairs, along a hallway of plain red tile, to a door painted a brilliant green. A deft turn of the key in the lock had them inside and in complete seclusion. Devin lit the lamp.

Harry stood by, her face twisted with nerves and discomfort.

"What's wrong, love?" he asked, concerned. *Is she worrying over what happened before? Did someone take advantage of her? Was she forced to sell herself?* The thoughts tightened his jaw, and he steeled himself for answers he didn't want to hear. *I have to accept whatever has happened to her. I have to comfort her with my understanding.*

"No, nothing," Harry said, shaking her head as though to clear it. "I just... I can't believe what we just did. How silly."

"Maidenly modesty, darling?" *Did I forget how charming a blend of curiosity and prudishness my lady has?*

"Something like that," she replied. "Did we really just..." her voice dropped to a whisper, "do *that* in the alley behind the club?"

He chuckled. "Shocking, isn't it, the way passion can overtake a person?" He slowly walked toward her. "Tell me any power under heaven could have stopped us though."

Harry shook her head. "No, I..." Her blush flared, visible even in the dim lamplight. "I... I had to."

"I had to as well," he reminded her. "I had to touch you. I had to claim you. To remind us both..."

"That there's nothing quite as amazing as us together," she finished for him. They stood a breath apart and Harry closed the distance, stepping directly against his body, her feet between his. He embraced her and gloried in the feeling of her arms sliding around his waist. "You really came all the way to India for me? I'm stunned. Devin..."

"What, darling?" he asked.

"You amaze me." She arched her neck so her warm brown eyes, damp and filled with adoration, stared up into his. "I love you."

"And I love you. I hope you finally realize your damned uncle was wrong."

She nodded. "Clearly." Then she sighed. "I suppose he told you the rest, too, didn't he? I mean, you had to confront him to find out where I was. Did you think I ran away?" Her eyebrows drew together, and her lips turned down.

Devin countered her worry with a kiss on her lips. "Not for a second. I knew you wouldn't run. Not after all the lengths you went to in ensuring we could be together. And to answer your question, yes. That is to say, he told me he's not actually your uncle. Is your Indian blood the dark secret you thought would make me unwilling to marry you?"

She nodded.

He shook his head. "And here I thought it was something important."

Harry regarded him in stunned amazement. "If I'd told you then?"

"I'd have reassured you in a moment. Listen, darling, my sister-in-law is Italian, and everyone loves her. Mother arranged her marriage to my brother, not that either of them minded. They're meant to be. Their daughter, the family's darling, is only half English."

"True." She touched his cheek. "But, Devin, even most English people don't have trouble with the mixing of Europeans. I'm Indian. That's considered lesser, and impure."

"Do you think so?" he asked.

She shook her head. "How can I? Apart from Mother, the only people who cared for me growing up were Indians. They have a beautiful, rich culture, a culture that is partly mine. I'm proud of it, even if I can't talk about it to many people. Even here, mixing is frowned on, despite that it happens often enough. I think it's the fact that my mother bedded an Indian, rather than the other way around, that sticks in people's craw."

Devin shrugged. "Humans can be stupid and inconsistent. Who knows why? Even if what your mother did was wrong, I don't see how that can be your fault."

"Mother wasn't wrong," Harry hissed, "unless people don't have the right to love."

"Remember I don't know the whole story, darling," he said gently, smoothing her hair away from her face. "I only have the parts told me by a hypocritical man who hates non-Europeans and loves his family, who probably takes his brother being cuckolded very personally."

Harry narrowed her eyes.

"I'm not defending him," Devin added quickly, "only giving you the perspective of the person who told me. He's not going to be fair, and I'd be hard-pressed to give him credit even for honesty."

Harry relaxed.

"Listen, I'm getting uncomfortable standing here. What do you say we adjourn to the bed? You can tell me the whole story. Also, tell me what's been going on since you disappeared. I mean, are you all right? You don't seem hurt."

Devin led her by the hand to the edge of the bed and sat down to remove his shoes. Harry followed suit.

"I'm all right," she said. "I think I must have a hundred guardian angels looking after me. Apart from being terrified and offended, the worst fate I endured along the way was to be cornered by some rat-faced idiot. My friend Ana lured him away from me before he could manage more than an unpleasant grab."

Devin wanted to ask, felt he needed to, but didn't know how to phrase the question. "It… I… Harry…"

She dropped her shoe on the floor and turned to him, one eyebrow raised in a silent question.

"I love you no matter what," he began again. "If someone forced you… if you had to in order to eat… I won't care. At least, it won't change how I feel about you, but I need to understand what you suffered during this ordeal. You just implied none of that happened, but is that true? In all these months among whores and whoremongers, no one took advantage of you?"

She tilted her head to one side and regarded him. "Are you certain you're real?" she asked softly. Then a soft smile creased her lips. "No one took advantage. No one forced me. Being surrounded by these ladies actually saved me. Why force the unwilling one when a rainbow of women can be had for a coin? She grasped his hand and laced her fingers through his. "No one has touched me but you."

Devin exhaled a huge sigh. *Blessed relief.* "That's good, love. I'm so glad."

"As am I," she replied. "I tried to prepare myself for my fate, but I couldn't do it, I just couldn't. Fortunately, ten years as a lady's maid provided me with a skill I was able to trade for money. I've been sewing my way across half the world." Her smile turned sad. "I was lucky. My friends have the most terrible stories. Women are too dependent on men to care for them. If more women had a skill, they would be less susceptible to harm at the hands of an uncaring world."

"It's true," Devin agreed. "Well then, I suppose that's one thing we both should thank Fletcher for, eh?"

Harry made a face. "If you say so. After all, he's also the author of this fine mess. If he'd just decided to mind his own business, we'd be five months married by now. Everything..." she trailed off, gulped, and tried again. "Everything would be so much easier."

"It's true," Devin agreed. "Why don't you slip that dress off, love, and get comfortable?"

"Why?" she demanded, looking shocked.

Devin laughed softly. "Because in a very few minutes, I'm going to ravish you again, love. I've already destroyed your undergarment. If I tear off your gown as well, you'll have nothing to wear tomorrow. We'll have to go back to Slade's and collect your clothing and settle things with him, and I'm sure you'd prefer to go dressed."

"Don't be angry with him, Devin. He was furious when he heard about what happened to me. He's adamant about willing girls, and about contracts. He even agreed to allow me to sew rather than... do the other kind of work." She blushed.

Actually, she'd been blushing since he asked her to undress, but it deepened now. *And she dodged the suggestion. Well, no worries. I'll coax her out of her restraint soon enough.*

"I'm not angry with him," Devin replied. "Now don't you worry about a thing. I'll figure out how do deal with Slade, but in the meanwhile, darling, let's enjoy the evening. This… this was so much more than I expected, and now you're here with me. Do you not want me to make love to you again?"

Harry bit her lip and met his eyes with a shy expression. "Do you love me, Devin?" she asked.

Not certain where the question had come from, Devin drew his eyebrows together. *Well, man, if your woman needs reassurance, reassure her,* he finally decided. "I love you, Harry. I love you with all my heart. I'll never let you out of my sight again, and I fully intend that we'll be married tomorrow if we can manage it."

She nodded. "Very well."

Rising, she shimmied out of her gown. He noticed she wore no corset. *Well, good. They might prove deadly in this heat.* Only a soft white chemise and matching pantalets, now ripped apart by his exuberance, covered her figure. Something about the shape of her struck him as odd. She was heavier than she'd been, her belly a round curve instead of the tiny convexity she'd had before. Her breasts strained the seams of her chemise. She met his eyes and drew off the undergarments, leaving her bare before him. Something teased the corners of his awareness, telling him her new shape had untold significance. *Slim legs. Slender arms. No sag under the chin. No fullness in the cheeks, and yet her breasts and belly are changed.*

"Devin," Harry began.

"Yes, love?" He could hear his blood circulating as his mind struggled to understand what he was seeing.

"I…ugh."

"Please, Harry," Devin urged, "this time just tell me. No more secrets, all right?"

She nodded. "I… I'm…" She swallowed and took his hand, laying it on the curve he'd been studying. "How I wish we'd married on the day we selected, all those months ago." She sniffled. "We made a baby together, darling, somewhere during those few days we spent in your home."

She stood before him, naked and trembling, looking vulnerable, scared and lost.

Sympathy filled Devin. *Alone, pregnant and frightened. My poor Harry. My darling girl.* He pulled her between his knees and laid his head against her breasts. With one arm he embraced her waist, with the other, he touched the place where their child lived and grew. "I love you, Harry," he told her. "I never stopped searching for you. I know you must have been terrified, but be at ease, my love. You and the little one will never be alone again."

Harry sagged against him, and he urged her onto the bed. Filled with tender desire for the woman who carried his baby, Devin removed his clothing. "Is it all right for me to love you now?"

She nodded. "The girls told me. They said there's no harm in it."

"I suppose they'd know," he replied wryly.

Then Devin laid his lips on Harry's, tracing gentle caresses across her skin in preparation for a long night of lovemaking.

Chapter 24

ARRY woke to a feeling of utter contentment. Though her night had actually been rather short, due to a protracted reunion with Devin, she felt wonderfully refreshed. Stretching her bare body full length on his bed, she savored each ache. *Well-loved? I should say yes.* He'd loved her enough to chase her all the way to India. He'd loved her enough to accept her even if she'd been forced into prostitution. He'd loved her enough to accept her Indian side without reservation. And then he'd loved her all night.

Slowly it dawned on Harry that what had drawn her from slumber was a banging on the door. The sound of voices filtered through her languorous haze.

"Good morning, Katerina. Did you need something?"

A sharp female voice responded in a shrill complaint. "Devin, how could you? After all this time, after coming so far?" The voice wavered.

"What are you talking about?" he asked sharply. "What is it you think I've done?"

"Christopher told me," she cried. "He came in last night so upset, saying you'd gone chasing after a loose woman and disappeared."

Well, this won't do, Harry thought, rising from the bed. Realizing she was naked, she pulled the sheet from the bed and wrapped it around herself before trailing to the doorway. Clutching the sheet in one hand, she wrapped the other arm around Devin's waist and rested her head against his chest.

"Good morning, Katerina," Harry said. Considering the scandalous picture she was presenting to her future sister-in-law, a wicked grin spread across Harry's face.

Katerina's gaze fixed on Harry and her jaw dropped, raised and dropped again.

"I'm fairly certain I don't qualify as a loose woman yet," Harry said with a considering air, "though if my current state of misbehavior calls that into question, I'll have to take immediate steps."

Devin chuckled and kissed her hair.

Katerina's flapping jaw settled into a croak.

"What's happening, love?" Christopher approached his wife and took her arm. Then he saw Harry and stared.

His appearance made Harry feel exposed. Showing up in extreme dishabille to tease Katerina was one thing, but she had not planned on Christopher, whom she barely knew, seeing her in a sheet. Her face flamed and she scooted behind her lover.

"All right," Devin said, "I know explanations are in order. What about we take a few minutes to make ourselves decent and then head down for some breakfast and a long chat?"

"I say that sounds like an excellent notion," Christopher replied, leading his wife away. Devin closed the door.

"I'll never be able to look at your brother again," Harry said, wondering how her idyllic reunion with her beloved had gone so terribly wrong.

"You're fine," Devin replied.

"I'm wearing a sheet," Harry protested.

"Pretend you're Roman," he teased. "Katerina is Italian. She'll explain it to him."

An undignified snort rose up in Harry despite her desire to suppress it. Her effort proved futile as peals of embarrassed laughter spilled from her until she slumped weakly on the bed.

"Get dressed, silly girl," Devin urged. "You look quite fetching—beddable—but it's a bit much for public."

That nonsense set Harry off again, until tears streamed down her cheeks. Devin held out her chemise and she lifted her arms, allowing him to cover her naked body. She stood and the garment slithered around her, covering her to the knees, but... "You ruined my pantalets," she reminded Devin.

He chuckled. "I haven't seen you in months, my love. I couldn't wait another moment to fumble with the knots. No one will know."

"I'll know," Harry replied, wrinkling her nose at Devin as he handed her the dress. She tucked herself into it, glad for the simple design that allowed her to fasten it without help.

"So will I," he replied, running a proprietary hand over her bottom.

She swatted playfully at him, and then sighed as he hauled her close for a long, wet kiss.

"Come on," she urged. "We have the rest of our lives to kiss, but right now, the baby's hungry."

"Well, if the baby's hungry, the baby must be fed," he replied.

Dressed and at least pretending to be presentable, they proceeded hand in hand to the restaurant where they joined Christopher and Katerina at a small round table. The older couple already had plates of food and cups of coffee in front of them.

"Sit, darling. I'll bring you breakfast," Devin urged. Harry sat, her face flaming as her eyes skated nervously away from Christopher.

"Did your uncle really have you kidnapped?" Katerina asked moments before she took a large bite of toast and washed it down with hot, milky coffee.

"No, he did it himself," Harry replied, "but let's wait on the big story until Devin's here."

"Good idea," Christopher said. *Good Lord, even the sound of his voice makes my face hot.*

"Here we are," Devin announced, setting a plate of everything in front of Harry and adding a cup of tea. "I remember you preferred this when we were together before."

"Yes, thank you, I do prefer tea to coffee. Probably due to growing up here," Harry replied. She inhaled the enticing aromas of sausage, tropical fruit, spiced potatoes and roti. A small scoop of chutney on the side of her plate drew her interest and she eagerly dipped the roti in the tasty mixture.

"What is that?" Katerina asked, eyeing the dark red mash doubtfully.

"Tamarind and date with spices," Harry replied. "I love it."

"I've never heard of tamarind," Christopher commented.

Harry smiled. "Try it. It's a tart, sweet fruit that grows inside a pod. It's so delicious I could eat it in place of candy."

"I'll have to try it sometime," Devin said. "But enjoy it while you can. There are no tamarinds in England that I'm aware of."

"Certainly not," Harry agreed. "The trees would be miserable in the cold, but don't fret. I can make chutney out of anything, even apples or peaches."

"You're in for it now," Christopher said. "I've eaten more garlic since I married an Italian than in the whole rest of my life put together. You'll be choking down spices until you die."

The group laughed. *How easily they accept, even joke about, wives from other countries. I couldn't have landed better.* She thanked the fate that led her to Devin, despite the wild path she'd had to follow to get to this place.

"All right, all food banter aside, what on earth happened, Harry?" Katerina pressed. "I had so hoped to become friends, and then you were gone."

"Not by choice, I promise you." Harry took another bite of her roti, this time nibbling a plump goat sausage to go with it. The sharp flavors of meat and seasonings brought back a wave of nostalgia. "Let me start at the beginning. Before my beginning, actually, back to my mother. When she was seventeen, her family encouraged her to marry Malcolm Fletcher's brother Andrew. She wasn't too keen on the match, but the family was desperate, the Fletchers were rich and young Andrew was headed off to the join the army in India."

Harry set her food aside with a satisfied sigh. "Mother succumbed to the pressure and went. India turned out to be her most natural environment. She loved the Indian people, their culture, and their religion. Even the plants and animals delighted her, and so her life was happy, but while she was the sort of woman everyone liked, and made many friends, she had one serious problem. Her husband. He didn't come home much, but when he did, he was usually drunk and inclined to violence."

Harry paused to sip her tea and sighed at the pleasing vegetal taste. *At least I can get this in England.*

"So what happened?" Katerina asked, clearly enthralled by the story. Something in her gaze told Harry she had more than a casual interest in this subject.

"He beat her sometimes, belittled and berated her often. She was always glad when he left. They never had any children, and he mocked her for that as well. One day he beat her and told her he would go find an Indian girl to carry his children, since his wife was so useless." Harry swallowed. "One of the servants, a young man named Kumar, found her lying in a heap, and treated her injuries." *This is it. If they're going to reject you, it will be now.* "Mother and Kumar became lovers," Harry explained, "and it is he, not Andrew Fletcher, who is my father."

"Are you sure?" Christopher asked.

Now, Harry discovered she could look him in the eye. "Unless Mother lied to her journal *and* to me, then yes, I'm sure. Besides, look at me. Andrew Fletcher was big and blond. Not like me. I look Indian."

"She does," Devin agreed. He laid his hand over hers.

"Of course, it was best for everyone involved if my true identity remained a secret, so Mother let Andrew think she'd finally born him a child. She also had dark hair, and Fletcher, being a bit of a drunken dolt, believed her."

She laced her fingers through Devin's and took a deep breath. "All was well until right around the time I turned fourteen. I don't know how Fletcher found out, but he seemed to become aware that not only was his wife unfaithful, but her lover was not even European. That seemed to be a huge issue to the Fletchers."

"I can attest to that," Devin added. "His brother is the same way."

"Yes," Harry agreed. "They had an altercation, and he hit her, hard. She fell down the stairs and her head hit the floor. She died a few hours later. Swelling of the brain, the doctor said. And since Fletcher told everyone it was an accident, and I was just a child, he was believed."

"Oh dear!" Katerina exclaimed. "That's just horrible. It's just horrible." Her voice wavered. Again the idea struck Harry that Katerina's reaction seemed far more than just casual commiseration, or even friendship. *I'll find out later.*

"What happened to Fletcher?" Christopher wanted to know. "How did you end up in England?"

"Kumar," she replied. "He brought me out of the house into the garden. There was a fire." She shuddered. "I think he probably started it, as revenge for the death of his beloved. Fletcher died in the flames." She frowned. "I hope he comes back as a cockroach and gets trodden in the street."

The table fell silent for a moment in honor of the sad story.

Then Harry heaved a sigh and continued. "I wanted to stay with my father, but our relationship was not and could never be acknowledged. Neither Indian nor Englishman would accept someone like me, so it had to remain a secret. He put me on the boat to England himself, made me promise not to worry about him." She looked down at the table, tracing the edge with her fingertip. "Unfortunately, Fletcher sent a letter to his brother in England. It arrived just before I did. The letter detailed the circumstances of my conception. Technically, Sir Fletcher was my guardian, but he saw me as an abomination. Rather than treating me as family, which I'm not, he put me to work. It wasn't bad, truly, and I adore Fanny, but his ugliness toward me never diminished."

"Is that why he had you sent away?" Katerina asked.

Harry nodded. "He took me himself, bound in a sack, tossed me on the boat, and forced them to remove me from England, just to protect Devin from my tainted blood."

Devin squeezed the hand he was holding. "I wish you'd told me. I thought some serious, terrible thing had happened to you, and you were keeping it a secret. If I'd known it was nothing more than mixed heritage, I would have understood so much better."

She lifted her eyes to his. He regarded her with utter sincerity on his face.

"I love you, Devin," she said. He smiled.

"But that doesn't make sense," Christopher said, interrupting their ruminations.

"What doesn't?" Devin demanded.

"If he hated her, why didn't he send her away years ago? If he believed her blood was tainted, that she was an abomination, why keep her around? He's protective of his daughter. Why expose her to that?"

Why did I never think of that? "You're right, Mr. Bennett," she said, "and I have no idea. I always supposed seeing me in a servile position made him feel magnanimous while at the same time allowing him to live out his prejudice."

"Not enough," Devin said. "If your so-called uncle didn't have a reason to keep you, he wouldn't have. Your food, your clothing, even your passage on the train required money, and the only thing Malcolm Fletcher loves as much as his children is money. You can't believe how many little nests of cash he has squirreled away. It took me ages to track down what all of them meant. Some I never could understand. Did you know he owns a share in Slade's businesses?"

"I found that out," Harry replied dryly. "Your brother raises an interesting question. Since he earns money from the brothels, why was I not sent to one immediately?"

"I have a theory," Christopher replied. "Devin, is it possible any of the mystery bits of money Fletcher controls might be an inheritance from his brother?"

"It might be," Devin replied, looking thoughtful. His words stretched out long and slow. "There was one that was only annotated *Andrew.*"

"But that would be Harry's money, wouldn't it?" Katerina demanded.

"It would," Devin replied. "Except that…"

"Harry is not Andrew's daughter," Christopher finished for his brother.

The implications seemed to sink into Harry's stomach like a lead weight.

Katerina made a choking sound, drawing all eyes to her. Rising unsteadily from the table, she bolted out the side door into an alley beside the hotel.

Christopher sighed. "I really must find a physician today."

Harry stared at him in alarm. "Is she ill? I thought the strong food might not have agreed with her."

"She's been ill since we set out," Devin replied. "We thought it was seasickness, but she never improved."

"Dear Lord," Harry said. Then a ghost of an idea began to germinate in her brain. "Let me go talk to her. Maybe I can get to the bottom of it."

"You're no doctor," Christopher pointed out.

"No," Harry replied, "but I'm a woman."

Without waiting for further comment, she rose from the table and followed her friend into the morning sunlight.

Outside, Katerina leaned against the smooth plaster, a few feet away from the mess she'd made. She rested her arm on the wall; her head on her arm. Harry handed her the handkerchief she'd plucked from Devin's pocket on the way past. "I'm sorry you're feeling poorly."

Katerina nodded.

"I can't believe you and your husband accompanied Devin all the way here," Harry commented, smoothing sweaty hair away from her friend's face.

"Of course we did," Katerina replied. "Chris wanted to support his brother since Devin was too upset to think straight, and I… well, I feared some harm might befall you, and having a woman to help you might prove important. You seem fine though."

"Yes, Harry replied, deciding to be blunt. "No one raped me, and because I know how to sew, I was able to earn a living without resorting to prostitution."

Katerina lifted her head and offered Harry a weak smile. "I'm so glad. So I suppose you'll be taking care of me, then."

"I think you're going to be all right," Harry replied. "I suspect I know why you're feeling ill."

"Please enlighten me," Katerina urged.

"Could you be with child?" Harry asked.

Katerina opened her mouth and closed it again. Her delicately arched eyebrows drew together. "You know, I don't know. Since Sophia was born, I only conceived once, about a year ago, but I miscarried. And after that, nothing… but… yes, that would explain a lot of things I hadn't put together."

Harry smiled. "I had a feeling."

"How did you know?" Katerina demanded.

"Let's say, I've had recent experiences myself," Harry replied, patting her belly. Katerina's eyes went wide.

"You wicked girl!" she exclaimed. "I knew you and Devin had been misbehaving in Brighton, but I didn't want to think about it." She laughed. "You two imps will have to marry immediately. Today, if possible. And don't worry. While Devin was flapping about trying to play the hero, I packed the marriage license and your dress."

"You are a gem, Katerina," Harry said. "I hope I can fasten the dress."

"You'll find a way," Katerina replied.

"Ladies, how is everything?"

Katerina's weak smile strengthened at the sight of her husband. She winked at Harry. "Wonderful, actually. Now, you two run off and try to find someone to marry you, would you? I'd like a moment with my husband alone."

"Come on, darling," Harry urged, dragging Devin out of the alley. "Let them be alone."

As they emerged on the crowded and busy street, Devin asked, "What are you two naughty girls up to?"

"Oh, nothing much," Harry replied. "I believe you're about to become an uncle again, as well as a father."

She laughed as his befuddled expression gave way to surprise. "Are you certain?"

"Yes, and if poor Katerina hadn't been trapped with two nitwit men, she would have had a lot less worry."

"Oh dear," Devin sighed. "Now what am I going to do? My woman has gone all saucy."

"Marry me at once," she demanded, walking backwards in front of him, practically skipping with good humor.

"Naturally, but how? We've had the worst luck finding anything we need in this accursed place."

"You're not looking properly," she shot back. Approaching a beggar outside the hotel's front entrance, she bowed to him. "Namaste."

He smiled, and she posed a question, which he promptly answered.

Devin approached from behind and took her arm, trying to move her back from the man, but she planted her heels and refused to move. "Give him a coin, darling. He's steered us right to our quarry."

Devin fished some money out of his pocket and gifted the beggar. "What did he say?"

"He said a missionary has just arrived from England. They've been enjoying scintillating conversations about religion and the nature of the universe. He says we can find this worthy gentleman at the little chapel two blocks down. And before you travel, darling, you should learn a bit of the local language and culture. Beggars in India are often holy men who have revoked the desires of Earth in hopes of escaping the cycle of rebirth. But for all that, they're friendly, wise and extremely knowledgeable."

Devin blinked. "If we'd had you along, our search would have been much easier."

Harry laid a hand on Devin's forehead. "You must have gotten too much sun. You're talking nonsense. If I'd been along, you wouldn't have needed to go."

"Ah, yes," Devin agreed. "I knew there was some flaw in my thinking. Well, let's go and find this mysterious missionary and see how quickly we can get all our issues rectified.

* * *

"Good morning," Devin said to the burly man he'd met two days prior. "Is Slade in, by any chance?"

"He's in," the man replied, "but you said you were coming yesterday."

"Plans change," Devin eyed him coolly. "Please let Slade know I'd like to speak with him about my wife."

The man's eyes widened, and he strode away from the bar to the private door through which he'd chased Harry two nights ago.

Squeals emanated from behind that door, and when Harry emerged, clutching an unwieldy bundle of fabric, two women trailed her. Devin recognized them from the other night as well.

"Who did you find, love?" he asked her.

"Devin, darling, this is Anastacia Alexandrovna Thomas. She's related to the royal family of Russia, as you can see." The blond tipped her head so regally he could almost believe the wild tale. "And this is Maria Jamison. These two were my particular friends and they protected me from people with evil intentions. Ana, Maria, this is my Devin. Can you believe he came all the way to India just to get me back?"

"So romantic." Maria sighed. "Bless you, sir. Harry was never meant for a life like this."

Devin smiled, though in truth the effusive praise left him uncomfortable.

"Do right by her," Ana said, in a voice as hard and cutting as the polished diamond she resembled.

"I intend to," he replied.

"Silly," Harry scoffed. "He already did. We were married yesterday morning by a missionary down the street."

"Send him our way," Ana said with a cynical laugh.

Maria squealed. "Congratulations, Harry. Your dreams came true! I'm so happy for you. What will you do now? You're leaving us, aren't you?"

Harry nodded. "We have to go back to England. Devin is a solicitor in Brighton, and we need to hurry back home. He's missed over four months of work already."

"You can't go! What will I do without you?" Maria grabbed Harry and dragged her over to the seating area where all three ladies subsided onto comfortable chaises to chat.

"Devin Bennett?" The sound of his name drew Devin's attention to a man not much older than Christopher, casually dressed in a flowing shirt and tight breeches.

"Yes, and are you Slade?"

A nod sent light brown hair dancing around the broad shoulders. "What's this about a wife?"

Devin indicated with his head. "I married Harry yesterday morning."

The man frowned, but more in consideration than anger. "Are you the one she was stolen away from then?"

"That's right," Devin agreed. "Damn her meddling uncle."

"Indeed," Slade replied.

Damn him too. I wanted to dislike him, but he seems surprisingly decent. "Just what exactly went on here?"

"She'll have to tell you most of it," Slade replied. "I got a wild story about kidnapping. How was I to know it was true? What I had a woman with no contract, which is strictly forbidden to all my captains. How she even got here is beyond me. But since she was here, I offered her a job, and she agreed to it."

Devin nodded. "All right then. Thank you for not forcing her into… that line of work. But what is this about paying passage? Harry is very concerned with the idea that she might owe you some debt."

Slade nodded. "The passage to India is far from free. The girls pay it off by giving a share of their profits back to the company. Harita has been sewing for us. The difference between what we would spend on ready-made clothing and her custom pieces forms her payment."

Devin narrowed his eyes at the man. "She owes you nothing. She truly was kidnapped, taken right out of my home."

"But, the money…"

"Extract it from the captains," Devin replied. "Do they work for you?"

Slade nodded.

"Do *they* have contracts about how the recruitment and transportation should take place?" At the second dip of the man's cleft chin, Devin went in for the kill. "Then they, not Harry, owe you for the passage. Every man who knew she was supposed to have a contract and didn't can pay you a portion of what you've lost. And if they prove recalcitrant, remind them that kidnapping is a prosecutable offense. A capital one."

Slade gulped. "I never authorized a kidnapping."

"I know. Malcolm Fletcher did that. You could order him to pay as well, since this whole damnable mess was his doing."

The man's lips turned down. "I rue the day I took money from that jackass. He's the one who caused all this trouble?"

This time Devin answered with a slow bob of the head.

"I think my association with Fletcher is about done. I don't need his money or his meddling."

"Good idea," Devin replied. *And I'll be dealing with him myself, once I have Harry home safe.*

* * *

"I wish you didn't have to leave," Maria said, her voice wavering.

"She should go," Ana reminded her. "Harry never wanted this."

"What will I do without you?" the brunette wailed.

"Get married," Harry suggested.

Maria's expression turned unreadable.

"What does that look mean?" Harry demanded.

"He bought my time again," Maria replied.

"To talk?" Harry guessed and noticed Ana's lips curve into a smirk.

Maria shook her head. "He made love to me. It was like nothing I've ever experienced. I gave him his money back."

Harry smiled, though the thought of parting from her friends made her eyes sting. *I shouldn't feel so conflicted about going home.* "You're going to be all right."

Maria pounced on Harry and nearly strangled her in a tight hug before running, weeping, for the hidden door.

Harry and Ana regarded each other, and Harry couldn't help but admire her friend's resilience. "Let him love you, will you?" she suggested.

"I'll consider it," Ana replied. "Be well, Harry. Be happy."

"You too, Anastacia Alexandrovna."

The ladies smiled at each other as Devin approached, helping Harry to her feet.

"Thank you for keeping me safe," Harry said, recalling how much Ana had sacrificed for her.

"Thank you for giving me hope," the lovely woman replied. "Godspeed."

"Goodbye, Ana. I'll never forget you."

Harry sniffled as Devin led her into the blazing Indian sun. "Well," he said, "now what?"

Harry wiped her eyes and regarded him. "What do you mean?"

"Well, it took us four months to get to India and find you. If we stay four days and then head back to England, well that just seems ridiculous."

"Well, we shouldn't linger too long," she reminded him. "Your practice."

"Who knows if I even still have one," Devin replied, "after your damned uncle is through interfering."

"He's not my uncle, thank God, but I do have one idea."

* * *

Two days later, Devin found himself in the last place he'd ever expected to be in his life. A sweltering, muggy rice farm. Though only a short distance from Bombay by train, Thane and its surrounding farmland felt like another world. The bustling city had given way to peaceful countryside where humpbacked cattle munched the vegetation and world-hardened men and women watched the passersby with hollow, hungry eyes.

Without Harry's fluency in the local dialect, they'd never have made it so far, but here they stood, amid the brilliant green of the rice shoots. To the left, a teenaged boy drove two bellowing buffalo through the field, a plow suspended between their shoulders. Their outward-curving horns made Devin uneasy, but the lad seemed unconcerned.

Harry smiled. "My father is rich. He owns two buffalo."

Devin regarded her dreamy face. *Enjoy this, love. I don't know that we'll get back here. Certainly not often.*

"Did you want to see us?" An Indian woman with a brightly-colored scarf draped over her salt-and-pepper hair emerged from the small house—a hut by Devin's estimation—and approached them. Though well into middle years, she had an otherworldly beauty.

"Yes," Harry replied. "I'm looking for Kumar Mangal. Is he around?"

"And who might you be?" The woman eyed Harry suspiciously.

"My name is Harita Fletcher Bennett. I knew your husband when I was a child. I came back to India this once, and I didn't want to leave without seeing him."

The woman gave Harry another cool look before turning back to the hut, emerging a moment later with a man in tow.

Devin regarded the Indian curiously. He'd been handsome once, though the sun had weathered his face and crinkled his eyes.

He regarded Harry in silence for a long moment and then said in a rough voice, as though his emotions were trying to escape, "Please leave us, Anuja. I will speak to this girl for a moment."

Anuja frowned but consented to depart.

Under a burning, cloudless sky, the man gathered Harry in his arms. "Harita, my darling girl. What are you doing here?"

"It's a long story, Father, and one that probably will do you no good to hear. Suffice it to say, I'm safe and all is well. I wanted to let you know that in person, lest my letter worried you."

"You know it did, beloved. But I'm glad if you're well."

"Harry, why is everyone calling you Harita?" Devin asked, breaking into the conversation.

She turned and he saw that her eyes were swimming again.

"Because it is her name," the man informed him. "Her mother and I named her. It means green, like something beautiful and alive. And so she is."

"It is a lovely name," Devin agreed, "but I was under the impression her name was Harriet."

Harry shook her head. "The Fletchers like Harriet because they can understand it. I think Andrew believed it was actually my name."

"That idiot," Kumar added, shaking his head. His movement, combined with the breeze, set his short, black hair dancing.

Harry opened her mouth as though to speak, and then closed it again.

Somehow, Devin knew she wanted to ask him about the fire but didn't know how. *Let it go, love. Just as there are some things he didn't need to know, this is something you'd be better off remaining ignorant about. Let it go.*

"I have to return to England soon. My..." she looked at Devin with affection in her gaze, seeming to understand the unspoken request. "My husband has been away from his work too long already, and the voyage is even longer."

Kumar nodded.

"May I write to you sometimes?" Harry asked.

He didn't answer for a long, painful moment, and then he shook his head. "My wife would not like that, Harita. She doesn't know about my past. Just as it is best for you to keep the truth in your heart, where it cannot harm you, I must do the same. Move forward, Harita. Take hold of your future. Our past is filled with darkness." His eyes bored into hers. "I will not regret anything I have done, but I will not be free of the wheel this lifetime, so perhaps we will meet in its next turning."

Harry swallowed hard and Devin laid a comforting hand on her shoulder. "I love you, Father," she whispered.

"And I love you, Harita, my flower." He turned to Devin. "Care for my child, sir."

"I will," Devin agreed.

"Farewell, both of you. Thank you for putting my mind at ease. Knowing you are well and happy makes my days brighter. Namaste."

He dismissed them with the traditional acknowledgment of the divine within each person and turned, stalking back towards his home.

"Namaste, Pitaaji," she whispered to his retreating back. "I'll never forget you."

She turned in Devin's arms and buried her face in his shirt, releasing India from her heart in a flood of tears, and embracing England and her future.

Epilogue

Ten weeks later

HE parlor of the Bennetts' London townhouse felt incredibly crowded with four adults in it, especially when two of them took up extra room due to their increasing shape. Harry smiled and took a seat on one of two red velvet sofas with daintily carved wooden arms, sighing as her weight ceased pressing down on her aching feet. They'd arrived the previous night, late, and tumbled into beds almost immediately upon walking in the door. Now, rested, fed and ready to face a new day, Harry couldn't stop thinking how strange it felt to be back in the weak English sunshine. All of summer, autumn and part of winter had passed. With mid-January's feeble sun trying to disperse a humid chill that had crept into the house and sunk into her bones, she felt as though a dream had wrapped itself around her and refused to let go. She regarded the small wood-framed window, adorned with scarlet draperies that matched the furniture and contrasted cheerfully with the white plaster of the walls while complimenting a dark wooden floor.

Katerina sighed and shivered. "I usually like winter, but I think my blood must have thinned a bit."

"I know mine did," Harry agreed. "It's rather nasty this morning, isn't it?"

"Feels good to me, Christopher said. "I found the heat in India oppressive."

"If you're cold, love, why don't you ring for some tea," Devin suggested.

Harry sighed. "Then I'd have to get up, and my feet don't want me to." Debating the relative merits of tea versus sitting, Harry found herself unable to decide.

The question disappeared from her mind as the cook-maid poked her head in the door. "Company, sir." No sooner had the woman spoken than the door exploded inward and a small, dark shape flew into the room like a cyclone and hurtled itself at Katerina. "Mama! Mama!"

"Oof," Katerina grunted as the child collided with her belly. "I've missed you so much." She drew Sophia onto a seat beside her.

Behind Sophia, a middle-aged couple stepped into the room. Harry gulped. The long-delayed meeting with Devin's parents was now upon her. She took a deep breath and her husband's hand as he helped her back to her aching feet. *Well, now that I'm up, I might as well ring for tea.*

"Devin, darling!" The woman with fading red hair exclaimed. She hugged him hard and pulled him down to kiss his cheek.

"It's good to see you again, Mother. May I introduce you to my wife? Harita... Bennett." He grinned.

He loves to call me by my new name.

"Harry, this is my mother, Julia."

"I'm so glad to meet you!" the woman gushed. "I've been wondering and wondering what kind of woman would finally capture Devin's heart."

"Good to meet you, ma'am," Harry said, but her proper words concealed a whirlwind roiling through her insides. *What a picture I must present, small and dark and hugely pregnant. She's going to hate me. Might as well get it over with.* Impulsively, she blurted, "My father was an Indian servant in my mother's household."

Julia regarded her with an unreadable expression for a long moment, and then she spoke in a quiet tone. "How fortunate for you."

Harry blinked. Not a hint of sarcasm marred the gentle voice. "Ma'am?"

"To know who your father was. I never knew. In fact, I'm not sure my mother knew either. Not that I know, as I never met her either. And please, call me Julia or Mother, as Katerina does. I'll accept either."

Harry's cheeks burned. *Well, no surprise after all. Devin must get his fairness from somewhere. Score another point for the Bennetts being the most broad-minded family in all of Britain.* "Very well then."

"Welcome to the family," Julia added with a smile. "I know we're a bit overwhelming, but you seem smart and sturdy. You'll adjust."

"I'm sure you're right," Harry agreed. She smiled warmly at her mother-in-law.

Julia turned to Katerina, who had her face buried in her daughter's hair.

"You naughty girl," she said, plunking down next to them. "You didn't tell me you were expecting before you left."

"I didn't know," Katerina replied. "In fact, this…" She trailed off with a wave at her burgeoning belly. "This didn't happen until we were underway."

"Nonsense." Julia dismissed the words with a wave. "You're bigger than her. By the look of you, you must be nearly eight months."

Katerina shook her head. "I've added it up over and over, and it can't be more than five."

Julia's face compressed in consternation. "Five? But you're ready to topple, Kat."

"I know," Katerina agreed. "I can't imagine getting four months bigger."

"We'll have to make an arrangement to get you to Mrs. Turner right away. You too, Harry," she added.

"Who's Mrs. Turner?" Harry wanted to know, not certain exactly what was happening.

"She's a family friend of the Bennetts," Katerina explained. "She was trained as a midwife before her first marriage and after her husband's passing, she took up the profession again. Now she's remarried to the manager of the cotton mill, but she still delivers babies for her friends. She delivered Sophia."

"All my babies as well," Julia added. "She's the best. If you want excellent care, look no further than Mrs. Turner."

Harry nodded. *Well, that answers a question I hadn't thought to ask yet.*

"Ladies, do you think you might wait to discuss all the squeamish details until the men are out of the room?" Adrian, Devin's father suggested.

"When have I ever done that?" Julia protested, drawing laughter from everyone.

Well, she was right, Harry thought. *They're a bit overwhelming, but it's all good-natured and accepting. I think this will be quite a fine family.* Another thought occurred to her. *Now that I'm a respectable married lady, I should send a letter to Fanny. I can't wait to hear what she's been up to in the last half-year.*

* * *

Devin watched his wife closely as the Bennett family enfolded her into its ranks. She relaxed, smiling, her hand on her belly.

I knew she'd fit right in. Smiling himself, he moved toward the door. "I have to run a brief errand. I'll be back soon."

"Where are you going?" Harry asked.

"To see Fletcher," he replied. "I'm overdue a conversation with that man."

Harry looked nervous but nodded. Devin put his arm around her and kissed her forehead. "I love you," he murmured. "Everything will be all right." He gave her a reassuring squeeze and stepped outside.

The cold, wet air bit at him right through his clothing, and he realized he agreed with both Christopher and Harry. India was too hot, but Britain in winter could be too damned cold.

Rather than walk several miles in the weather, Devin hailed a hansom cab, black and shiny and pulled by a brown horse with white stockings.

Arriving at the spacious London mansion, he knocked and presented his card.

A bowing, gray-haired servant of painful dignity ushered him into a room that, like Fletcher himself, found a way to be overwhelmingly impressive, even though it lacked significant size. Two wing-backed chairs, upholstered in a deep blue fabric Devin's trained eye immediately recognized as inferior, flanked a small table. A frayed but colorful rug covered a wooden floor with more than a few scuffs. *Fletcher isn't as imposing as he wants people to think.*

The door opened and the little rooster of a man stormed in, fury radiating off him the way steam had from the chilly horse's hindquarters. *An apt comparison for this horse's arse,* Devin thought with an irreverent smile.

"Well, Bennett, what the devil do you want? You disrupted my entire life, and now you have the effrontery to turn up at my home?"

Devin raised an eyebrow, unimpressed by the smaller man's blustering. "With all due respect, Sir Fletcher, you disrupted your own life by being a meddling bigot and a thief. And you managed to turn mine upside down as well. Now, you and I have a serious problem to address, and I suggest you settle down and sit. I won't be leaving until the air is clear between us."

Devin's calm defiance seemed to startle Fletcher out of some of his fury, and he dropped into a chair, his forehead gathered into a mass of startled wrinkles.

Devin settled beside him, turning his chair to face the man who'd made his life—and Harry's—a living hell.

"Well, Bennett, out with it!" Fletcher spat. "What do you want?"

"First of all, I need to know. What have you been telling people about the situation?"

Vertical wrinkles joined the horizontal ones as Fletcher drew his eyebrows together. "Nothing," he replied. "I'm not a damned gossipy old woman."

"Good," Devin replied. "Let's keep it that way. For my sake and for the sake of my wife."

Fletcher's eyes bugged out. "You actually married that half-breed tart?"

Devin's hand closed into a fist. He could see, in his mind's eye, those oversized knuckles colliding with Fletcher's face. *What a satisfying moment that would be.* Regretfully, he released his grip. "Harry is no tart, and I'll thank you to refrain from any further comments on the subject. My wife is dear to me and protecting her is my primary goal."

Fletcher pursed his lips. Every movement made him more closely resemble a fish, until Devin had to fight down a shout of inappropriate laughter at the image.

"I ought to tell everyone," Fletcher muttered. "Tell them you married a half-Indian slut." He laughed bitterly. "You'd lose your license then, and you'd be out on the street. It would be no less than you deserve."

"Really, Fletcher," Devin snapped, rolling his eyes. "How is my marriage to your former employee grounds for so much venom? Her heritage doesn't bother me, so why should it bother you so much? Just let it be. It's nothing to you now anyway."

"Nothing?!" Fletcher shot to his feet. "My daughter abandoned me over Harriet. Eloped with her damned doctor two days after the chit sailed. You lost me my child, Bennett."

"No," Devin countered, remaining seated. "You did that yourself. Only you think Harry—Harita, not Harriet, as you well know—is so terrible. Everyone else, including your daughter, finds her charming."

Fletcher muttered something Devin couldn't make out. *Probably for the best.*

Again he considered hitting the man but restrained himself. *Can't let this turn violent. Have to take care of business with as cool a head as possible, for Harry's sake.* "So she married her William after all."

Fletcher frowned. "It's only thanks to my lucky stars your contract held despite the elopement.

Devin shook his head. *Still thinking of his daughter's welfare despite his contradictory attitudes. What a confusing man.* "Well, that's good then."

"But she won't speak to me. She's furious, thinks I've done something wrong. You and your *wife*," he pronounced the word with an ugly sneer, "muddled her thinking so badly, she no longer knows what's right or trusts my wisdom to guide her."

Good. I knew Fanny was smarter than she pretended to be. "Well, Sir Fletcher, it seems we have a serious problem," Devin said, returning to the topic. "You think I deserve to have my career and reputation ruined and I simply don't agree. However, I think I know a way we can both have something we want. You see, if you spread rumors about my wife, about her heritage, I will have no choice but to put information into the ears of some influential people I know. How do you think it would go over if the advocate for hyper-moral living was proven to be part-owner and financial backer of several whorehouses all over India? Places where British girls can go to ply their trade in the tropics? Or that a young, innocent woman had hands laid on her by yourself and was placed on a ship headed towards such an establishment against her will? And do I need to remind you that kidnapping is a prosecutable offense?"

"You can't prove kidnapping," Fletcher snarled.

"No, but I can bring charges. Remember, sir, that I'm trained in creating legal documentation. You might not be convicted, but do you really want to risk the scandal?"

Fletcher stilled, clearly pondering Devin's words, and his face paled. "You can't tell them anything I told you in confidence. What the hell kind of solicitor are you anyway?"

Devin laughed. "A damned good one—you said so yourself—but if you create a furor, I won't be a solicitor anymore. You know how it works. So, if I'm not a solicitor, I'd feel no inclination to guard your privacy. And by the way, it won't hurt me one bit. My father owns a huge business and is always in need of employees. He's been asking me for years to give up law and work for him. It's not what I want, but I'll do it if I need to."

Even from several paces away, Devin could hear Fletcher's teeth grinding. "So, what then?"

"So we agree to keep silent about what we know. You don't ruin me, and I won't ruin you."

"I won't lie," Fletcher insisted.

"No one is asking you to. The official story about Harry and me is true… if not exactly complete. No one will ask you if she's Indian because no one will think of it, so let it be."

"Exactly what foolish fabrication are you expecting me to endorse?" Fletcher snarled.

"Just this," Devin said in a calm, uninflected voice. "In the course of our professional association, I made the acquaintance of your daughter and her companion, who is a poor family connection and your former ward." He regarded Fletcher. The man wore a sour look but appeared to be listening. "Harry and I found a deep resonance and it developed into love. We married quietly and made a voyage to India, where she was born. What else really needs to be known?"

Fletcher wrinkled his lips to prunish pucker but tilted his chin a bare fraction of an inch.

"Now about Harry's inheritance."

"Damnation, Bennett!" The man rocketed to his feet. "She has no right to that. She's not even his!"

"You wouldn't want it to get around that you robbed your orphaned niece, would you?" Devin asked, his voice mild as he examined his fingernails.

Fletcher made no response, but Devin could see the gears turning in his head as he looked for a way to circumvent the agreement.

"Half," he grunted at last.

Devin curled his lips into a malevolent grin. "No. That's her dowry, along with years of back pay, if you need a justification."

"She has no right to it!" Fletcher snarled. "Only a natural relative should receive his life savings. You know that. The chit must be a witch as well as a slut, to have duped a proper English gentleman."

"No proper gentleman would allow slights to his wife to go unpunished," Devin said. His mild tone drew Fletcher's gaze to him, just in time to receive Devin's fist directly to his sulking mouth. Devin had the satisfaction of feeling the skin split beneath his knuckle and watching blood trickle down his chin.

Fletcher wiped the blood from his lip with the back of his hand. His eyes narrowed to slits so tiny, Devin wasn't sure how he could see.

Casually, he drew himself up to his full height, stepping forward and crowding into the other man's space. Both fists clenched, causing his biceps to bulge. His mild look faded, allowing the barely leashed rage to show.

Fletcher's firm expression faded to uncertainty as the imbalance of power in the situation finally sank in.

Devin projected a silent message through his posture and gaze. *Your adversary is just as smart and wily as you. I have resources that match yours, in terms of influence, and I have much less to lose. I'm also taller, stronger and younger than you. Is this a fight you want to take on?*

"Very well," Fletcher hissed from between clenched teeth. "I'm sure you'll understand if I don't bring any more of my legal needs to you, you blackmailer."

"Oh, Sir Fletcher," Devin laughed, an ironic chuckle, "that was far from blackmail. Only a gentleman's agreement to protect the innocent and the private."

Fletcher looked like he'd been chewing lemons, but he spat out, "Fine, I agree," in a sulky voice. "Now get out of my sight, Bennett. Be gone."

Recalling the greeting he had observed in India, he pressed his hands together and said, "Namaste," just to irritate the man. Then, turning on his heel, Devin left smiling. Despite the gray sky and chilly wind, he felt a lightness in his spirit that made him want to shout and dance. *I can't wait to tell Harry the good news. All is well in our world, and we can relax and settle into our marriage, prepare for the birth of our child. That little cottage by the sea is waiting. Fletcher won't back out of our agreement. He has more to lose than we do, so Harry's reputation is finally safe.* He thought of his wife, of the joy of their relationship, and how far they'd come in less than a year, and all the beautiful, hopeful, amazing things ahead.

In the sky above him, the somber gray clouds parted, and a warming shaft of sunlight fell on his face. A broad smile curved his lips as pure joy welled up from every corner of his soul.

He recalled several bits of Hindu philosophy Harry had revealed over their time together. *In the end, we return to the beginning. We began with joy and hope for the future, and that's where we have returned. The turning of the wheel has led us right where we want to be—home.*

Dear Reader,

Thank you for taking time to read *Devin's Dilemma*. If you enjoyed it, please consider telling your friends or posting a short review. Word of mouth is an author's best friend, and much appreciated.

This story has been special to me since I was very young—high school to be exact. Back then, I used to imagine being swept away from the bullies and the stress of everyday life and caught up in a grand adventure. It's the source of most of my oldest stories.

This particular tale was inspired by a song we learned in choir, which happened to be in Hebrew. I imaged the hero chasing his lost love to the far ends of the earth, and that particular scene outside the club has been with me since I was almost too young to understand the mechanics of it.

Things have certainly changed since then. India made more sense than Israel, and in recent years, the stigma biracial people face has become of particular interest to me, so I allowed the book to change into what it is here, and I'm happy with it. I hope you were too.

Love Always,

Simone Beaudelaire

P.S. if this story did delight you, be aware that it is book 2 in a series. Book 1, Keeping Katerina, has been available for ages. Check it out (see the link below). And the final book in the series, Colin's Conundrum, is coming soon.

Other Books by Simone Beaudelaire

When the Music Ends (The Hearts in Winter Chronicles Book 1)
When the Words are Spoken (The Hearts in Winter Chronicles Book 2)
When the Heart Heals (The Hearts in Winter Chronicles Book 3)
Caroline's Choice (The Hearts in Winter Chronicles Book 4)
The Naphil's Kiss
Blood Fever
Polar Heat
Xaman (with Edwin Stark)
Darkness Waits (with Edwin Stark)
Watching Over the Watcher
Baylee Breaking
Amor Maldito: Romantic Tragedies from Tejano Folklore
Keeping Katerina (The Victorians Book 1)
Devin's Dilemma (The Victorians Book 2)
High Plains Holiday (Love on the High Plains Book 1)
High Plains Promise (Love on the High Plains Book 2)
High Plains Heartbreak (Love on the High Plains Book 3)
High Plains Passion (Love on the High Plains Book 4)
Devilfire (American Hauntings Book 1)
Saving Sam (The Wounded Warriors Book 1 with J.M. Northup)
Justifying Jack (The Wounded Warriors Book 2 with J.M. Northup)
Making Mike (The Wounded Warriors Book 3 with J.M Northup)

You might also like:
Beautiful Rose by Simone Beaudelaire

To read the first chapter for free, please head to:
https://www.nextchapter.pub/books/beautiful-rose

Devin's Dilemma
ISBN: 978-4-86745-604-0

Published by
Next Chapter
1-60-20 Minami-Otsuka
170-0005 Toshima-Ku, Tokyo
+818035793528
3rd May 2021